THE VANISHING TOME

THE NETHERWORLD ARCHIVES * BOOK 1

Stella Fitzsimons

This is a work of fiction. Names, characters, organizations, places, events, and incidents are either products of the author's imagination or are used fictitiously. Any resemblance to actual persons, living or dead, or actual events is purely coincidental.

THE VANISHING TOME

Copyright © 2024 Stella Fitzsimons

Cover Design by Dan Fitzsimons

All rights reserved. No part of this publication may be reproduced, distributed, or transmitted in any form or by any means, electronic or mechanical, including photocopy, recording, or any information storage and retrieval system, without permission in writing from the author.

Published by Butterfly Electric Press

www.stellafitzsimons.com

For my mother, Anna
You are always with me

THE VANISHING TOME

The Netherworld Archives

"I'm beginning to hear the teachings of my blood pulsing within me. My story isn't pleasant, it's not sweet and harmonious like the invented stories; it tastes of folly and bewilderment, of madness and dream, like the life of all people who no longer want to lie to themselves."

Hermann Hesse

Chapter 1

"I'm not an open book. In fact, I'm unreadable even to myself." I shot a grin at the Arcane Investigations Bureau recruiter. "That's why I read others. I want to know how their stories end. I was made for this."

A bit aggressive, Tess, but I stated my case as best as I could without getting into details.

The woman across the desk, her eyes polar icebergs, stared me down for a short eternity before offering the most theatrical yawn this side of Broadway. And... there went another job interview spiraling down the drain, courtesy of my sparkling response to the question, "Do you possess unique skills that would make you a fit for the unusual challenges of paranormal investigation?"

And just like that, Recruiter – 1, Tess Hilliard – 0.

Let's slice it thin and serve it cold: at twenty-six, I was already stuck in the underbelly of this business, my name at the very bottom of the employee list at the Shadow Chasers Agency, taking on the cases that no one else would touch with a ten-foot pole, scraping by with meager paychecks, and dealing with colleagues who'd finish dead last at the *Camaraderie Olympics*.

And maybe I deserved it all, considering my top selling point as a supernatural snoop and ghoul-hound was, uh, a Napoleonic chip on my shoulder caused by my nearly complete lack of the paranormal power possessed by all the big-time Chasers.

I took a deep breath. It was no surprise I'd failed to impress her with my self-professed genius level ability to bluff my way out of any jam and spin trite sayings like plates of life-altering wisdom. Tempting as it was, I couldn't spill my whole can of beans and lay out the truth entwined in my words—in fact, my life depended on the zipping of my lips. Being alive, after all, was essential to all my career goals.

Standing outside my Agency, I couldn't help but notice its dingy contrast with the flash and prestige of the Arcane Bureau. Sadly nestled between a laundromat and a falafel wrap takeout joint, our offices were in a nondescript two-story brick building with a cracked wooden awning that had paint peeling off it like sunburnt skin. The elements had had their way. The neon glow of an OPEN sign still flickered in the early morning haze.

A washed-out gold plaque on the door read:

SHADOW CHASERS AGENCY INC.
Drawing back the shadows.
Mysteries <u>solved</u>. Items <u>found</u>.

Treasures <u>won</u>. Curses <u>squashed</u>.
Give those suspicions a HOME!
Understand the inexplicable!
Exorcise the paranormal!
Budget-friendly consultations.

Unlike the Bureau, all hush-hush and operating entirely under the radar, we were face forward, out in the open paranormal investigators, a beacon for those fragile souls drawn to the eerie and unlikely. Our neon light lured the gullible believers convinced that the creaking of their old homes was proof of poltergeists, that their neglected yards and fields were hotspots for alien abductions, or that their former neighbor's grouchy spirit wanted a word.

You know, people who were looking to chit-chat with the dead, or needed a bargain basement exorcism to chase away demonic rats, or a seer to divine the location of misplaced priceless heirlooms, that sort of thing. When the Arcane Bureau were generous enough to offload surplus cases our way, meaty cases involving supernatural perps or unexpected visitors from the multiverse, well, those cases hardly ever landed on my desk.

No, I was pushed to the end of the bench, my unofficial title as Assistant to the Lead Investigators inked in permanent marker. I was stuck sorting out crackpots and lost possessions, while my teammates got to play on the fringe of the big league every now and then. Today promised to be like any other day in the life of Tess Hilliard, pseudo-professional ghost whisperer and amateur treasure hunter. Same as it ever was.

But you know what they say about hindsight? *They* being the vaporous ectoplasmic tendrils of the human hive mind. Unfortunately, we live life moving forward. Looking back is not advised. Regret feeds the dark energies. I would say I wish I knew then what was coming, but that kind of thinking always ends with a bucket full of bad juju.

The familiar hum of fluorescent lights and the reassuring aroma of cheap coffee welcomed me as I stepped inside the doors of 405½ South Few Street.

Just down the hall, our Director, Abraham Pankowski, sat in his office looking uncomfortable in a now too tight suit. While he was growing thicker, his hair was growing thinner, forcing him to comb the remaining strands over bald spots. He was engaged in a conversation with his Chief Investigator.

Gideon Crawford. Tall, all glower, sharp lines, and an attitude to match. Guy had the charisma of a piranha and the cordiality of a… well, piranha.

They paused their conversation as I strolled by, Gideon's eyes narrowing in a glare. He made no attempt to conceal his disdain. I returned the favor a hundredfold. I took my saccharine smile and moved on.

My desk was cluttered with a hodgepodge of case files and unwashed coffee mugs. I settled in and rifled through a stack of papers, zeroing in on a new report resting on top of a half-eaten cinnamon muffin.

"Hey, Tess. Yet another dud," Izzy announced, dropping a manila folder onto my desk. Her steaming mug radiated warmth that cut through the chill of the office.

Her magic trickled into me as I raised my focus from a particularly lurid file detailing a demonic possession that turned out to be nothing more than a bizarre fraternity hazing ritual. My nose twitched, threatening a sneeze. Izzy's etheric aura always had that effect on me. My gaze momentarily snagged on the myriad of scars that crisscrossed my hands—an unwelcome reminder of my brush with the darker side of the supernatural. It was the other strange thing Izzy's magic did to me. It revealed my meticulously hidden scars—thankfully to my eyes only.

I surrendered to the sneeze and hummed the word *calyptio* under my breath. A veil of illusion wrapped around the scars, concealing them again. Izzy Everett was a skilled empath, and I could assimilate her etheric aura into mine within seconds, a secret I was keen to keep. This was why I found excuses to turn down every one of her social invitations. I couldn't afford to get close to anyone, especially not an empathic mage who might sense my strange, not to mention outlawed, ability.

Izzy was on the short side, but her fit, solid build and intense green eyes demanded your complete attention. Her curly hair was a fiery spectacle, not just red but a living blaze. Strands of deep auburn twirled with flashes of copper and scarlet that flickered with every tilt and turn of her head.

Her physical presence may have exuded strength, but it was her uncanny ability to sense and absorb the emotional energy around her that kept people in the office on their toes. With Izzy, a lie was as transparent as glass, and that made our co-workers tread carefully.

I gestured to the empty chair across from me. "Yep, that

dude was totally not a pyromancer. Not even a little. I doubt he could rub two matches together and get a spark."

The moment I arrived at the scene of the literal dumpster fire behind O'Malley's Emporium, I knew that no magic was involved in the failed arson. The location had given off an initial whiff of the paranormal—after all, the Emporium had a reputation of attracting rogue mages and aspiring spell conjurers—but I would have sensed a *fever print* lingering, that heightened supernatural pheromonal scent that pyromancers leave behind.

"I knew you knew," Izzy agreed. "You always know. They should give you bigger cases. I wish you had been wrong though, because a rogue spell spinner would be a far more exciting Tuesday than a nut job with a shabby pipe bomb."

"So, they pulled the plug on the investigation?" I said, twirling a pen.

She nodded. "Afraid so. It's now strictly a police matter."

"Got anything else with a pulse?"

Izzy, our resident empath, juggler of emotions and assigner of the less complex cases, eased into the chair I'd offered. The leather creaked beneath her as she set down her coffee and opened a worn notebook, its pages covered with hastily scribbled notes. She glanced up and bared her teeth, sheepishly.

"Go ahead," I encouraged her through a sigh.

"It's a, um... a haunted house," she said, almost bracing for my response.

Before I could advise her where to shove that haunted house, Director Pankowski approached with Gideon Crawford at his heels. They both had a puckered look, like they'd been sucking on lemons.

"Just had an interesting call from an associate, Tess," the Director said, adjusting his midnight blue tie. "They work over at the Arcane Bureau."

Uh oh. That icy bitch. So much for confidentiality.

Pankowski seemed to be clearing his thoughts and, thankfully, failed to notice my apprehension. "They curiously asked about you, they requested *you* specifically to consult on a case."

The hostile glare in Gideon's eyes confirmed that this was no prank. My confusion matched both of theirs. A case from the Bureau. For me. My trainwreck of an interview must have made an impression.

Ah, I see. They are trying to read my reaction.

"Sleeping your way to the top, Hilliard?" Gideon hissed.

"You're so predictable, Crawford. It puts me to sleep."

He mean-mugged me, revealing his teeth. They were almost as pointed as his tongue. Pathetic. The big bad mage was trying to scare me.

Intimidation was Gideon Crawford's game. He was a kinetic mage who could absorb, store and release energy at will. It made him a formidable adversary in physical combat, like a wrecking ball in a tailored suit. I'd seen him punch through walls and blur across rooms in a blink.

His talents didn't end there. Gideon possessed persuasion magic and was known to bend wills when the circumstances were right. He could toy with a person's psyche to incite fear, trust, or anger. A handy little trick, especially when he wanted to throw someone off balance. Too bad it never worked on me, a fact that frustrated him daily.

I had no idea why Pankowski chose to trust Gideon. I mean, would he even know if Gideon planted that trust in him or not?

"I'll be off," I said. "My talents are needed elsewhere."

"You're the one," Izzy said, her face beaming. "Show out, sis."

"Make it quick," Pankowski called after me as I grabbed my jacket and headed for the door. "I expect a full report!"

Just for that, I'm taking my sweet time.

Chapter 2

THE FOUR-STORY BUILDING LOOMED above, a monolith of gray concrete and black glass, standing stark against the foggy backdrop of Lake Mendota. The Bureau knew how to make an imposing impression.

I pulled my jacket tight. Madison in mid-November was a city held by winter's cold grip, the chilly wind a biting reminder of the freezing waters that would soon become the icy surfaces of its many lakes.

The façade bore the inconspicuous name *Mendota Research & Development Institute*, but this was no ordinary research center. Beyond those ominous walls, the Arcane Investigations Bureau guarded the library portals that bridged parallel realms. They kept tabs on the fraying threads of the multiverse, safeguarding our world from the nastiest entities in dimensions near and far, threats both heinous and clever, both visible and veiled.

Climbing the stairs was like trudging through a stream of sticky molasses. My scars tingled, a sure sign of overflowing power mojo in the air. I wrapped a shield around my magic core to keep it from gulping down all that magic like a bad drunk at a cocktail party. Security wards, concealing endless spells and enchantments, formed an intricate web that turned the Bureau into an impenetrable fortress. Not even a sly thought could slither past this place's defenses. It was less like walking into an office and more like trying to slip past a sleeping dragon—one false step and you were a kabob. Literally. But everyone has to earn their living, even those who flirt with dimensional gateways over morning coffee.

Two agents breezed past me on the second floor. My nostrils twitched as I caught a whiff of their power, but I managed to hold back the sneeze: an electromancer and a sorcerer. Very on brand for the Bureau.

I reached my third-floor destination. I paused, hand hovering over the brass doorknob, as I read the name on the metal placard: *Special Agent Miles Donovan, Paranormal Investigations and Interactions Division Coordinator.*

I double-checked my phone, half-hoping for a mistake. Room 309. Nope. This was happening. I thought I might run into him in these halls one day, but him being my liaison for a case... that was a twist I had never imagined.

This was going to be interesting, yet dread sunk into my bones. Every instinct warned that I was opening a portal into a world of trouble.

How would he feel about partnering with me? I had ghosted him without a single word, and he had not taken it well. He'd demanded answers via texts, DMs, and even telepathic messages he sent through a seer, until he had finally accepted that silence would be my only response.

It's been two years, Tess. He's obviously over it. Get a grip!

My heart jackhammered in my chest. Was *I* over it?

Oh, hell. A deep breath. I knocked.

"Yeah, come in."

The easy command of his deep voice soothed my nerves. I imagined him leaning back in his chair, the embodiment of confidence and grace.

I pushed the door open.

His friendly eyes welcomed me without a hint of surprise. "Tess," he said with a handsome grin. "You can unclench your jaw. I promise not to bite."

Biting was not my concern. Miles was a powerful elemental mage. If he harnessed earth, wind, fire or water energy while in a sour mood, well, not much in the neighborhood would be left standing.

"You got promoted," I said. My tone was frostier than intended.

"Does it surprise you?" he said, tapping a folder on his desk.

"*Surprise?* No. I just never pegged you as a pencil pusher."

"A pencil is a reliable weapon. You can count on a pencil. It quite literally hangs on every word."

I felt my defenses tighten. *Don't let him drag me onto memory lane.*

He was the devil incarnate, not just in his sharply cut features and penetrating black eyes, but in his impertinent swagger and effortless charm. He hadn't changed a bit. Not physically, not in his wickedly cool attitude—and not in the way he regarded me, as if he knew me better than I knew myself.

"I was sure my interview was a disaster," I said. "Wasn't it?"

He raised his eyebrows. "You interviewed with the Bureau?"

Ah, there it was, a spark of genuine surprise in his eyes, but something else there, too. A sly hope that I was trying to worm my way back to him.

As if.

"If not that, then why am I here, Miles?" I shot back, not in the mood for any of his games.

"Didn't they tell you? I requested you consult on a case."

"Me? Come on, you're the bigshot kingfish of paranormal investigations. You have your pick of agents."

His eyes flickered, unapologetic. "I need someone I can trust."

"Or someone who won't ask questions," I countered, not missing a beat.

"That, but also the trust thing. Complete discretion is required." He pushed back from his desk, rising with a grace that was almost predatory. The perfect lines of his suit hugged his sinewy form, a shade of dark that matched his slick black hair, a look so polished it was sinful. "You will talk to no one about the case but me," he said, as if all had been decided. "Something's off with the Bureau. We need to get to the bottom of it. If my hunch proves out, this will be trouble for all the worlds and time's not on our side."

A multiverse crisis. Of course. Together again for another shit show.

Contact with parallel universes was becoming as common as morning traffic in Madison, and the Bureau was the bulwark against all those worlds spilling into ours. What chaos such a spillover would bring was anyone's guess, and trust me, nobody wanted to find out whose guess was right.

Our eyes met from inches away. I took a step back. Too close for comfort, his powerful stare. I couldn't shake the feeling that this was about more than a case. It was a challenge, an invitation to duel, a chance to prove my mettle.

And damn his arrogance, he knew I would accept.

His composure seemed tightly held. I knew him too well to miss the coiled tension in his shoulders, the vein popping in his rigid neck. Or was it all projection? The past could cloud one's judgment. Either way, I was all in.

"Sounds serious," I said. "Are you sure I'm the wingman you need?"

"You're the only one, Tess. Most people are goddamned useless in a crisis—you're not. Believe me, I wish there was someone else."

Not exactly glowing praise. Sheesh.

I stared at him. "My powers are unsubstantial, they're on par with a stray mutt stealing magic breadcrumbs."

He gave me that half-cocked, *oh-please* look. "First, why do you always sell yourself short? Second, I might need those breadcrumbs."

"Do share that opinion with my Bureau interviewer. Third try and I'm not sure she even knew I was in the room."

"You're holding back, Tess. That much I know."

If he learned the truth, which of us would be left standing?

"Then you know nothing, Miles. Not one crumb."

His expression hardened. "Don't be coy. I was there when you took down that ten-foot-tall Gryphalion at Hawthorne Library before it could stampede out onto East Washington Avenue, remember? The abundance of power you summoned was no parlor trick."

That's because you were there next to me, you fool. I siphoned a chunk of YOUR power juice.

"Pure adrenaline, Miles. Survival instinct. It was either that or become breakfast for a hungry lion. And, actually, it was a *Gryphatiger*."

He looked down at me. "Shadow Chasers may not be the Ritz of paranormal agencies, but they don't hire amateurs."

Ah, the emotional landmine. "Let's be real. We both know the only reason I got the gig was the fact Mom and Dad worked there when—"

...when they were alive.

My parents were wind mages, the real deal. Director Pankowski figured I was a chip off the old block—potential yet to be tapped. Little did Miles or Pankowski know I was an illusion mage. Little did they know that when I stood next to a dynamo like Miles, I was immediately filled with elemental magic and only pretended to be tapping into a feeble wind energy resource inherited from my parents. Made me look almost competent but not flashy. The problem with the Gryphatiger situation was I unleashed a tad more energy drawn from Miles than I should have.

Blame the adrenaline.

I was playing a deadly game of hide and seek, a game I one day expected to lose. I clung to my anonymity, because the day my secret got out would be the day my life under 24/7 surveillance as a VIP member of a watchlist would begin. And that was a best-case scenario.

Illusion mages were not just watch-listed—they tagged us as the highest possible threat. We could absorb magic like a sponge, then twist it, weave it into anything we fancied and spit it out as our own, and that included some magic from other dimensions. The Bureau recognized our value but also that we were too hazardous to be handled without gloves. By law, our whereabouts must be known. One mistake, one impulsive outburst of power, and we may never walk free again.

I could hardly blame the Bureau. When illusion mages let their guard down, they quickly got drunk on magic and mayhem soon followed. Every now and then, one went rogue and nearly blew the cover off the magic world.

One mage practically made the Statue of Liberty dance the Macarena for every Joe Schmoe to see. And the Alice-in-Wonderland transformation of the Vegas Strip caused enormous headaches. Thousands of tourists, thinking they were tripping out on spiked drinks, suddenly needed a memory wipe.

Because, no surprise, our only true innate ability is crafting illusions.

Except, unlike the rest of my kind, I wasn't born this way. No, I was an anomaly. An illusion mage had forced this high-risk, high-reward gift upon me after killing my parents. It came with a slew of bodily scars and a warning to stay silent or others I cared for would die too.

Why had he done this to me? I had not one foggy fucking clue. Either way, I was stuck with powers and secrets I did not want.

Surfacing from my pity party, I shifted gears. "So, what do you think you're sniffing out? An insurgency of rowdy unicorns? A backdoor portal to the island of lost Bogeymen?"

He exhaled, shifting back to business mode in a nanosecond. "I wish it were something that absurd. We have a rogue beast hopping library portals. The eggheads in tracking have it slated to pop up over at Sun Prairie Public…" He checked his phone. "T-minus fifty-five minutes."

"Wait, what type of beast? A furry bigfoot or a scaly cold-blooded—"

"Something like that," he said, his eyes narrowing. "We've only got a blurry heat image from the other side, but it's massive, it's nasty, and it's coming this way."

He laughed, apparently finding my concerned face amusing. "I'm sorry," he said, getting serious. "It's a pomdor."

"*A pomdor?* You just said it was massive. Those critters are pocket-sized. *Oh.* You were trying to be funny. Which part was the joke, because pomdors are five realms away and there are no direct portal nexuses between their dimension and ours."

"It's a pomdor. How could it portal jump that far?"

I shook my head. "It can't."

A pomdor taking a multi-dimensional road trip and surviving the portal strain was as likely as a chicken penning *The Grapes of Wrath*.

"Someone's driving this," I calculated. "Pomdors stumbling through one secret portal is a fluke, but five? That's a planned invasion."

His eyes met mine. "Right. And so, we need to find out who's doing the planning, because I, too, hold a low opinion of pomdor intellectual capacity."

"Someone who would enjoy the sinister absurdity of enlisting pomdors as foot soldiers," I offered.

Miles reached for his coat—the material a posh blend of fine wool and cashmere. Broad lapels and silver-lined cuffs and collar screamed authority and old money. Even the buttons offered the kind of refined detail that only came with a hefty price tag. Miles was insecure despite his good looks and forever adorned himself in high fashion.

"Still remember how to seal and unseal portals?" he said.

Memories flashed of lessons under lamplights, practicing in hidden corners of the city outside official Academy hours. Miles guiding, coaching, demanding perfection... and then declaring his feelings for me.

"I remember."

There was a challenging glint in his eyes. "Am I right to trust you?"

The sharp jab caught me off guard. "Okay, sure, I woke up one day and broke it off. That's it. Nothing more."

His gaze didn't waver. "People grow apart, I get it. You were young, maybe you met someone, maybe you lost your nerve. Doesn't matter. When it comes to the job, I trust your determination and discretion. This is a professional commitment. It's not personal. Friendship is not a requisite."

His words hung in the air like a dull ache. "Does the Bureau Director know I'm shadowing you today?"

He grinned, leading the way to the elevator. "I have broad authority, Tess. I operate above and beyond any office politics."

We descended into the underground parking. Miles had suggested there was something nefarious afoot at the Bureau, but my every instinct suggested that he, too, was not himself. He claimed to trust me, but should I trust him?

If only I could get him into a room with Izzy and borrow her empath skills, then I could get to his truth, discover what really was at the center of Miles Donovan's heart. You know... regarding the case.

Chapter 3

As the door of the Sun Prairie Public Library opened, a surge of portal energy prickled across my face causing a sudden but familiar shiver. The well-lit space with its striking vaulted ceiling had been completely redecorated. Miles noticed it too. An explosion of color, accomplished by an abundance of new plant life highlighted by vibrant peace lilies and Chinese evergreens, created the lush silence of a vast, empty forest.

Looks like the library has battled a greenhouse to a draw.

"This cost them some money," I said under my breath. "It's as if Mother Nature had a super sweet sixteen party."

Shuffling portals around was never a good idea. Even a minor relocation, the slightest shift in the dimensional axis, could spell havoc.

Miles shot me his signature *stay focused* glare, then fixed his gaze on two librarians chatting over coffee behind the front desk. He leaned in close. "I'll keep these two busy. Go find the portal and seal it."

He glided over to reception with a smile that appeared every bit as sincere as it was not. "Excuse me, ladies. Sorry to interrupt. I find myself a smidge turned around within this dazzling new setup. Would you be kind enough to shepherd me over to the reference section? I've a hot list of architecture and engineering books burning a hole in my pocket."

The librarians looked flustered. One even dropped her eyes to his pants pocket expecting it to start burning. *Sheesh. They never had a chance.*

I wove between aisles, scanning for a ripple or even a spark that could guide my way. Portals were usually nestled behind musty, thick tomes or tucked in the nooks between rarely disturbed shelves, but thanks to the library's revamp, I had to quickly reorient myself.

Time ticked away in my head—each second amped up the urgency. We had less than thirty minutes before our furry friend made an entrance, and I was in no mood for an interdimensional meet-and-greet.

I closed my eyes. The faint frequency of a rogue energy tickled along the concealed scars gracing my arms, nudging me... to the left. *Gotcha.*

Miles still held the rapt attention of the librarians. That man could sell a furnace to Hades. Charming two bookish women with his words was a far easier challenge, especially dressed in his wool and cashmere ensemble that oozed a certain *rugged chic* style.

But that was only his surface. What lay beneath was quite another Miles. The vast difference between what you see and what you get with him I felt as sharply as a knife to the heart.

His etheric aura, his magic, his *vibe*—all resounded with an intensity both mesmerizing and unsettling.

Why was I thinking about him? The past, our past, what could have been done differently, how I could have fought to safeguard him instead of setting him free... these were all tired lyrics from the shit song that used to play over and over in my head. The mental anchors that tried to pull me down.

Not the time, Tess, you've moved on, remember?

I snapped out of it. The reality was Miles had edged too close to the truth, becoming a potential liability, an untenable risk in my world of riddles in which I was forever entrenched. Our increasing intimacy threatened to paint a giant bullseye on his back. After the Gryphatiger incident, severing ties had been inevitable. Before the walls of my isolation crumbled completely under the weight of his persistent scrutiny, I had to end it.

History would not repeat itself. I had to be fine alone. That was why I kept Izzy at arm's length, despite her friendly hope to crack open my fortress of cynicism. Bringing her into my chaotic sphere, especially given how fond I was of her, was a line I refused to cross.

Right now, a crisis barreled down the tracks, heading our way. Madison had long been a hotspot for portal hopping—that's why the Bureau had set up shop here in the first place. But lately, incidents had been popping off like a string of firecrackers. We were suddenly the flashing neon *Open 24/7* sign at the heart of the multiverse. Because of our efforts all over the Earth, notably cities built on a natural isthmus like

Seattle, Auckland and Corinth, the world at large remained blissfully unaware of magic and the parallel worlds. It was our job to keep it that way. *Forever the one. Forever the many.*

I spotted the portal. It settled, nearly imperceptibly, between the dense volumes of an alchemy anthology and tales of the Bermuda Triangle. To the untrained eye, it would seem nothing more than motes of dust caught in a light beam, but when I gently blew on it, a faint glowing halo ignited—a gateway craving activation.

I waved my hand, summoning the *Codex Portallis*—the quintessential guidebook for those who tread the paths between worlds. The thick, leather-bound tome materialized on the shelf before me.

The Codex was our map through the cosmic wilderness—without it, we might as well be navigating blindfolded, at the mercy of the multiverse winds. I opened the book, carefully flipping one heavy page at a time. Each one contained the key to a different dimension.

My hand suddenly froze. A page was missing. It had been deliberately ripped out. In my years dealing with portals, I'd never come across a severed link inside the Codex. This was clearly a calculated act of sabotage, a rogue element shutting down access to another world.

The portal began to surge and sputter, then went into full spin mode. I returned the Codex to the shelf and hurried to draw upon every shred of training, knowledge and magic within me.

I thrust my hand into the portal, channeling my core power

into the sealing spell.

Claudatur ostium ad alias mundi!

A silver radiance encased the portal, beginning the laborious process of locking it down.

My hand recoiled from a sudden shock. I slammed back into the shelves behind me, barely staying on my feet. I refocused and forced the spell forward only to get flung back a second time.

Something on the other side fought to keep the portal open.

Not good. So much for being discreet. That ship was crashing.

Miles!

The portal blew wide open. My attempt to tap into Miles's arsenal of elemental magic hit an invisible barrier.

I shouted out his name again. *Miles!*

Where the hell... he better not be banging a librarian in the bathroom.

I resisted with everything I had, but my opposition pushed harder.

Relentless bastard! They really wanted in. I could feel the desperation.

The pomdor burst through the portal, flying right at me. The vibrant orange furry blur collided into my chest and neck. I breathlessly enclosed the small creature within both hands. It fought my grip at first, baring tiny teeth in a display more cute than ferocious, then thought better of it and quickly started to lick my fingers. It shivered waiting for my approval. Its large, dark eyes sparkled with a mix of curiosity and mischief.

I petted its head.

The pomdor and the portal both quieted down.

Miles!!!

I debated if I should squeeze the pomdor back into the portal before sealing it, but with all the interdimensional unrest that had been happening, who knew where it might end up? And this furball might hold vital answers, or at least pathways to evidence. Decision made, I gently herded my grateful new friend into my backpack.

A wave of unfamiliar magic washed over me, immense and pulsating, expanding in the air like a giant spiderweb. I couldn't detect its signature which meant I couldn't assimilate it—not that I would want to. Untraceable magic was either precariously obscured or came from a source beyond this realm. Both possibilities promised trouble.

I heard a rustling behind me, the sound of shuffling books. Through a gap in the shelf a man's intense gray eyes stared at me. His stormy, predator-like gaze and angular features unnerved me. He never blinked.

He slid out of sight and reappeared instantly at the end of the aisle. At just over six feet tall with wide shoulders and an impressive build, the man seemed to lean slightly forward, coiled and ready like a boxer. Both his physical and supernatural essences teemed with unspoken threat.

If he came at me, I'd stand little chance without access to a nearby human reservoir of magic, and right now, there was none within reach. At five foot five and 120 pounds, I wasn't exactly his equal in a wrestling match. Sure, I kept up with physical training, hit the gym regularly, but let's be honest, in hand-to-hand combat he'd crush me like a soda can.

His thundercloud eyes engaged me. The puzzling magic pulsing from the portal (*or from him?*) grew in intensity. It struck suddenly with a devastating blow, knocking the wind out of my lungs.

The man grinned. Whether the magic's source was him or something beyond the gateway, he was enjoying its painful effect on me.

An invisible force pulled me toward the portal. The air itself seemed to thicken, charged with an electric current that tugged me toward the eye of this tempest.

The man pressed a finger to his lips, urging me to stay silent, before he faded from view as if swallowed by the shadows.

I was helpless, immobile, and my heart raced. The magic swirled around me, raising the fine hairs on my arms and nape. The portal intensified, becoming a powerful vacuum sucking me into its void.

My feet scraped backward across the floor. I felt myself surrendering, but then I sensed an imperfection, a tiny opening in the magic wave. Seizing the opportunity, I absorbed a sliver of its essence, an engulfing, arcane power that strained my senses.

Reality dipped, my stomach turned, and I reached out into a blurred chaos, grasping at whatever scraps of enchantment I could use to anchor myself amidst the storm. The portal's vacuum grew hungrier, eager to swallow me whole.

I channeled every spark I had absorbed into the sealing spell, struggling to enunciate the words.

Claudatur... ostium... ad alias... MUNDI!

The portal's voracious appetite abated. Its veil of power dissipated until it winked out of existence and the portal was sealed.

I stood there, panting, a cocktail of adrenaline and apprehension twirling through my veins. Someone had orchestrated this meticulously, tearing vital Codex pages, breaching portals, unleashing clandestine magic.

The spell should hold for several weeks, in theory at least, unless someone used a cheat code, an anti-spell of sorts to unravel it. The truth was I had no idea what dark forces lurked out there in those unmapped dimensions. But that was the job, taking on and subduing any manner of hideous instrument of fracture or annihilation that came our way.

I heard footsteps and whirled around. It was Miles.

His expression was surly. "What's taking so long?"

Gods. Remain calm, Tess.

"You better be joking, Miles. I was literally yelling for you. Where in the seven hells have you been?"

Fuck calm.

He inhaled sharply and sniffed at the air as if he could pluck from it all the answers he needed.

"Didn't hear anything," he finally said, his gaze dropping to the floor. He squatted down and scooped up dust onto his fingertip. "Warding ash residue. This whole section must have been shielded from the rest of the library. What happened here, Tess?"

I shrugged. "I'm still not sure. There was a strange man."

"A strange man? What man?"

"I don't know… Tall, short chestnut hair slicked back, gray eyes, fit. Likely supernatural." The words flew out unfiltered. "He had a messy look, but confident eyes. Rather alluring, I suppose."

Miles arched an eyebrow. "You suppose, huh? And how do you suppose that's relevant?"

"He kind of had that whole vibe."

"What vibe?"

"Like he might be one of yours."

He shook his head. "No Bureau agent could block me out like that. Their embedded connective pathways are always open to leadership."

That vibe. The blind confidence.

"The pomdor?" he said.

"Safely in my bag. Thought you might want to hand it over to the experts."

He nodded. "Good call. The Cross-Realm Monitoring Division will be completely geeked about this little pest." He chuckled.

"Something funny?"

"No. I just remembered pomdors love ice cream. Give them some and they'll do anything."

"You can't be serious."

"A hundred percent. Seems… Pomdoria is sorely lacking in frozen treats."

I rolled my eyes. "Maybe you shouldn't attempt comedy."

He turned to go. My hand latched onto his arm.

"Miles, wait. There's something else."

His eyes opened wider as he turned to me.

"The portal tried to suck me in. I was nearly gone."

A glint of concern shaped his features. "Tess, you should have waited for me. That's why we send two. Are you okay?"

"You were busy being charming. I'm fine. Really. Miles, there's a bigger issue. The Codex—it's missing a page. Maybe more than one. I didn't have time to examine the whole book."

"That can't be."

"I know what I saw. A gaping tear where a page should be."

He regarded me tenderly. "Are you sure you're okay?"

"I said I'm fine. Go ahead, you can check for yourself." My gaze drifted towards the now dormant portal. "The Codex has reverted to stealth mode and, frankly, I'm in no mood to summon it again, but, hey, you're more than welcome to give it a shot. Or... you could just take my word for it."

"I trust you, Tess, but this is... unprecedented."

Your face is unprecedented.

Okay, my internal monologue is not always mature or even logical.

"Could the Bureau have done this to cut off access to a particularly nasty dimension?" I pondered aloud.

"We keep tabs on realms that pose a threat, we don't tear pages from the Codex. That's a desecration of every principle of our methodology. We seal dimensions, we don't erase them. Our eyes are open. We are ever vigilant. We do not willingly blind ourselves."

"Yeah, I thought so. Just spit balling. You tell me, what's our play here?"

"I'll take the lead on this. Don't worry, I'll handle everything."

"You'll handle everything?" I raised my eyebrows. "You and your Bureau? What does that mean, because I'm pretty sure I will include this anomaly in my report to Pankowski."

He looked befuddled.

Oh, c'mon.

"He's the director of my agency," I clarified. "You don't even know his name. Of course. You and your Bureau cronies are so arrogant."

His expression hardened. "No, don't tell him. Not yet," he cautioned, noting my apprehensive look.

"This is too fucking serious, Miles."

"And that's why we need to tread carefully. At this point, we don't know who's an ally or a spy."

"Funny, I was just wondering the same thing about you."

"Look," he said, softening his approach, "there's an emergency briefing at the Bureau tonight. We'll go together. Your perspective could prove invaluable. It's better to have us both there, listening in, discovering what we agree on and what we disagree on."

This is not how Miles thinks or talks.

His words accomplished one thing, making me certain something big was brewing.

I knew his soft touch was really an attempt at control, but I wanted to crash that briefing at the Arcane Investigations

Bureau, so I decided to play along for as long as it took. I needed to know. I've always needed to know. If you want my weakness, that's it.

"With all this talk of secrecy, they're just going to let me waltz in?"

"I'll list you as my investigative shadow. Come on, let's see what unfolds, then decide our next steps together."

Together? I had to fight not to laugh in his face.

"Izzy would be the real asset here," I found myself muttering.

That piqued his interest. "Izzy?"

"She's an empath and a friend." I immediately regretted trying to pull her into this hot mess.

He could not have hated the idea more. "Empaths and the Bureau don't mix. She'd never clear the scanners."

Ah, those pain-in-the-ass scanners. The little dance I did with my illusion magic just to get through the door without triggering alarms was very slowly becoming routine.

"It's so full of lies, huh?" I teased.

"It comes with the territory. Caution is the prime virtue in the clandestine arts. Remind me another time, we could leverage your friend's skills outside the Bureau's walls. So, what will it be? Can I count on you tonight?"

I nodded, more sheepishly than intended.

He grinned, a flicker of victory and possibly a spark of his old warmth in the sly curve of his lips. "Great. See you at seven sharp."

Chapter 4

FATIGUE GROUND INTO MUSCLE and bone like a dull blade. I felt as if I had been beaten from head to toe. Every tender joint stung when I moved, the price for absorbing those tiny fragments of peculiar magic at the library. What would have happened if I'd been able to fully assimilate that toxic torrent of energy into my core? Bad stuff. I'd rather not entertain the thought.

My every fiber yearned to inform the Bureau about the portal's pulling force and the vanishing page from the Codex, but I'd promised to hold off until after the briefing. I'm a mage of my word if nothing else. Miles had made it crystal clear from the jump that this case demanded utmost discretion.

I decided to walk directly home from the Bureau rather than returning to my agency for a workday wrap-up. The thought of facing Pankowski's prodding questions filled me with dread. My patience was worn too thin—one wrong word and I might snap.

The clean, crisp air filled my lungs as I set a vigorous

pace. The rhythm of the walk grounded me in the here and now... the pitter patter of my foot falls, the barely happening breeze, the pale remnants of color from the withering autumn flowerbeds. *This city is my soul.*

I lived on treelined, shrubbery possessed Jenifer Street in a quirky American Foursquare house built in 1897. What had once been a grand home for a single well-to-do family had been partitioned into quaint, snug apartments.

Living in this vibrant, hipster neighborhood was the one good thing I had going for me, even if my space was only marginally larger than adjoining walk-in closets. It was a brisk, six-minute walk to the agency and a leisurely twenty to the Bureau, offering both convenience and tranquility at a price I could almost afford.

The house itself had a certain old-world charm, with its two sturdy stories crowned by a whimsically angled half-floor complete with lookout windows. That top unit was my domain—bedroom, a basic shower and a modest living room that doubled as a makeshift kitchenette with a sink, a mini fridge and one electric burner. Not made for two but quite nice for one.

There were five more units below, and while I mostly kept to myself, exchanging the occasional hello, I was pretty sure I was the only tenant whose everyday life didn't revolve around the University campus in one way or another. That suited me fine. Living in this tiny bubble of academia added another layer of anonymity to my rogue existence.

Right now, a hot shower was more than a simple desire—it

was an urgent craving. I could practically feel the steam wrapping around me, melting the grimy residue of magic from my body.

I trudged up the front steps, two at a time. I kicked off my boots and locked the door behind me. Home sweet home.

Snug as a bug in a rug.

The room glowed with the soft light filtering through the high arched back window that offered a glimpse of Lake Monona through the stark, leafless branches of century old oak trees.

Why didn't I tell Miles that the mystery man at the library carried signature-less magic? Maybe because admitting I could ID all magic signatures like I had penciled them myself would trigger a few alarms. But really, who and what was that guy? What game was he playing? How could the mere thought of him send a chill to my core?

I made a beeline for the shower, shedding my nagging thoughts along with my clothes. The hot water soothed my aching muscles and frazzled nerves like a healing balm.

I turned off the water and wrapped myself in a towel, my thoughts as hazy as the steam fogging the mirror.

My eyes snagged on my murky reflection. I usually avoided mirrors. They always felt like a challenge, threatening the intricate illusion veil I kept active around the clock. I did not want to see the unsightly scars marring my skin, the unvarnished monstrosity I kept hidden beneath layers of deception. I wanted to see only what the world saw.

With a sigh, I let the towel drop to the tiled floor and

squeezed my eyes shut, pushing away the growing dread coiling in my stomach. As a child, I had envied my mom's emerald-green eyes, but perhaps it was a blessing in disguise that I'd inherited my dad's deep brown eyes instead, the sole trait I got from him. Everything else was mom's—the warm, sun-kissed tone of our Mediterranean skin, the auburn hair that curled just so at the ends, the determined set of my chin, the charming slight gap between my front teeth that Miles once confessed mesmerized him after first seeing me smile.

My eyes opened. The illusion veil fizzled and dissipated from my head down to my toes. My reflection blinked back at me, the left side of my face a roadmap of dark, jagged scars. They began at my hairline, splitting my eyebrow in half before weaving down my cheek and jaw like a vine, then tumbling over my neck and collarbone, where they spread out into sinister rivulets and twisted branches that curled around my torso—both back and front—and trailed down my arms and left thigh. By some miracle my right leg and all ten toes remained thankfully untouched.

Some scars were superficial enough that generous amounts of a good concealer would mostly camouflage. But others were vicious, raised ridges of purple flesh, and deep, jagged hollows that no amount of makeup could hide.

Extensive energy went into maintaining the illusion veil cloaking my skin, but by now it was second nature, worn as effortlessly as a silk scarf.

I went to such lengths not out of vanity but necessity. Those scars bore the distinct signature of the illusion mage who had marked me when I was eighteen. To flaunt them would be idiocy, broadcasting my dangerous secret to every magic user who crossed my path.

Curiously, the sadistic bastard had warned me about that as well. The memory came flooding back every time I dropped my illusion shield.

I was eighteen, studying advanced warding spells in the dimly lit library of my childhood home in McFarland just south of Madison. Rain lashed against the windows, drumming a relentless pitter-patter against the backdrop of the storm-tossed waters of Lake Waubesa.

A dusty tome lay open before me. The arcane symbols on the vellum pages swam before my eyes as the night stretched into the early hours.

The illusion mage emerged from the shadowy portal that ripped open right in the middle of our family library without any telltale signs—no ripple of displaced air, no shimmering energy—slicing through my parents' carefully woven wards like they were cobwebs.

He was a daunting figure, shockingly tall and broad, dressed in a black trench coat. A dark mask obscured his face, two sinister eyes glistening through the eyeholes like black coals. Lightning struck outside the windows, flashing off the dagger clutched in his right hand.

The air crackled with an ominous energy as he strode forward, each step deliberate and heavy, his very presence a suffocating force that pressed down on me, a primal predator in human form.

"Where are they, child?" His voice rumbled, firm and drawn out, as if he had all the time in the world.

The library door burst open. My parents rushed in, alerted by the hostile surges of dark magic shredding their wards. Their eyes were wide with terror; my father clenched his jaw, a small tornado already spinning on his fingertips.

The mage leveled his dagger at them.

"Erin and Thomas Hilliard, First Order wind mages of the Madison Chapter," he hissed, his words slithering through the air. "Transgressions against the natural order have been detected on these premises. You've been meddling in affairs beyond your ken."

He flicked his wrist, and a bonding force slammed my mother and father back, pinning them against the bookshelves. My mother shrieked as the invisible restraints tightened.

I tried to lunge to protect them, but he tilted a finger my way, entombing me with a force that rooted me in place. My frustration swelled—a white-hot hate ignited inside my restricted core.

My father strained against his bonds, his eyes blazing with defiance. "We have committed no crime. The wind is ours to command, by birthright. The air is our domain, but you, dark mage... you are an abomination."

The mage's roar shook the room. "You bend the pure elements recklessly, without regard for consequence. You are a blight, and I am here to purge you."

The air around us stirred. Bookshelves rattled as wind kicked up within the library. My father's face contorted as he mined the depths of his geostrophic power, calling upon the currents of the night sky.

My mother's hair whipped about her face, caught in the grip of a forming cyclone. She slammed her palms back against the bookshelf, muttering a spell. Emerald runes ignited on her skin as she wove a shielding ward around me.

She offered her strength to the growing storm, her magic a silver thread intertwining with my father's power. The hurricane howled, breaking the mage's restraining bonds. Book spines snapped, pages wiggled into a frenzy, tomes flew off the shelves.

For a moment, the mage wavered. His billowing coat thrashed violently as the hard-bound tomes swirling in the air pummeled him.

With a snarl, he flung out his arms, invoking a counter ritual as he fought to assert dominance over the elemental fury. One raised hand clenched into a tight fist. The cyclone groaned as its furious momentum faltered. The winds my parents had summoned abruptly reversed course, slamming back into them with bone-jarring force. Books rocketed back into their places on the shelves as if reality had been set to reverse.

Thunder shook the windows. My mother's scream did not make a sound, her agony muffled by the shield she had cast around me. The air grew heavy, stagnant, succumbing to the mage's will. His power—the very power he had leeched from my parents—became a dark vortex that sucked the air from their lungs.

They clawed at their throats. Their eyes bulged. The vacuum stole every breath. The tears in my mother's eyes crystalized to salt rather than roll down her cheeks. My father fell... to his knees... lifeless.

"No!" I scrambled towards them, clawing at the flickering shield, but my mother's wards held true. I could not move. I could not do anything.

Fear raged, hot and acidic, burning in my throat. I reached out with my crude, fledgling magic, a feeble gust that dissipated as soon as it hit the shield.

The towering mage loomed over my parents' broken forms, the air shimmering with the heat of his stolen power. "Such a waste," he muttered.

I opened my mouth to scream, but my throat was stripped dry. My heart collapsed into jagged shards of shooting pain.

His head snapped about quickly like a hungry bird. He scanned all the bookshelves, then began a more methodical search, trailing his long fingers over the book spines. He plucked random volumes, files and papers with no discernible pattern and piled them on the floor.

A lit match appeared in his right hand. He tossed it on the pile, setting it ablaze. The flames hungrily devoured the knowledge and history packed inside those cherished texts.

His gaze darted to me. He considered me for a long breath, as if I was worth considering. The cruelty in his eyes emptied me of everything.

He raised two of his long fingers to produce a scalpel of raw energy that sliced through my mother's protective shield with surgical precision.

At last, my lips came alive. "If you mean to kill me, fiend, at least explain yourself. What crime did my parents commit? What laws have they transgressed to deserve such brutality? Huh, psychopath?"

"Silence, child," he said, his voice devoid of any inflection.

His magic struck me everywhere at once like a thousand pins piercing my skin, each one a red-hot point of pain. Guttural incantations ripped from his throat that felt like barbed wire scraping not just my flesh but into the very essence of my being, each word branding me with sizzling, swelling marks.

When the torture subsided, he regarded his handiwork with reverence.

"Commit this pain to memory," he hissed. "Consider it a doorway. I have bestowed upon you an immeasurable power. Yet it will not save you from the wrath to be unleashed should you be foolish enough to ever speak of me or this night's deeds to a single living soul."

The portal behind him yawned open again and swallowed him back, then vanished like a lost dream, leaving behind only the metallic scent of blood.

What entity could maneuver a portal with such ease and land it smack dab in the heart of our library? Until then I thought portal-walking within the confines of our own world was impossible.

Why was I spared? Why bother branding me with twist-ed illusion magic? I deemed him psychotic, his choices no more than a perverse form of revenge, an ultimate retribution against my parents, a sadistic legacy forced upon their only child.

He would be coming back for me. I felt sure of it. Why else would he forge me into this illegal weapon if not for his own nefarious games?

I was so much stronger now, hardened, and a portal-walker myself. The list of my skills was almost as long as the list of lines I was willing to cross for justice... okay, for *vengeance*. I could easily absorb magic, channel it and redirect it in controlled bursts, but what that asshole had done, the way he had reversed the fundamental essence of the wind into a suffocating void, blatantly defying both natural order and magical laws—that level of manipulation was out of my reach. I was still David. He was still Goliath.

He was leagues ahead of me in the power department, but power wasn't everything. My wrath was a weapon onto itself, a wellspring of untamed potential waiting to be tamed and directed.

Somehow, some way, I'll carve him into bite-sized morsels.

Eight years had passed, eight long years of hiding beneath veils of illusion magic. I pulled on an old, oversized t-shirt and loose black jeans and moved to the window. I pressed my forehead against the cool glass.

He never answered my question. What crime did my parents commit?

I wanted to sink into my sofa, dive into a cup of chamomile tea and bury my face in that slice of lemon cake I'd bought at the gas station last night, but the hour was already slipping away and soon I had to powder my nose and trudge my way back to the Bureau and all its tangled webs.

41

Chapter 5

THE ARCANE BUREAU'S BRIEFING chamber was a far cry from the high-tech conference room with panoramic lake views I had envisioned. Instead, I stood in a sterile windowless room with a long table bolted to the floor flanked by the kind of rigid plastic chairs designed to induce leg cramps. Three smaller tables huddled against the walls, one boasting an unappealing selection of tuna wraps, turkey subs and powdered donuts. Two steaming stainless-steel carafes offered some hope for decent coffee.

The real kicker though? The wards. Layers upon layers of them, woven so intricately that not even a whisper of air could slip through. Impressive, sure, but also a major headache waiting to happen. The room crackled with the reverberations of contained magic, a potent stew of supernatural energies swirling in the air like exhaust fumes. I'd have to focus every ounce of my defenses against inadvertently guzzling it all down in one toxic gulp. Getting drunk on magic wasn't on my bingo card. Not tonight—not if I wanted to maintain my anonymity.

"All these wards in a secure room inside an impenetrable fortress..." I muttered under my breath.

Miles didn't even throw me a side glance. "How about one more for your mouth?"

Prick.

The chamber prattled with hushed exchanges. I scanned the room, taking in the sixteen agents who already surrounded the table, presumably the Bureau's finest. Miles led me to two empty seats, his voice turning velvety as he exchanged pleasantries with a leggy, blonde blood sorcerer. *Of course.*

I mentally weaved through the throng of magic signatures: at least one telekinetic mage, a chronomancer, and four sorcerers of combat disciplines, their signatures tightly coiled springs. There was definitely a healer in the mix, a geomancer, a fire mage, an aeromancer, and something else—a seer with a distinct aura of precognition. Standard Bureau fare, for the most part, except for a discordant note: the cloying, cold taint of necromancy.

Across the table, the necromancer idly flipped a lighter between her fingers. She had youthful, almost delicate features and midnight hair pulled back in a tight braid. Her snug black dress did little to conceal the lean lines of her body. There was a slightly purplish tinge to her pallid skin, the result of too much time spent in subterranean crypts communing with the dead. Her pale blue eyes scanned the room with a detached intensity.

I would not touch her magic with a ten-foot conjured pole, let alone attempt to absorb or use it. Some lines were best left uncrossed.

All chatter died down when the Bureau Director strode into the chamber. Imani Harris was a woman who needed no attention but received it anyway. She was in her early forties, but toned and broad shouldered. Her flawless bronze skin stretched over sharp features, and silver streaks highlighted her otherwise black cropped hair. All of that created a breathtaking frame for her intense eyes that swept over each of us in turn as she settled at the head of the table.

She was a telepath, the most formidable I'd ever encountered. Her invasive energy slammed into the room like a physical wave, probing every mind for useful knowledge and guarded secrets.

As if the wards weren't taxing enough, now I'd have to scrape up every drop of discipline to shield my tangled thoughts from her scrutiny.

The aeromancer to her right, a lanky man with bleary eyes, stood up clutching a wooden clipboard. She snatched it without looking. The clipboard slammed down on the table with a dull thud.

"All division coordinators currently present?" she said. Her tone left no question as to who was in charge.

"Yes, Director," the aeromancer confirmed.

She gave him a curt nod. "Let's proceed through the agenda with a similar efficacy."

A holographic projection hummed to life in the center of the table as the first item blazed into focus.

The aeromancer cleared his throat. "A construction project in Seattle will commence within walking distance of the public library's Capitol Hill Branch."

Director Harris leaned forward. "A new tower breaking ground in close proximity to an interdimensional portal nexus is a recipe for disaster. Structural integrity and magical safeguards are paramount. Have the appropriate measures been implemented?"

Eww. That Capitol Hill Branch was infamous for housing not one but two active portals. The dilemma of high-rise structures popping up near portals had become a logistical nightmare in our line of work. Downtown Seattle, like Madison, was wedged between bodies of water and, therefore, teeming with interdimensional gateways. The more urban one of these water-wedged cities became, the more infrastructure headaches for Bureaus across the country.

Seattle's skyline, ever evolving with its rampant growth of skyscrapers, flirted dangerously with the stability of these portals. Skyscrapers, with their towering ambition, seemed to disrupt the delicate equilibrium between realms, stirring unrest and anomalies, more than any other human intervention. The juxtaposition of such high-rises and portals was akin to mixing fire with gunpowder—an equation ripe for combustible surprises.

The geomancer, a tall, tanned man with deep-set eyes, chimed in. "The Seattle Bureau is employing a dual-phase enchantment grid to stabilize the foundation. It's a complex operation, but within their capabilities."

Director Harris nodded, almost absentmindedly. "Do they only build behemoths there? That is a dozen or more in recent years and another dozen in the decade before that. Are they Babel fetishists? We all know how that ended. Let's reach out and make sure they have enough resources to prevent hundreds of portals rupturing. They have experience, but their resources are not limitless. What's next, Agent Louis?"

"Our underground links with the Singapore Bureau are fraying," the aeromancer said.

One of the sorcerers leaned forward into the light of the projection. "A proposal to enhance our ley-line transmissions has been drafted. It should offer us a more reliable connection, cutting through geo interference."

A flicker of something unreadable crossed the Director's face. Annoyance? Frustration? The Bureau's dealings with their Singaporean counterparts must have been less than smooth.

She tapped the clipboard with an impatient finger. "We press them harder. Singapore owes us cooperation, and Director Cheng will be reminded of that fact in no uncertain terms."

International cooperation—always a potential minefield of political posturing and veiled threats.

The third item on the agenda popped up on the holographic projection.

Lumina (World-328)

"We're seeing an uptick in error rates within Lumina," Agent Louis clarified. "This isn't just your standard technical glitch—it's a rift waiting to happen. We must address it."

A middle-aged man, his face etched with deep lines, tugged at the silver talisman hanging from a leather cord around his neck. It was designed in the shape of a swirling vortex. All portal mages wore such talismans. The tiny gemstones embedded on this one represented different elemental planes, which meant he was Edgar Rice, the head of Portal Operations. "Our team is on it, Director," he said. "We suspect a misalignment in the dimensional anchors. A recalibration is underway."

One would hope. Error rates meant breaches, and breaches in Lumina, a volatile place on a good day, meant potential interdimensional pandemonium. The last thing the Bureau needed was packs of carnivorous butterflies crossing the veils between the worlds.

"Speaking of error rates, our budget is stretched thin," Director Harris said. "The recent portal disturbances and increased surveillance demands are bleeding us dry. We need to reallocate resources—wisely."

A collective nod followed her statement.

"Right, let's prioritize our efforts towards stabilizing Lumina and bolstering our communications with Singapore," she concluded, seemingly ready to bring the briefing to a close.

Wait, what? This isn't even close to wrapping things up. What about the pomdor I practically handed over to them?

Miles's hand clamped down on my wrist under the table before I could open my mouth.

The chamber door flew open. An agent burst through with the alert energy of a predator on the hunt. He spotted Director Harris and made a beeline for her, leaning down to whisper into her ear.

Whatever he said, it turned her face into granite. "Thank

you, Agent Reynolds," she said, her voice clipped. "Assistants and shadows, please move to the front of the room."

Two men and a woman rose from their seats and herded themselves near the door with practiced discipline.

I stole a glance at Miles. His hands were now clasped in front of him, strong and sure, like the roots of an ancient oak. In his eyes I saw a... shrug.

Frustration boiled over inside me once again. Miles quickly cut me off with a glare. Resignation and defeat kept my anger at bay as I joined the other assistants. Were investigative shadows just glorified furniture? No, unglorified furniture would be more accurate. Did they expect me to just sit there like an end table while serious shit went down?

C'mon, Tess.

What did I expect? That they'd turn to me for suggestions?

"Detective Hilliard, in your infinite wisdom, would you care to enlighten us with your expert opinion on, oh, I don't know, how to charm a particularly grumpy portal into submission?"

Director Harris swiped a hand at the holographic projection. An energy shift pulsed through the air as a thick curtain of wards slammed down in front of me and the other shadows, effectively severing us from the rest of the chamber. Well, that explained the oddly Spartan room décor. Wards within wards, especially at this level of complexity, devoured neutral, colorless energy like a starving yeti at a buffet.

The Director launched into an exchange with Agent Reynolds, but all that reached my ears was a distant buzz. We were completely cut off. Might as well have been banished inside a broom closet.

Did Miles know this might happen? *The schmuck!* He had to have known. He'd dangled the Bureau briefing like a juicy carrot, knowing full well I wouldn't be allowed anywhere near the real meat of the matter. A small cruelty to amuse himself, no doubt. Shame on me for expecting more.

If only there was a sensory mage in the room, I could have used their heightened hearing to eavesdrop.

The room bubbled with tension. This wasn't just another briefing anymore—it was a full-on feud. The agents started to argue, gesticulate, abandoning their docile deference to their director.

This was pointless. They could have their playground squabble without me standing there doe-eyed like an idiot, watching through a translucent wall of wards. Comparing notes with Miles afterwards was the whole point. This was a complete waste of time. I should be on my sofa eating lemon cake.

I turned on my heel and reached for the doorknob. It budged with minimal resistance. They hadn't bothered keep-ing the door locked then. *Good.*

Slipping through the doorway, I stepped out into the car-peted hallway. My stomach rumbled. The Bureau might have its fair share of irritating bullshit, but it was also reputed to have a decent selection of adult beverages. A stiff drink with a strong kick was exactly what I needed right now. There was a bar somewhere in this bureaucratic labyrinth.

I set off down the hallway, scanning for any sign of the

elusive Bureau watering hole. Where was that blasted bar?

Rounding a corner, I spotted a man strolling leisurely toward me. My reflexes kicked in, sending a jolt of wind magic up my arm. I readied a few quick excuses on the tip of my tongue—*lost, bathroom emergency, missing file*—just in case he decided to grill me about my solo mission down the Bureau halls at this hour.

But then I got a better look at him. This wasn't your standard-issue Bureau agent, all crisp suits and tightly leashed magic. No, this man was something else entirely. He had an easy swagger and teasing eyes—the enigmatic stranger from the Sun Prairie library, the one who'd vanished into thin air, leaving me alone to deal with the portal chaos. *No fucking way.*

The sinewy strength visible in the broad set of his shoulders and the thickness of his neck hinted at years of disciplined physical conditioning. The bastard was more handsome than I remembered, his features a teasing mix of sharp angles and devilish allure. High cheekbones, full lips, a strong jawline, and a scar that slashed across his left cheek like a lightning strike, deep and jagged as if stitched in haste with brutal efficiency rather than delicate care, perhaps a battlefield souvenir. The scar lent a dangerous edge to his features, a hint of savagery simmering beneath the surface.

A wide grin crossed his lips as he met my confused gaze.

"You're still breathing," he said. "Wonders never cease."

"Yeah, no thanks to you."

He went stoic. "Self-reliance is everything."

"Spare me the dime store philosophy. You were at the Sun

Prairie library at the exact time that portal blew up. Timing is everything."

He raised an eyebrow. *"Je suis accusé?"*

"Yes, very much so! And you're not charming. You were involved in all that chaos, clearly. What were you doing at the library? And don't tell me you were there learning French."

He leaned in close, his breath cool and minty. "I was there to save your petite derriére. I'm the only reason you're standing here talking your shit instead of being enslaved or consumed in another dimension."

This dude. How delusional!

I bit my tongue. Confronting him about his magic lacking a signature would be the equivalent of waving a giant red flag emblazoned with *Human Magic-Signature Detector Here!* right in front of his face.

"No, really, why were you there?"

"Why were you?" he shot back.

Ugh. "Why do you think? To seal the portal."

He considered me for a moment. "The Bureau sent you?"

"That's so hard to believe? We're literally in the Bureau."

He shrugged. "We are, but you seem a little, um, unseasoned."

"Who should they have sent? Someone like you?"

His quick laughter pushed back his head. "They couldn't afford someone like me, sweetheart."

"Call me sweetheart again and I'll make sure you're consumed in another dimension, you arrogant chauvinist."

His eyes twinkled with amusement. "Feisty. I like them feisty."

"Oh, you do? Do you like them knocking your teeth out?"

Why am I threatening this rabid bulldog with violence?

I always felt ridiculous when I refused to back down, but I almost always refused to back down. I loved and hated that about myself.

He tilted his head, slowly assessing me. "I welcome you to try. It's amusing conceptually. Might I suggest another approach? Keep threatening me and see if it makes me laugh to death. That's your best shot, *sweetheart*."

I was about to go stupid with rage when a familiar voice thundered down the hall. "Step away from that douche!"

Miles. Of course. The goddamn epitome of perfect timing. His hand clamped down on my arm.

"Always the buzzkill, Donovan," the mystery man drawled. "Relax, your novice Bureau honey trap is perfectly safe. And not for nothing, she needs more training. You have a brand to protect, big guy."

I yanked my arm free. "First of all," I hissed at Miles, "take your hand off me. Second, we were just talking. I've encountered his kind before."

I haven't, but I enjoyed saying it.

And why was I not blurting out that this smug guy was the one who'd been lurking around Sun Prairie library? Was I starting to mistrust Miles?

Miles sneered at the stranger. "Killian Tierney never *just* talks, isn't that right, Tierney? There's always a deeper play lurking, always an angle."

The stranger smiled. Every word we said pleased him.

Killian Tierney... where have I heard that name?

"Perhaps the company man is right, little shadow," he told me. "Be sure to apply a cold compress to your bruised egos. Enjoy your clubhouse meeting." With a lingering glance in my direction, he sauntered away, his sure steps leaving a trail of unanswered questions.

I shook my head at Miles. "There's no need for the chivalrous Knight act. I can handle my own business."

"Tierney is toxic."

"Ya think? Then why, dear Knight, is he strolling right through your Bureau at night?"

Miles snorted. "It's complicated. As much as we want him far from Madison, we can't afford to drive him away."

"That chump? Why not?"

His voice dropped to a whisper. "Killian Tierney isn't your average everyday chump. He's an elemental warrior. His kind might be our last defense against a full-blown interdimensional invasion one day. And he's the head man of a whole damn clan of them." His phone buzzed in his pocket. He held up a finger. "Hold that thought. I need to take this."

That's why I knew his name. I only ever heard bits and pieces about them. Elementals were like urban legends. Most of us went about our lives never expecting to meet one and so never felt entirely sure they really existed.

We knew elemental warriors were in the history scrolls and that they were some serious, scary dudes. In the modern world they were no more than whispers, sad unicorns—reclusive, feared and shrouded in secrecy. When in their massive warrior forms, they were ominous forces of nature, walking battle machines capable of leveling city blocks with both physical and elemental might. The most powerful among them were said to possess the ability to morph into multiple elemental forms.

I remembered an old campfire tale of a warrior from a bygone era who could assume ten separate forms, each a manifestation of a primal element—a razor-sharp vortex of wind, a raging inferno capable of melting steel, a furious tidal wave, a creature made entirely of stone. When battling such a being, there would be no warning, no time to prepare. It would already be too late. The Elemental would cut you down with the untamable forces of nature.

I'd have given anything to get a taste of such power, a chance to channel that raw, untamed magic. I know, such desires were pure vainglory and an obvious gateway to breaking bad and becoming a villain, but just the idea of amassing that kind of transformative magic inside my body was intoxicating.

Power absorption is a compulsion that can become an addiction, a drug unlike any other. You get a high off the stolen energy, a sense of control that is both thrilling and terrifying.

I never expected to be in the presence of an elemental warrior, but based on the usual logic, I should have been able to snag a trace of his power, or at least a residual echo of his magic. And if not, I should have been able to sense the intricate weave of his defenses. That would have impressed me to the point where my guesses would have included Elemental Warrior.

I got nothing from Killian Tierney. Not a flicker, not a tremor. He could have been a human with a library card. I never heard of any prohibitions of elemental transformations or special concealment protocols. So why and how? The puzzle kept growing and more pieces were missing.

Information was the lifeblood of any illusion mage, but my knowledge of elemental warriors was about as deep as a city puddle. And, keeping it real, my knowledge of illusion mages was also limited, even though I was one. Having not been raised by an illusion mage, I was mostly self-taught, cobbling my education together from scraps—dusty volumes in forgotten corners, whispered rumors in murky alleys, my own mage instincts, as well as a bit of trial and error. Right now, my instincts screamed that an energy source as potent as an elemental warrior should have scraped my core like nails on a chalkboard. I mean, I could pick up faint echoes of magic from the other realms, but not from a guy standing two feet away.

There were two ways an illusion mage might fail to gorge on a magical smorgasbord surrounding them. The first was if the person in question was powerful enough to actively shield their power, a kind of magical lock designed to keep prying fingers at bay. But that would require instant recognition of an illusion mage's presence, which, considering the entire Bureau's blissful ignorance of my true signature, seemed unlikely. The second way... well, the second way was an ancient practice undocumented in the archives. There was a single mention of it, a single cryptic line about a *negation signature*, but that line was in a tattered, unreliable scroll filled with gibberish, recipes and rhymes written by a condemned man.

I needed to snap out of the rabbit hole. This distracting enigma wrapped in a chiseled rogue package was eclipsing the looming interdimensional crisis as my primary concern.

Miles finished his call. "Sorry about that."

"Was the pomdor discussed in the meeting?" I asked. "When do we tell them about the portal and the Codex?"

"No need. They knew already. There was a similar incident in Corinth."

Corinth. Another isthmus city, this one in the heart of Greece, a portal magnet since ancient times, strategically placed on the thin lines between worlds. If something was happening there and here, it was time to panic.

"How similar?" I pressed Miles.

He hesitated, running a hand through his hair. "Another Codex page torn out. Just like Sun Prairie."

I felt sick. I had clung to the flimsy hope that the portal malfunction might be isolated, a small glitch in the system, something the Bureau could easily fix. But now everything felt like dominos, a chain reaction about to happen, a shadow campaign orchestrated to dismantle the safeguards that kept our world safe. In my mind's eye I imagined the high-rises of Seattle falling against each other one after the other. Babel on steroids.

"There's a pattern here," I said, stating the obvious.

"A pattern," Miles echoed, his attention elsewhere, scanning the hall.

"I blame the giant, sentient hamburgers that flew out of the janky portal and exploded into confetti," I deadpanned.

"Nice image," he said. "Let's eat at the Nitty."

"Miles, what's up? Are you high? Have you seen a ghost?"

Director Harris rounded the corner, in perfect stride with a tall mage sporting a tightly braided beard.

I have always sucked at taking a moment for myself. Wherever I try to hide, people show up like it's World War Z.

Imani Harris begrudgingly considered me for a brief second, a faint acknowledgment I suppose, then turned to Miles. "Agent Donovan, a word?"

Miles nodded, pulling on a perfect mask of professionalism. "Of course." He cast me one last look. "Later, Ms. Hilliard."

I watched them saunter away and disappear round a corner. Something prickled at the back of my neck, that unsettling sense of being watched.

Killian Tierney lurked right behind me, just three feet away, leaning on the wall like he'd been there for a minute. A glint in his eyes made me want to give him a loud slap. The guy was not all there, he seemed manic, wild. He winked at me, then mouthed something incomprehensible.

My eyebrows shot up. *What the fuck?*

He repeated the words, slower. *We. Don't. Belong. Here.*

Chapter 6

THERE WAS QUITE POSSIBLY one thing worse than waking up from a restless night to find your fridge barren and your coffee pot bone dry, and that was Director Pankowski shouting in your face the moment you stepped into his office in front of his lead investigators—the snake Gideon Crawford included.

"What happened at the Bureau?" Pankowski barked. "What did they want with you?" The man had a talent for making an already dreary morning seem like day one of the apocalypse.

I shrugged. "Just a portal glitch. Standard Bureau business. They had me sign an NDA."

"NDA my foot! They slash our funding, then have the nerve to gag you?"

He was on his own thing now. My job was to listen.

"I received an email this morning. They're cutting budgets. Our commission's been gutted. Maybe they're only cutting ours. Yeah, they said budgets in the plural. I call bullshit on that. Smoke up our ass, probably. I don't know what to be-lieve." He crumpled up a sheet of paper and slammed it onto his desk. "Believe this, we're fucked. We couldn't run a lemonade stand on this pittance." He pointed his meaty finger at the crumpled document.

His eyes bore into me as if I somehow caused the problem.

I held my hands open. "Don't look at me. I was there to assist on a portal issue. I didn't hear diddly about money."

Pankowski glanced around his dim office at the dim furniture and the dim faces of his bored investigative team. "We are important to the Bureau," he proclaimed, trying hard to believe his own words. "We handle the cases they don't want to handle. We do the goddamned dirty work. Why would they hamstring us like this? Do you know how many sub agencies they work with?"

Before anyone could answer, he barreled on. "Not many, that's how many!" He hung his head, out of steam.

I knew his question was rhetorical, but I couldn't resist. "Correct, sir. Just three sub agencies in all of Wisconsin."

Pankowski's gaze snapped back up to me. A half-assed smile replaced his initial confusion. "That's right, Hilliard. Only three. They need all of us. And us more than those other two. At least more than Chippewa Falls. They can't afford to lose Shadow Chasers. We do damn good work. Now, get back to it, people! Meeting adjourned."

That was... quite the pep talk. Especially since we were in no way as essential as the other two sub agencies. They covered completely different parts of the state. We were just a few blocks from the Bureau.

I ducked into our breakroom to grab a can of cold seltzer. Might as well get one while the getting's good. Drinks would certainly be a budget cut.

Miles had not responded to texts, and my calls were going to voicemail. Was he ghosting me as some lame payback for our break-up two years ago, or was it because of whatever was distracting him last night?

Gideon blocked my way to my desk.

"I see you, Hilliard," he said. "Seems like you managed to slither your way out of questioning yet again. You fooled that old nitwit Pankowski, but I'm not buying it for a second. You said *diddly*. No one says that. Except liars."

"Is your sole purpose just to fuck with me, Gideon?" I said with zero energy. "Because you should really shoot for more."

I tried to skirt around him, but he shifted positions with preternatural speed to block my path. I could never win this duel. His kinetic magic granted him an unfair advantage when it came to reflexes. As tempting as it was to tap into his power and zip past him, I knew better. Revealing my illusion magic because of my temper would be my downfall someday, and I wasn't quite ready for that curtain to fall.

"I will find you out, whatever it is," he said. "And when I do, I will come to you and—" He laughed. "Nah, that would spoil the surprise. I'd rather you not see it coming."

The snarky retort that sprang to mind died on my tongue, replaced by an inkling of curiosity. "You're one sick puppy. What's your issue with me? Your paranoia is super extra. You need to go that way and knock on HR's door. You shouldn't let someone as insignificant as me live rent free in your mind."

He scoffed. "Don't flatter yourself. It's not about you, it's a principle. I loathe it when the unqualified try to worm their way into places they don't belong. You're leeches, sucking away resources from the qualified."

"Wait, am I a worm or a leech in this story?"

"You're a liability to the whole company."

"Sucking away resources, huh? Just look around you, Gideon. We're not exactly rolling in the dough. And your tacky leopard cufflinks probably cost more than my entire monthly paycheck."

I didn't wait for a reply. I *knew* they were *cheetah* cufflinks. With a shove that shocked even me, I rocked him back a step, my elbow hitting his ribs. Why did I even bother with him? Gideon Crawford was central casting for toxic male co-worker and not above using his power to manipulate.

I slumped into my chair, fuming. The radio silence from Miles grated on my nerves. My fingers hovered over my phone, the half-typed text message on the screen taunting me. I wanted to fire that text right off, but a rational impulse interceded. Another text wouldn't solve anything. It would only make me appear desperate.

I needed a distraction.

Pushing myself to my feet, I stomped over to Izzy's desk—as always, a microcosm of organized chaos. Scribbled notes shared space with a bag of torn open gummy worms, half-disassembled gadgets and three miniature potted cactuses. Izzy was hunched over her keyboard, her brow furrowed as she typed with furious abandon, a perfect match for her fiery red hair that was pulled back into a messy bun.

"That bad, huh?" she said without even looking up.

Oh shit. She sensed my foul mood. My carefully constructed core shield felt like it was made of Swiss cheese right now. I shoved some extra energy into the cracks, slamming the metaphorical door shut, before Izzy, the ever-perceptive empath, could glimpse any deeper. "It's whatever," I said. "What's new in the Izzy-verse?"

She finally lifted her gaze, her eyes widening at the sight of my face. "No deflecting. I can see by your eyes you're morphing into a raccoon. The night was just as bad, huh? Silly sleepless girl. Taking everything too seriously."

I nodded. "Everything's ridiculous."

She leaned back in her chair. "Starting with you, yes. Tell Izzy everything and then start fresh after that. It's only morning. The day will bring you unexpected gifts. My mother liked to say that."

"Your mother never met Gideon."

Izzy erupted into full-blown laughter. "Thank goodness for that. Even she couldn't turn that guy around. He's stuck on scuzzball."

No argument there. I wouldn't wish that self-important amoeba on anyone's mother. I should, literally, reduce him to a single-celled organism—it might help deflate his ego. But alas, magic ethics and all that.

"Any new cases today?" I tried to feign curiosity but failed.

Izzy reached out and patted a cactus with a tenderness

usually reserved for a purring cat—or perhaps a cuddly baby porcupine. "Sorry, hon, nothing exciting came in. Let's see, we got a run-of-the-mill case of a—" She paused as she rummaged through a pile of disorganized notes. "Yes, here we go, an elderly lady convinced her neighbor's geraniums are practicing mind control."

A thrilling case of floral telepathy. Hard pass.

"Guess I'll catch up on some paperwork then," I said with a sigh.

Izzy shifted in her chair. "You know, for someone who supposedly can't lie, you're a real enigma. I can track a person's emotional state from a block away, but you? You're an emotional black hole. No mood deviations, no sentimental ripples—just static." A playful grin lit up her face. "Tess, are you an A.I. or are you actively blocking me? I have politely never asked."

Uh-oh, landmine detected. I plastered on a smile. "Of course not, Iz. Shielding isn't exactly my strong suit. If I was blocking, you'd know."

She wasn't buying it. "I remember your first day here. Pankowski boasted that you aced all your Spells and Shields courses at the Academy, both offensive and defensive. Doesn't scream weak shield wielder."

Ugh. Pankowski and his motivational speeches.

"It's not that I'm shielding others. Maybe I'm shielding myself against even *having* deep emotions. Being numb inside gets a bad rap."

"Everyone has emotions, Tess. Trust me, I often wish they

didn't." She tapped her head. "Empathic emotional overload in here sometimes."

I shrugged. "I'm not still in shock about the night my parents died or anything like that. I choose to be this way. I am actively isolating myself from being annoyed, let down and betrayed. I'll choose a life of reason over a life of madness every time."

Izzy's playful demeanor vanished. "Tess, I didn't mean to—"

"It's nothing," I said. "The day's just begun, you're right."

I waited for her breezy response, but she hesitated. Confusion and concern shaped her expression.

"I'm weird, but you knew that," I said to fill the air.

"Everybody knows that," Izzy said, giving me my space. "So, what plans do you have for Thanksgiving?"

"Hot date." Wow, I was on autopilot.

"Right. So, that's basically nothing."

Ouch. Direct hit.

"Yaz and I are having a small gathering at our place. We'd love to have you and your plus one," she said.

"My *plus one*? You're mean."

"Luckily, you don't have feelings. But, also, I was serious. Don't just joke about it. Go on a date. Even A.I. robot girls need a distraction. That's what this whole conversation was about, right? To give you a distraction. A date would work better."

The thought of a homecooked meal and companionship was undeniably appealing, but... empath... illusion mage...

alcohol... a recipe for disaster.

"Can I come without a date?" I said.

"Don't be dumb. Just come. It's nothing fancy, just mounds of food, questionable humor, and not a single mind-controlling geranium. Seriously, consider it, you freak. It'll be fun."

"Okay, maybe. I'll think about it. Thanks."

Izzy sighed. "Tess, I'm not daft. I know you're not going to do that. Your response is always the same—*I'll think about it.* Having dinner with friends doesn't mean you'll get hurt, hon. Relax a little. You might enjoy yourself."

I saluted her in a mock military fashion. "Yes, ma'am."

How pathetic am I?

Growing uncomfortable, I headed for the door. She had me cornered and I wasn't sure how to handle it.

"Hey, Tess," she called out.

I paused, turning back on my heel. "What is it?"

"Everything okay over at the Bureau?"

"Yeah, just a case. It's classified."

"Should I be worried?" she said, her eyes locked on mine.

"Why would you think that? The Bureau is handling it as usual."

The words sounded unconvincing. I hoped my shield was up and running because I sucked at lying, and Izzy could sniff out a falsehood faster than a bloodhound. I started to realize she could do that even without her powers.

MOST OF THE MORNING I sorted through paperwork, but my mind kept circling back to Miles, to Killian Tierney and the missing Codex pages. The shrill ring of the office phone shattered that disturbing loop.

The Caller ID read *Arcane Investigations Bureau*. I lurched for the receiver, my heart hammering against my ribs. "Shadow Chasers, can I help you?"

The female voice on the other end was clipped, efficient, devoid of all pleasantries. "Detective Hilliard? This is Administrator Moore from the Arcane Investigations Bureau. This call is to inform you that your services will no longer be required. Effective immediately. The case has been reassigned. We appreciate your involvement. Have a good day."

The line went dead before I could utter a sound.

Chapter 7

THE PLAY OF TREE branches outside my window sent the morning light flickering across my small kitchen table. That usually helped keep me calm as I ate breakfast and anticipated the day ahead, but it was day two of waiting for any contact from Miles and now those spastic flashes of blinding morning sunlight unnerved me.

I called the Bureau five times. The first three attempts went straight to voicemail, then someone answered only to inform me there was no Arcane Bureau at that number, just a *Research & Development Institute*. The fifth call finally yielded a female voice acknowledging I existed. "Detective Hilliard, how can I assist you?"

"I need to speak with Special Agent Miles Donovan," I said, laying on my sweetest sugary voice. "It's important."

The response was swift, not a hint of hesitation. "Coordinator Donovan is not currently available. Perhaps you could try again tomorrow?"

And... she hung up. Their customer service was sorely

lacking, but then again, I was more of a stalker than a customer.

If I had a gold doubloon for every time someone at the Bureau withheld information, obfuscated the truth, or flat-out lied, I'd be a pirate by now. No way was I backing down without a fight. The whole thing reeked of a coverup.

Nine o'clock sharp found me strolling up to the Bureau's front entrance. The security guard, a mountain of a man with a shaved head and a fixed scowl, took one look at me and wagged his index finger *"no"*.

"Turn around, ma'am. Building's closed to visitors."

Wow, they blacklisted me already? Okay, if they want crazy...

"I'm here to see Special Agent Donovan," I protested.

The guard's scowl somehow deepened. "Make an appointment."

"I have an appointment."

He grunted and turned to the comms device strapped to his shoulder.

"Wait, look, I technically don't have an *appointment* appointment," I conceded, "but there was an implied appointment."

"I don't know what that is, but it's not an appointment."

"Trust me, he'll definitely want to hear what I have to say."

"If true, it'll be easy to schedule an appointment."

"So, he's here, sounds like?"

"That's privileged information, ma'am. You'll have to leave now." His voice boomed with a level of authority that promised to physically remove me if I did not comply.

I mumbled and retreated to the safety of a park bench across the street. From there, I had a clear view of both the front entrance and the parking lot. Miles would come or go eventually, and I would be there when he did.

Settling in for a long and tedious stakeout, I pulled out my phone. Foresight had never been my forte. I should have grabbed a thermos filled with steaming coffee and a good detective novel.

It wasn't too long before a familiar silver Audi sedan with tinted windows darted into the parking lot. Gideon Crawford slithered out of the driver's seat.

What's the toxic twat doing here?

Honestly? I couldn't care less. This new development was a particularly fortuitous stroke of luck. I left the park bench, eyes tracking Gideon as he trotted up to the entrance. I lay in wait, then trailed behind at a safe distance.

He exchanged a few terse words with the security guard, then flashed some kind of credential. The moment the door swung shut behind him, I hurried after. I needed to keep as close onto Gideon's trail as possible if I wanted to tap readily into his magic. Gideon was gifted with both kinetic and persuasion powers. It was the latter I needed.

The guard's face flashed a *"you-again"* expression when he spotted me.

I plastered on a smile that must have landed somewhere between manic Tasmanian devil and deranged Hello Kitty. My illusion radar stretched outward, searching for Gideon's distinct dual signature. *Got it.* Latching onto his magic core, I pulled just enough persuasion magic to nudge the guard in the right direction to let me through the door.

"I'm late for an appointment with Coordinator Donovan," I said, my teeth flashing my forced grin.

The guard was uneasy on his feet. "I'll... I'll call your name in."

"Don't bother. I've already texted him I'm here."

The guard stared at me, unsure. I could picture the gears in his brain skipping and locking. I flashed my Shadow Chasers' badge as if that was all the confirmation he needed.

He nodded sheepishly. "My apologies, Detective Hilliard. Go ahead."

"Aww, you're a doll," I said with a wink as I hurried past.

Assist... Gideon. I guess he's not completely useless.

Once inside I took a steadying breath, then searched for Gideon's dual signature. That persuasion mojo is good magic to have when busting into hostile territory. Once the initial enchantment faded, that security guard would realize his lapse and come looking for the intruder.

The Bureau teemed with a churning sea of signatures crashing against my senses in chaotic waves. A whole tsunami of them stormed my magic core all at once, Gideon's included. The sneeze I let loose was loud enough to wake the ancient vampires rumored to slumber in the Bureau's sub-basements.

Vampires didn't bear a signature since their supernatural state wasn't innate like ours but acquired. You could, however, count on a necromancer or two skulking in their vicinity. For better or worse, the cold tingle of necromancy was never difficult to discern—a sickly, unsettling signature that raised the fine hairs on the nape of my neck.

I reined in my core's defenses to filter out the excess energy flooding my system and focus in on Gideon's magic.

As I approached the signature sensors leading deeper into the Bureau, I offered the next security guard another semi-deranged smile. With a subtle pulse of persuasion magic, I diverted his attention just long enough to skirt around the scanners unimpeded. No need to tap into my illusion magic. For now, I would ride Gideon's coattails.

The reception area was staffed by a somber, round-faced woman whose name tag identified as Anita Sommers. Her head lifted as I approached, followed by one meticulously groomed eyebrow arching inquisitively.

"I'm trying to locate Special Agent Miles Donovan," I told her. "Could you direct me to his current whereabouts?"

Her expression turned impassive as the enchantment took hold. "Agent Donovan hasn't been in since Tuesday evening. That was..." She pursed her lips, struggling under the strain of the persuasive compulsion. "Yes, two days ago," she concluded as if solving the world's most elusive math equation.

Tuesday night... I knew it. I wasn't going crazy. Everyone was aware of his absence. Where the hell had he disappeared to? Did the Bureau send him somewhere? Had something happened?

The Bureau clearly knew more than they were willing to share. If that was how they wanted to play, I had no choice. Unconventional times called for unconventional methods.

I had told myself I wouldn't push things, yet here I was, pushing like a madwoman on a bulldozer. I dug deep into Gideon's reserves and borrowed a hefty dose of persuasion before he slipped deeper into the labyrinthine building and out of my reach.

"Would you be so kind and point me in the direction of the Director's office, Anita?" I asked the bewildered receptionist.

Anita's gaze faltered for a beat before refocusing. "Director Harris? Of course! One moment." She produced a glossy visitor badge. "Let me stamp your clearance."

A few keystrokes later, the printer whirred to life, dispensing a sticker inscribed with *LEVEL 5 CLEARANCE* that Anita applied to the badge.

"Take the elevator to the fourth floor," she said. "The Director's office is at the end of the main corridor, through the double doors."

"You're an absolute gem, Anita."

I clipped the badge to the lapel of my faux leather jacket, turning on my heel to hurry to the elevators. By the time I reached the fourth floor, I had lost track of Gideon's signature. It was all on me now.

I pressed onward down the hallway, keying into the strongest paranormal signature radiating from the upper level—the Director's unmistakable telepathic signal. If Imani Harris knew what Miles was up to, her thoughts would be a fountain of information, and I was more than willing to use her power to take the plunge and drink from the wellspring of her mind.

At the end of the hall, I stood in front of a pair of oak double-doors that loomed like imposing sentries, carved with elaborate warding runes.

I pressed the security push button. A harsh buzz resonated.

"State your business," a voice demanded through the speaker grill.

"Here to meet with Director Harris," I said. "I have clearance."

The silence was so protracted I hit the button again, but in the same moment the heavy doors swung inward with a low groan to reveal a tall woman in a charcoal pantsuit regarding me with disdain. "You have no appointment scheduled nor do you possess the necessary clearance."

And yet you came to the door for this. What are you people hiding?

The woman was a basic spell conjurer, her abilities limited to rudimentary wards and summoning incantations. There was nothing in her core arsenal I could use to get past the door.

Screw it. I'm down to moxie.

"I've got an urgent message from Special Agent Miles Donovan!" I boomed, hoping my words rang out loud enough to travel past the doorway and deep into the warded office. "There's much at stake. I must speak with the Director."

That did the trick. The same mage with the braided beard that had escorted Director Harris when she came looking for Miles slid past the pantsuit lady. His pale eyes expressed a similar extreme doubt.

"A message from Agent Donovan?" he inquired.

My mouth felt dirt dry. "Yes, how many times do I have to say it? It's urgent. I must deliver this to Director Harris herself."

He chewed on that. I sensed my bluff crumbling. He turned and walked back through the doorway, leaving it ajar. His disembodied voice found me as if from a dream. "Follow me."

That actually fucking worked. Wow.

I stepped into Director Imani Harris' luxurious office. Dark mahogany bookshelves lined the walls, overflowing with hardbound tomes and antique artifacts. An enormous, rounded, floor-to ceiling bow window consisting of six panels overlooked the shimmering expanse of Lake Mendota.

Director Harris sat behind her desk—an impressive slab of flawless, polished cherrywood. She pinned two cold, severe eyes on me. "Yes?"

"I'm Tess Hilliard. An investigator with Shadow Chasers. Agent Donovan—"

"Right. Brought you in to assist on a minor portal matter," she finished my sentence for me. "I'm aware."

"I wouldn't call it a minor—"

"I understood your services were no longer required," she said, speaking over me once again.

"About that, I have a message for you..." *What exactly could that message be? What would Miles want me to say?*

All signs of patience drained from her face.

"Agent Donovan insisted that I be reinstated immediately."

"Did he now? And did he do that from the grave?"

The words slammed into me like a physical blow. I stepped back.

I heard that wrong. I must have.

"He called me last night…" I realized I didn't know what I was saying.

"Ms. Hilliard, whoever communicated with you was not Miles Donovan. His body was recovered for an autopsy yesterday morning. He died of natural causes in his sleep the night of the special briefing you attended with him."

She's lying. I'm being played.

"Natural causes? No. No way. He's as strong as an ox, a picture of health…" The protest died on my lips, replaced by an aching dread.

Her words drilled into my skull, refusing to be dislodged. *Miles… dead? Why is she saying that? It can't be…* The walls began to tilt and close in. *If Miles is gone… what does it all mean? Someone must be responsible. A healthy young man doesn't just die without violence… an accident… a killer…*

Director Harris leaned back in her chair, scrutinizing me with those piercing black eyes. "Ms. Hilliard, I must ask… why are you really here?"

I settled on the only truthful answer I could share. "Miles went dark after the briefing. I came looking for him."

"You and Agent Donovan… were you close?"

It's all a fabrication to throw me off track. But if her mind harbors key evidence… if there's even a shred, I will find it.

My shield flickered, opening my core's pathways. The Director's powerful signature churned. I pulled her telepathy to me, then redirected it deep into her own mind. I hit a barrier—a dauntingly potent energy shield. Pushing harder, I extended my illusion power like a fishhook, piercing her defenses.

Her memories overwhelmed me, a torrent of unbearable pain. My magic shrieked in my ears, or perhaps it was the ragged scream of my own sanity fraying. I became a singularity, an all-consuming rage.

Fragments flashed into my mind—faces, snippets of conversations, reports, security rosters, case file reviews... and the stark, visceral image of Miles's mutilated body.

The backlash of that certainty crushed me, severing the connection like a snapped cable. The pain destroyed me, body and soul. Miles was not only dead—he'd been savagely, mercilessly butchered.

The enormity of it all emptied my lungs. My knees weakened. I became absently aware of Director Harris watching me with increased suspicion.

She may have pondered I had turned her own power against her, but I don't think she would let herself believe it. The fact that everyone sold me short was one of my superpowers.

With the tattered scraps of composure I had left, I made it to the door.

"Ms. Hilliard?"

"Sorry for the interruption."

I floated through the office spaces, down corridors, around corners, into the elevator, out the main door. I was disconnected from my legs, my arms, the world around me, myself.

The world blurred. I wiped tears away like they were not my own. I kept going, kept moving, wanted nothing to be static or certain or permanent.

Miles was gone. That would never change, never move, never end.

Chapter 8

The silky surface of Lake Mendota mirrored the crisp autumn morning sky. Walking the length of Tenney Park Beach usually cleared my mind, but today my thoughts were a tangled mess. Miles had reentered my life when I least expected it only to be viciously ripped away forever.

The muted thrush of passing cars on Sherman Avenue buzzed like a frenzy of dive-bombing bats. How many bridges had I just torched? I had for sure incinerated any goodwill Director Harris might have possessed. Would I even be allowed to set foot inside the Arcane Bureau again?

Where to from here? It's all so pointless.

A tickle of unease crept down my spine. A trail of magic, too faint to identify, hung in the air behind me. I was not alone.

Play it cool, Tess.

I forced my legs onward, fighting the urge to spin around. If I stopped or looked back, the stalker would know I was on to them. Without breaking stride, I flexed my left calf to feel the reassuring shape of the dagger sheathed inside my boot. Miles was the reason I carried it. He made me practice the cross-body draw motion more times than I could count. My blade would land in their throat before a thought could land in their head.

The possibility of violence felt like a warm embrace.

I quickened my pace, shoving my hands deep into my jacket pockets. A lone jogger bobbed past, offering a polite nod.

The tree line along the lakeshore path thickened. I darted behind the thick trunk of a bur oak. Pressing my back against the rough bark, I listened closely, my breath misting in the chill morning air. Each rustle of leaves, each distant bird cry, amplified in the tense silence.

There it was again. That uneasy feeling. *Eyes watching.* I took a slow peek. Nothing seemed out of place, yet the phantom energy signature lingered.

An orange flicker confirmed my fear. A tall figure solidified from thin air, the remnants of a concealment spell swirling around his feet like smoke.

My reflexes kicked in, my hand a blur as I bent my knees, gripped the boot dagger and hurled a heat-seeking underhand throw.

The blade glistened green with bonshek, a rare, gooey toxin capable of shutting down one's magic for a few crucial moments instantly upon contact. The blade ricocheted off the intruder's thigh before sticking into the trunk of a Slippery Elm.

The man yelped and stumbled backwards as blood trickled from his sliced open pants. The viscous toxin seeped into his superficial wound. I took advantage of his shock to barrel into him, spinning away to reach for the elm tree. I retrieved the dagger and swung it around to press up against the soft hollow of the man's throat.

Engaging a mystery magical foe was a gamble at best, but right now I had entered the zone of not giving one single solitary fuck.

"Speak fast," I hissed, pressing the cold steel against his skin.

His pupils dilated with uncertainty as the bonshek did its work, draining him of his magic. "Wh-what did you do to me?"

"Gave you what you deserved, stalker."

I studied his face—young, barely out of adolescence, with a mop of unruly dirty blond hair, tall, a lanky frame and a raw, almost comical bewilderment. Doubt tugged at me. He wore a worn denim jacket, cheap jeans and beaten sneakers—not the typical gear of an assassin or a Bureau operative. This dude made me think of skateboards and vape pens. Was I really strong-arming some hapless kid right now?

"Let go!" he spat through gritted teeth.

Holding the knife to skater boy's neck gave me a creepy vibe, but releasing him could prove disastrous, especially if the bonshek's effect wore off and he turned out to be a supernatural thug. Once again, I was operating blind. His magic had no signature—an alarming, all-too-common occurrence lately.

Ugh.

"Bonshek," I said, enunciating each syllable. "Ever heard of it?"

He said nothing.

"It's a toxin that neutralizes magic." *No need to mention the brief nature of its effects. Leverage is king after all.* "Helps level the playing field."

"Lady, I'm unarmed, and your blade is at my throat. Not exactly level."

Fair point. "Answer my questions, and I'll consider reversing the spell."

His eyes narrowed to slits as he calculated the variables. "What? I don't have answers. Someone wants to talk. My job was to get you there."

"Get me there? That's called kidnapping, bro."

"Kidnapping? No. I have something to show you. That's it. This was supposed to be simple. Not paranoid *knife ninja* shit." He inched his fingers toward an inner jacket pocket.

I kicked him. "Uh-uh. You'll lose those fingers. I wasn't born yesterday. Whatever you got in your pocket, I'll be the one taking it out."

He threw his hands up in surrender. "Fine, go crazy."

Keeping him pinned with the dagger, I slid my fingers into the worn fabric of his pocket. Paper crinkled under my touch. "Take it out," I told him.

He fumbled with an envelope, his fingers stiff and uncooperative. Finally, he extracted a photograph and held it before my eyes.

The image staggered me. Miles lay sprawled out on a bed of wet leaves, his pale face covered in blood and bruises. His fashionable clothes hung in tatters, revealing a horrifying glimpse of mangled flesh and bent bones. Bile scorched the back of my throat; my thoughts crumbled, refusing to fully make sense of the stark brutality of the murder scene.

I clawed out a few syllables. "Who sent you?"

He flipped the photograph over. A single letter, *K*, was scrawled in thick, crimson ink on the back.

Killian Tierney.

Why did that psycho send a boy? Unless... Was this skinny brat one of the elemental warriors in Killian's clan, his unfathomable power anchored to the primordial forces of nature? That would explain his cloaked signature.

My dumb luck... I was ten minutes from the comforts of my loft and twelve minutes from crawling into my bed where I could bury myself in a tangle of blankets and pillows.

That path is ash on the wind now.

I sheathed the dagger in my boot, the weight of the hilt nestled against my calf once more. "Lead the way."

Was I walking into a trap? More than likely. I didn't know shit about Killian Tierney, but one thing remained certain—the man never did anything without cool calculation and dead-eyed precision.

I heard Miles in my head, warning me about him. *Toxic... always an angle...* But I couldn't walk away. I'd unearth the truth about his violent end, one bloody fingernail at a time. I'd never stop digging, even if it meant traversing the darkest of paths... even if it proved to be my own grave I was digging.

THE TUNNEL SNAKED ENDLESSLY, our boots thudding with each plodding step. Humidity beaded on the polished stone walls, catching the flickering light of mounted torches lining the passage.

My dread mounted as I followed a complete stranger down a secret stairwell and into a damp, subterranean labyrinth beneath the historic University of Wisconsin Armory known as the *Red Gym*, a 19th century castle-like structure made entirely of red-brick complete with crenellated towers. The claustrophobic passage widened into a vast grotto.

The vaulted ceiling soared some thirty feet overhead, a magnificent dome crafted from the same aged stone as the walls. At the center of the grotto, wide steps led down to a steaming sunken pool. The pool easily spanned 50 feet in diameter; its turquoise waters radiated a preternatural luminescence.

"Behold the last remaining bathing chamber of the legendary Therian King," a smooth, baritone voice announced.

My gaze snapped towards the sound, landing on the lone figure sprawled languidly on the steps at the far end of the pool, bottom half under water. Even from this distance, an unmistakable aura of power and menace clung to Killian Tierney like second skin. His lean, muscled frame was a study of sharp angles and rugged symmetry.

I tamped down the sliver of alarm that skittered through my core. If this cunning bastard held any answers about Miles's fate, I would play along with his twisted games as long as necessary.

"I'm assuming Donovan told you who I am," he stated. He rose from the steaming waters stark naked, carelessly draping a towel around his hips.

I raised my chin to avoid directly staring at his exposed manhood. "No, he seemed unimpressed and uninterested."

He scoffed. "Woof... your acting will need to improve if you are ever to become even a minor asset in the clandestine arts."

Oh, the arrogance!

He circled the pool with a predator's easy lope, closing the distance between us with measured strides. His wet skin glistened over sinewy ropes of lean muscle. The jagged scar on his left cheek was not his only blemish. Deep furrows and poorly healed gashes sketched a violent history on his powerful torso. Claws, I realized, serrated blades, axes... the brutal legacy of battles fought with medieval savagery, worn like insignias of high honor.

Oh boy. "Would you mind putting on some clothes?"

A wolfish grin played across his lips. "That was my intention."

In a practiced motion, Killian shed the towel and swept a pristine white ceremonial silk robe around his shoulders, tying the belt at his waist. In the flickering torchlight, his features remained unreadable, his eyes radiant with a glowing hunger.

The man's presence was flammable, threatening to ignite.

Proceed with caution, Tess.

My young escort sidled up to Killian and whispered in his ear.

The shift in Killian's expression was instant as he emitted

genuine surprise. "Bonshek? You used the magic-eater? Really? How did you get your hands on that?"

"Family heirloom. Limited edition, single ampoule."

"And you wasted precious drops on poor Aiden here?" He clucked his tongue in mock disapproval. "You're a dangerous little thing, aren't you?"

Little? Don't rise to the bait, Tess... Don't smack the satisfaction right off his pompous face...

"That's Investigator Hilliard to you."

His mouth curved into a half-grin. "I do relish a woman with teeth."

"Dude, I didn't come to this creepy basement to trade adolescent barbs with a toxic warlord, or Therian King, or whatever the hell you like to call yourself, playing dress-up in his secret bathhouse. Let's cut right to it. You knew about Agent Donovan... how?"

"When a top dog supernatural is murdered, it's my business to know."

"Yes, but you know details. The Bureau's cover story is that he died suddenly in his sleep."

"Unimportant. What's important is to uncover the identity of his killer. That's where our interests align, Investigator Hilliard."

I mulled that over for a moment. "You're after the identity of the killer?"

He nodded.

"Why? You made it very clear that you loathed Miles."

Killian Tierney assessed me for a few breaths. "My feelings

for the victim are irrelevant. My gut tells me someone's playing a very dangerous game and trying to pin this murder on my people."

I blinked. "Your people? You mean elemental warriors?"

Who in their right mind would mess with elemental warriors?

Besides the possible exception of me.

Whatever. Killian Tierney had my undivided attention.

He arched an eyebrow. "You're sweating, Investigator Hilliard. Don't be shy, the water is perfect. You can shed those constrictive clothing layers and have yourself a spa break."

Jeez, dude.

"I'm just fine."

It is *fucking humid and hot in here.*

"Were you his woman, by the way?" he asked with studied detachment, as if the question held no more weight than an inquiry about the weather.

His new title... King of the Chauvinists.

"I'm entirely my own woman, Mr. Tierney. And why exactly are you gifting me with all your close-held truths? What's the angle?"

"The Bureau won't let me or my people anywhere near the evidence surrounding Donovan's death. Clearly, they have not crossed us off their suspect list. You, however, might have a little more wiggle room."

"Wiggle room? I'm afraid I'm persona non grata at the Bureau just now. I have zero wiggle."

"Ah. But when you get your resourceful little claws out,

anything's possible. Like today when you waltzed into the Bureau. And, also today, when you used rare and potent toxins on unsuspecting youngsters... Tsk tsk tsk... for shame, Investigator."

Okay, maybe asking to be addressed by my job title wasn't my best idea.

"How did you know about the Bureau? Did you have me followed?"

That wolfish smile stretched wider. "Just since Donovan's unfortunate demise. You see, you are the only person of which I'm aware who cared two shits about the fallen Agent. And you clearly possess the will and the wiles to access restricted areas like the Morgue."

Of the two insinuations, caring for Miles struck a deeper nerve, rekindling a hollow ache. "Come on, Miles had people and I wasn't one of them."

It can't be true, can it? Miles had always been fiercely private about his personal life, but he had people. Of course he did. I realized I had never even asked him about that.

Killian spread his arms in an expansive, all-encompassing gesture. "Well, if he did, he kept them hidden."

Change of subject, please.

"If I start snooping around the Bureau, I'll become a suspect myself. That might work in your favor. In fact, that's probably what you're hoping for with all this. Frame the new girl. I'm an easy target, right?"

A flicker of irritation tightened the austere lines of his face. "*You?* And where would you be hiding beastly claws capable of inflicting such butchery? You'd never be the suspect for this, Investigator."

He extended his hand, that damning photograph gripped between two fingers like one might hold an old receipt. The horrific image of Miles's ruined body assaulted my senses.

"So, *you* must have claws capable of it," I countered, "if they consider you a suspect."

In a display of impossible transformation magic, his hand began to elongate and distort with a series of sickening pops and snaps. Smooth tanned skin morphed into thick, overlapping plates of scarlet scales. Knuckles swelled grotesquely before erupting in a shower of arcane sparks. In their place, a series of curved obsidian talons punched through flesh, each one nine inches of razor-edged lethality.

The monstrous manifestation of an elemental warrior's true form should have triggered primal terror. Instead, I found myself gaping at him in unsettling fascination, a nauseating vertigo twisting my gut as Killian flexed and unfurled his partially transformed extremity, the movement as effortless as stretching his fingers after a long day.

What dark wonders this world holds.

Before I could process the implications, my hand shot out. My fingertips brushed against the dragon scales, seeking the telltale fever print that would reveal his magic signature. An elemental warrior of Killian Tierney's colossal power could easily mask their essence even from an illusion mage like me, but it was possible my touch could cut through it.

The torrent of magic fueling this partial transformation

seared my own magic core. Touching him exploded light through my mind's eye, like I was witnessing the birth of a supernova at point-blank range.

I gasped, yanking my hand back as if scorched by molten lava.

My reaction transfixed Killian, his unnerving human eyes sparkling against that monstrous dragon hand.

"To fight monsters, you must become one." He flexed his talons with a soft crackle, then his hand seamlessly morphed back into human flesh.

He reached out, a single finger tilting my chin, forcing me to meet his stormy gaze. "Tell me, ingénue investigator, what kind of monster are you? No mere mage can pierce the essence of an elemental warrior while in flux."

Shit, he knows. He felt me probe his elemental essence.

I stumbled back, shaken. It was beyond fear, though there was plenty of that. I was astonished. The visceral power I had sensed in his transforming state was vast, a primal awareness of a cosmic force held barely in check.

And now he was toying with me, putting on a deliberate display of overwhelming dominance.

Transformation magic to my understanding was a gradual process, requiring immense focus and meticulous energy control. Killian Tierney had just shifted into that chilling hybrid form on a whim without so much as breaking a sweat.

My survival instinct swelled. I fought off the impulse to turn tail and run—to put as much distance as possible between myself and this self-proclaimed dragon king holding court in a steaming throne room.

Then again, considering I was in the lair of a man who seemed more at home conducting business half-naked in a bathhouse than fully clothed in a boardroom, a warlord directly descended from the Primals and who could transform into the rarest of elemental forms, a freaking red dragon, combining air, fire and kinetic powers, perhaps blind escape wasn't the best course of action.

Under his intense scrutiny, my secret felt more fragile than ever. If he discovered what I truly was, if he even suspected, he might decide to dispose of the dangerous aberration, or cage me as a novelty pet, or do who knows what to me.

I had to throw him off my scent. Cooperation might be the only way out.

"I can't make any promises," I said, swallowing down the knot lodged in my throat, "but I'll see what I can do."

He winked. "There it is. That's the old college try."

How old does he think I am?

"Right. Yeah, okay, so... time to get to work, I guess," I said. "And one more thing: no more following. It's a dealbreaker."

"You have my word. Aiden will escort you out."

He snapped his fingers. Aiden appeared like a conjured genie.

Killian stroked his chin thoughtfully. "Perhaps I should confiscate that bonshek knife." His lips quirked in a sardonic smile. "Oh well, I'll trust you not to resort to such intimidation with my young liaison in the future."

I shook my head. "Aiden will receive no harm from me." My

gaze swept over the grotto one last time, taking in the glistening stonework and the pool's ethereal glow. "I'm curious. How old is this place?"

"Tamelin the Fierce, the first Therian King, commissioned the construction of these bathing chambers in the early eighth century BC. There have been several renovations since."

"Therian? As in therianthropes? The original shapeshifters?"

He let out a derisive snort. "Inferior primitive forms, lacking the potency and control of true elemental mastery. Erratic. Unreliable. No finesse. We're the true Therians."

Touchy touchy.

"And does that make you the new Therian King? Should I call you *Your Grace?*"

He shrugged. "If you wish. *Killian* works just fine. I'm not one for archaic honorifics." A playful glint surged in his storm-colored eyes. "You're more than welcome to try the waters, by the way. Quite replenishing, I can assure you."

Was an insinuation buried in there somewhere? "Appreciate the offer, but roasting in saunas isn't really my thing."

I didn't wait for his response. Turning on my heel like my ass was on fire, I marched towards the tunnel entrance where Aiden waited. I shot a glance back over my shoulder. "What is Aiden's elemental form?"

Killian's grin stretched wider. "Embers. A work very much in progress, I'm afraid, still learning to control the flame within."

I followed Aiden's lanky frame through the tunnel and out

of that stifling cavern, the image of a half-naked Killian Tierney bathed in a luminescent glow preserved in my mind with disturbing clarity.

Embers, huh? How does a man go about turning into embers... oh, the dragon, how could I forget about the dragon?

Chapter 9

KILLIAN'S MONSTROUS DRAGON HAND and its razor-sharp claws played on an endless loop in my mind. Why reveal his primal elemental form to me? His choices confounded me as I found myself back on the familiar bench across from the Bureau. I scanned the faces filtering through the entrance. A different guard stood at the checkpoint today—a small stroke of luck.

After the unexpected help I got from Gideon yesterday, I figured it would be a matter of time before another useful signature popped up on my radar, and I was ready to bend all rules, cross any line to get to the truth.

An unsettling realization took root—Miles had stumbled upon an ugly truth, a deadly secret that ended his life. Someone powerful stood to lose everything and killed to protect their high station in life. The list of suspects was long, including rogue supernatural factions, high Bureau officials, even Director Harris herself.

My phone buzzed. Pankowski. I'd called in sick, again.

I silenced the call.

A middle-aged woman in a sharp pantsuit and high heels crossed the parking lot. *Jackpot.* Invisibility magic.

I jumped to my feet and tailed her, dipping between two parked SUVs like a shadow as she approached the security guard.

Against every sense of self-preservation, like a mindless moth drawn to a deadly flame, I channeled my clandestine magic to conjure the slightest of illusions—a vibrant arc of light, not exactly your standard rainbow, because I could never remember the color order, but close enough. It stretched across the ground like a bridge of orange and red and green and indigo light, settling in the space between the invisibility mage and the guard, shimmering with an almost hypnotic pulse.

"How can this be?" the woman said, startled.

The guard turned his full attention to my faux rainbow.

It was the opening I needed. I latched onto the mage's core like a leech, extracting tendrils of her invisibility power, absorbing it like a sponge. The stolen magic coursed through me, melding with my own essence.

I watched, both awed and appalled, as my hands glistened and faded, morphing into liquid mercury. In the blink of an eye, the refractive effect rippled up my arms, torso and legs until I vanished completely from sight.

It took longer than I hoped, three or four seconds. If my transformation was noticed, I would soon be in a cell deep in the sub chambers of the Bureau.

Invisibility magic was the ultimate illusion. It didn't truly turn you invisible—rather it manipulated light to create a deflective dome that steered people's eyes away from you. My own illusion powers couldn't sustain the integrity of the deflective dome for long without constant infusions of invisibility magic.

I sprinted up the wide steps and slipped unseen through the Bureau's front doors, falling seamlessly into step behind the mage who unwittingly shared her magic with me. I skirted the security scanners and made straight for the visitors' lobby, searching for the building directory. Killian had hinted at a restricted Bureau morgue, and what better place for it than the vast basement levels underneath my (*very invisible*) feet?

The directory was a confusing mess of acronyms and opaque official jargon for most departments, but the entire underground section was labeled with a succinct "B", an absurd understatement given the sprawling expanse of the basement levels. Navigating what was below wasn't going to be easy.

The only way down was the staff elevator at the back of the lobby. Time was of the essence. The fragile invisibility illusion wouldn't hold much longer. The mage veered away from the reception area. I drew closer to siphon a fresh dose of invisibility.

My heart hammered in my chest as the mage left and I made my way to the elevator. I lingered back until it arrived and slipped through the opening door, pressing myself into the rear corner to avoid any unintended contact with the other two occupants—a hydromancer and a conjurer. As the door closed, I leaned against the cool metal wall. A small security camera in a corner was fixed on us like an unblinking eye.

The elevator shuddered to a halt and the doors slid open on Basement Level Two. A long, sterile corridor with white, uninviting walls stretched out before me. The grooved metal flooring of the elevator gave way to reinforced concrete. The oppressive, harsh glare of the light fixtures overhead seemed intentional, as if coordinating with the rest of the stark décor to set the tone for an industrial-scale detention facility.

Solid metal doors with small viewing windows stared across at each other down the hallway at regular intervals. At the far end, a large red sign marked the location of a staircase. I padded down the hallway with soft, measured steps, glancing at the doors to my left and right—offices, labs, storage rooms. Nothing obvious to suggest a morgue.

I hurried down the flight of stairs to the next level. More bleak and silent corridors. A door swung open revealing a brief glimpse of a lab before snapping shut again as I clung to the wall waiting for a hydromancer to pass.

My invisibility veil flickered. I drained every scrap of magic left to maintain the illusion just a bit longer. Without another magic signature around to latch onto, my options were dwindling.

Another flight of stairs led me deeper underground. The air grew colder with every step. The echoes of my light footsteps whispered off the walls.

Every floor and every turn revealed more identical passages, each indistinguishable from the last. Up ahead, a healer mage in crisp white scrubs moved toward an unmanned security checkpoint. He swiped his ID card after a retinal scan and handprint verification. I quickened my pace and slipped through the checkpoint right behind him, close enough to snag a second ID badge clipped to the side of his pocket.

I ducked into a small alcove behind a file-laden trolley, pressing my back against the concrete wall. My borrowed invisibility flickered once… twice… three times, then sputtered out completely. Relief washed over me as the tremendous strain of carrying all that excess energy left my core.

My attention jumped to the badge in my hand. High clearance.

Yes! Let's eat.

With a dash of illusion and a pinch of nerve, I swiped my hand over the printed name morphing it to mine. Using illusion magic inside the Bureau, let alone inside their covert underground lair, was pushing my luck. But, hell, I was in too deep, and luck was all I had. Walking out of the Bureau undetected would likely be a fool's errand, but slinking out empty-handed would mean I'd risked it all for nothing.

If I fail, I'll fail spectacularly.

Badge prominently secured to my jacket, I straightened up and stepped out of the nook. Scanning the hallway, I caught a glimpse of the healer mage's white coat disappearing around a corner. He was my most promising lead yet, so I trailed after him at a safe distance.

He turned down a narrow passage leading to a reinforced steel door. Stark red lettering screamed a warning.

Morgue – Authorized Personnel Only.

A sudden chill as I neared the door gave me a shiver.

The healer mage keyed a code into the keypad lock. The door slid open. Charging in after him, badge flashing, wasn't an option. He'd for sure expect me to input my own code, and even with the stolen badge, he'd likely question my identity and assignment. Without telepathy, hypnosis or persuasion signatures around, I had no chance to talk my way past him.

The heavy door shut behind him, leaving me staring at the steel barrier like a chump. All that effort, all that risk, and I was still locked out. Knocking seemed like a spectacularly stupid idea and fiddling with the keypad was a guaranteed security alert.

"I can help you with that," a female voice said, startling me.

I whirled around. My hand reached for the dagger in my jacket. A woman stood there, her features partially obscured by a gray hood, but the energy her signature radiated was unmistakable. The necromancer from the briefing. Her ice-blue eyes dissected me with a detached yet razor focus.

I eyed her warily. "You surprised me... have we met?"

Her lips twitched, as if suppressing a smile. "Really? Are we playing that game? Okay, let's play. We met at the Bureau briefing. I'm an associate agent, a forensics consultant specializing in the Archives of the Undead." She shook her head. "That's not an official title, no one's ever called me that, let's just say I'm the resident expert on all things undead and spooky."

I laughed, trying to act social. "I bet you've seen Nightmare Before Christmas a lot."

What the hell am I saying?

"Twenty-seven times straight through," she said, proudly. "Also, the Corpse Bride. Anything involving Tim Burton, really."

"Wow, that's a lot," I said like the least social person ever. "Is this your gig, then? The morgue? Doesn't get any spookier than that."

"It does get spookier than that, but it's not, no. Not my zombies."

"Okay, well—"

"Don't worry, I'll get you inside. You've come a long way to sneak a peek at your friend's corpse. Nothing is more intimate than that. No judgement."

My eyebrows shot up. "My friend?"

"That type of news travels fast. Every Bureau agent knows by now of your... complicated history with the late coordinator. You're all the buzz."

Brilliant. As if I needed another office fan club who secretly despises me.

"So, you must run the Bureau's rumor mill, too, then."

"Only on Fridays. Ms. Hilliard, don't you worry about what other people think. That's no way to live. Now, let's get you the rest of the way in. We wouldn't want to look suspicious standing outside the door."

I tightened my grip on the dagger. Every instinct urged me to leave. This was clearly a trap. I knew my new *bestie* couldn't be a necromancer. Although with my life lately, that sounded about right.

I nodded. "Yeah, sure, lead the way."

Fuck it. Might as well go down in flames.

She pushed back her hood to reveal striking purple hair with silver highlights shifting like shadows under the light—not the midnight black ponytail I'd seen at the briefing. With a swift motion, she punched a series of codes on the keypad, and the door groaned open.

"After you," she said, extending her hand toward the entrance.

I stepped through the threshold into a chamber far larger than I expected. The clinical whiteness of the walls contrasted with the deep green linoleum that covered the floor. A row of stainless-steel tables ran down the center of the room.

The air carried a sharp antiseptic tang that did little to mask the underlying scent of blood. Embedded in the right wall were ten refrigerated body drawers. Along the left wall clear-view cabinets were filled with medical instruments and forensic tools, each item labeled and placed with precision.

My stomach twisted a little at the austerity of it all, but I choked back the looming nausea and followed the necromancer to the reception counter.

The clerk glanced at our IDs (*thanks again, healer mage*) and tapped away at his tablet.

"The subject rests in room 38. Go right ahead," he said, moving quickly on to other work.

We shuffled past the rows of tables, our steps quiet, almost reverent. At the far end of the room, a flight of stairs descended into a smaller chamber. A lone healer mage hunched over a computer terminal. Multiple screens displayed data points, graphs and what appeared to be autopsy reports. Harsh fluorescent lights cast an unforgiving pallor across the chamber, reflecting off another series of examination tables.

"He's here," the necromancer said, gesturing at the place with a sweep of her arm. "Not exactly a cozy psychologist's office, but this is where the dead tell tales if you know how to listen."

Two figures lay sprawled on separate tables. The first was vaguely serpent-like, its scales shimmering with a metallic sheen that changed tint as the light angle shifted. Multiple limbs sprouted from its torso, each ending in delicate, hand-like appendages. Its eyes were closed, but the size and shape suggested a vision adapted for a darker, perhaps underwater environment.

The second creature bore a more humanoid form but with skin that appeared almost translucent. Beneath its surface, a network of blue veins wove an intricate, mesmerizing pattern. Its head was devoid of any hair, and its open eyes, oversized and unblinking, were a vivid violet that stared vacantly at the ceiling.

Both lifeless forms, clearly rogue visitors from another dimension, were preserved for study. Their presence underscored the Bureau's extensive interdimensional operations, with the morgue serving as a central hub where specimens from beyond our world were studied and catalogued.

Why, then, is Miles's body here?

We halted in front of a heavy-duty steel door.

A long horizontal handle stood out, designed for easy operation even with gloved hands. A small, double-paned window was frosted over from the icy internal temperature.

The necromancer tugged at the handle and ushered me into a compact room constructed entirely of metal. A covered body lay motionless on a table bolted to the floor.

Arctic air hit me like a punch in the face. My teeth chattered. I rubbed my hands quickly along my arms to keep warm. The necromancer handed me a thermoguard—a silver, heavily insulated but surprisingly light suit, designed to fit snugly and maintain body heat.

I quickly slipped into the suit, the material hugging my body like soft wool. "Any leads?"

"That would be above my paygrade."

The idea of Miles lying there underneath that gray sheet made my entire body ache. I knew it was irrational, but I wanted to swaddle him in blankets to protect him from the cold.

"Where was the body found?" I said.

"That's privileged information, but you might find something interesting under that sheet if you stole a peek while I'm not watching."

My breath caught in my chest. I would have to look at the body.

Of course, Tess. Why else are you here?

"Were you close?"

The question caught me off guard. "Once upon a time."

"Didn't work out?"

I shook my head.

She nodded, understanding—or pretending to. "You've got five minutes."

I stared at her. "Why are you helping me?"

"Someone's framing this as a vampire job. It wasn't."

Interesting. That's exactly what Killian said of elemental warriors.

"How can you be certain?"

"There's a glaring inconsistency in the evidence. The wounds mimic a classic vampire attack—claws slashing through muscle and down to the bone, teeth gouging out chunks of flesh, it's all there, except no major blood vessels were punctured prior to death—no arterial spray patterns that typically accompany such ferocious attacks. Even pet vampires who control their urges would at least have a taste. But here, there is absolutely no sign of blood drainage. If I were a betting woman, I'd wager they'll point the finger at vampires first, necromancers next. I'm not about to let my kind be the fall guys, and I can't act on that information, because I'm bound by blood oath not to oppose the Bureau, but..."

"But *I* can," I finished her thought. "I've heard that before."

For the first time irritation flashed onto her pale face. "I thought you wanted to get to the truth. If you need anything, come and find me."

"How? I don't even know your name."

"Rae Van Zelst, but you can call me Raven. It suits me, don't you think?"

I rolled my eyes internally. *Cute.*

She handed me a folded paper. "This is my number. It's untraceable. You might need a friend, Tess, someone you can trust."

Trust a necromancer. What could go wrong?

Necromancers kept vampires as pets, for fuck's sake, and even those supposedly unbound vampires maintained a powerful connection to the necromancer who helped birth them. How many of these *pets* did my new friend Raven keep in her basement?

The door thudded shut behind her. I was alone with Miles, my heart hammering in my chest. I steadied my breathing and peeled back the sheet. What lay beneath was a patchwork of torn flesh haphazardly stitched back together, dark hematomas and mottled contusions, bones visibly snapped in half. His face, that once handsome, familiar face, was unrecognizable.

If not elemental warriors or vampires, then what vicious entity could have taken out Miles, the most formidable of elemental mages, with such brutal efficiency? It was not possible for a single adversary to overpower him to this extent. There had to be multiple assailants. Why didn't he fight back? Where were the signs of his magic? Shouldn't there have been another body or two that he took down during the battle? The pieces just didn't fit.

I resisted the urge to run away and held back my welling tears. I picked up the clipboard lying beside the body and flipped through its pages.

Miles was found on the trail leading out to Picnic Point just before midnight on November 14th. The estimated time of death placed the attack between 10 and 11 pm.

Amidst the clinical notes, there was mention of *LPS residue* and a *modular brand*—terms that eluded my understanding. On page three, someone had hurriedly scrawled a note about an *unknown signature on site*.

Not much to go on, but it was a start.

What could have compelled Miles to venture out to Picnic Point in the dead of night? Was he there on Bureau business?

I traced the body with my gloved fingers, searching for residual signature remnants, though finding residue after so much time had passed seemed unlikely at best. As my fingers brushed against his right biceps, I registered a faint wave of energy radiating from it—illusion magic and it wasn't mine.

Someone left their slipper.

I pulled the illusion magic to me, unraveling it like threads of silk. The veil dissolved, revealing deep, jagged scars running from his wrist to his elbow. These were different than the rest. They were older, healed scars identical to mine... hidden beneath layers of illusion magic... just like mine.

I don't understand.

Who had done this to him? And did this magic belong to Miles? Could he, like me, somehow wield illusion magic? Or had he enlisted the help of another to conceal his scars? Either way, it had to be recent. During our time together, I'd seen Miles stark naked under the glare of bright lights. There were no scars then, no veils of illusion—I'd have seen right through that.

I carefully examined the rest of his body, searching for anything hidden beneath his injuries. There was nothing, only endless brutal wounds.

Could my old nemesis, the very same illusion mage who marked me, be responsible for all of this—the vicious attack, the branding, the illusion veil? He definitely could have overpowered a mage of Miles's caliber, but for what possible motive? Even if he'd uncovered my connection with Miles, what did he stand to gain? Miles knew nothing about my past.

The more I pieced together, the less the pieces fit.

Miles's death was likely made to look like a savage assault to cast suspicion on vampires, elementals or even beasts from other dimensions. The question was, to what end. If the goal was to cover their tracks, wouldn't a simple staged accident have been far less conspicuous?

The list of suspects was growing—rogue elemental warriors, bloodthirsty vampires, the Bureau and, at the top of the list, the sinister illusion mage himself.

Most of that list had already tried to convince me of their innocence, but why me? This was not my case. I held no great significance to anyone.

I'm just me. I'm Tess. I'm no one.

Chapter 10

Picnic Point peninsula jutted out nearly a mile onto Lake Mendota. When you walked its wooded trail, it narrowed the farther out you went, so eventually you saw the lake through the trees to your left and the lake through the trees to your right and the lake just ahead as you neared the tip of the peninsula.

It was singular and spectacular and profoundly life affirming. How could they kill and mutilate Miles here? Here where we used to rendezvous on the same stone bench on which I now sat hunched. We came here on cold winter nights to train when the trail was quiet. We harnessed the harsh wind elements whipping across the lake, a skill I was supposed to have inherited from my parents but had utterly failed to master.

Back then, I was a wide-eyed student at the Runestone Academy, and Miles was a charismatic guest instructor specializing in using elemental magic to secure interdimensional portals and, ultimately, travel through them, not to mention making every girl in the class swoon—including yours truly.

It was impossible to forget the first time I saw him. Miles entered the lecture hall wrapped in a sharply tailored suit and a roguish grin. His raven dark hair was immaculately combed back, not a strand out of place. He looked less like a seasoned mage and more like a GQ model who had stumbled into the world of magic—the irony, of course, being that beneath that charming façade lurked a man capable of immense destruction.

Elemental magic flared around his fingers like mischievous will-o'-the-wisps. If you brushed against him while he harnessed the elements, you could suffer frostbite or third-degree burns or worse, depending on his mood, which, as I would soon learn, could turn on a dime.

The lake still smelled the same, the trees still rustled the same, but nothing would ever be the same again. I closed my eyes.

Miles Donovan, may you find peace on this very path where you were savaged while the city all around turned its eyes away.

The bitter frost of the stone bench seeped through my jeans, biting into my bones. Time seemed to slip and twist and stretch like an amorphous blob. Seconds bled into minutes... minutes into hours. The possibility of sensing his etheric aura at the murder scene paralyzed me. I didn't want to get too close.

No amount of magic could call back a life, no spell would bring back a soul, no incantation would whisper breath back into his lungs. I wasn't in love with him anymore, but the memory of love carries its own wound.

A faint dusting of snow swirled. I felt the cold in my bone marrow.

Drawing in a deep breath, I pushed myself off the bench to walk on stiff, frozen legs. The trees along the path, now mostly bare, reached up to the gray sky. The crisp air carried familiar scents of damp soil and decaying leaves.

A few feet shy of the peninsula's tip, I stopped cold in my tracks. Miles had never reached his destination. Instead, he had been ambushed at this very spot. They found his body right here. I had no doubt about it.

The scene was near pristine. No traces of blood, no odd scents in the air. There were no uprooted trees, no cracked earth, no seared foliage. No signs that Miles had put up a fight, not a single hint of his elemental magic. Yet something was off. If I wasn't so finely attuned to subtle supernatural echoes and prints, I might have walked right past it.

The leaves, those last defiant clusters of autumn oranges, reds, and yellows, were too neatly gathered on the ground, like someone had painstakingly raked them into a pattern, then pressed on them with unnatural force to keep them glued together.

I crouched down to brush aside a few fresh leaves to inspect closer, searching for any lingering magic residue. Director Harris had likely dispatched a cleaning team to sanitize the crime scene, but they'd focused on the physical evidence and didn't bother with a micro scrub of all possible magic prints. They couldn't have anticipated that Tess Hilliard, the human signature sensor, would come sniffing around.

And there it was, pulsing faintly—a fever print, several fever prints, too weak to pinpoint a specific source or signature, but undeniably foreign, possibly nonhuman. An unfamiliar brand of magic, a puzzling calling card left behind by his killers.

I mapped the scene in my head. The residue patterns painted a grim picture. The attackers had approached from the point, their path converging on Miles here. The fact that he hadn't attempted to fight, shield himself or flee suggested that he knew his attackers. Maybe they were who he came to meet. Yes, they lured him here, peacefully, then cut him down.

I could almost picture him standing under the moonlight, his face contorted in disbelief as they came at him from all sides.

The residue trail led me to the Point where it hit me like a Mack truck. A magic signature unlike any other, stronger, more pervasive, suffocating and... strangely familiar... especially since I'd felt it for the first time only yesterday.

It was the unforgettable aero-pyro-kinetic-who-knows-what-else power signature of Killian Tierney. But how? Had he come to investigate the crime scene? But then, how did he know this was where it happened? According to him, he had no access to the Bureau's reports. Unless... unless he was the attacker, he and his army of elemental minions, in which case, what the hell did he want with me? Was I some sort of pawn, unwittingly doing his dirty work for him? Well, yeah, I was that either way.

The hairs on the back of my neck prickled. If the Therian King was involved in the murder, bringing him to justice would be a suicide mission. Miles would have counseled me to stay as far away from Killian as possible, he would want me to snap out of it, get smart, be careful, but how the hell was I supposed to turn a blind eye when the evidence pointed a giant, red arrow in his direction? There was no way I would ever back down.

I do have a morgue report to share with Mr. Dragonhand.

The eerie whistle of the wind through tree branches startled me. I turned and marched back down the path. Snow fell in thicker clumps now, filling my vision with swirling white. My fingers ached and I couldn't feel my nose. I'd been out in the cold too long.

By the time I reached The Red Gym, dusk was settling, my breath came in short pants and my entire face had numbed from the cold. The goliath Armory and Gymnasium building with its Gothic gables and turrets held the promise of warmth, looking as inviting as a crackling fireplace beside a Christmas tree.

Quickening my stride, I pushed the door open and stumbled into the entrance hall. A wave of warm, heavy air overtook me, shocking my frozen body, making me shiver from the clash of hot and cold.

I kept moving, navigating the main hallway that branched off into various offices and classrooms.

My heart thrummed a nervous rhythm in my chest as I closed in on the narrow, spiral staircase that led down to the basement. My fingers brushed against the cool, rough stone walls as my eyes scanned for the door Aiden and I had used to access the hidden tunnels and bathhouse grotto.

The air down here was colder, the light dimmer. I went past some old equipment to the spot where the door should have been, but there was no entrance, no passage—just a damp, stone wall.

I surveyed the space again, noting the familiar column adjacent to a pile of wooden crates thickly coated with dust. This was definitely the right spot. I ran my hands over the wall again, searching for any lingering magic echoes.

Nothing.

The door we went through wasn't your typical portal, of that I was certain, but it might have been enchanted. If it was sealed with Fae spells, well, I was out of luck. My sensing abilities didn't extend to detecting or unraveling the elusive, often capricious Fae magic.

Damn this cursed day! Am I always to be at that psycho's whim?

I stormed out of the building back into the biting evening air, my nerves frayed. The streetlights came aglow one after the other, casting long shadows over the thin film of snow blanketing the sidewalk.

The prospect of trudging the city streets back to my place was becoming a grim reality. *A car.* Gods, my kingdom for a freaking car.

Grim and dim and shabby and cruel. This world.

My whole life was defeat. All my thoughts were surrender.

Fuck surrender. You know where you can find a car.

I shook my head, getting more pissed by the second.

No, I don't.

Something with functioning heat and a working radio.

Shut it, you irritating voice of inconvenient truths.

With each step, my frustration grew. I started to feel eyes on me. Every shadow seemed to hold a hidden threat.

Killian's presence loomed like a monstrous storm hanging over my head. The man oozed raw power and whispered violence with every breath. Reaching out to him felt like a deal with the devil, but I was out of smart options. I needed answers, no matter the cost.

A man leaned against a tree up ahead, blocking my way. Snowflakes swirled around him in a mystical dance. He wore a black t-shirt and skinny jeans clinging to lean but toned legs, his denim jacket slung over one shoulder with casual defiance of the cold.

He tracked my every step. I was so tired and cold my sensors were shot. I hadn't registered Aiden until he was practically in my face.

My gaze snagged on his left arm. It pulsed with a smoldering glow—embers, his elemental form on full display.

What now? A magic flex-off? Is he jealous that his king showed off that dragon hand to me?

I must be some sort of magnet for the disgruntled, a designated dumpster for damaged magic egos.

He took a step back, eyes narrowing.

Ah, he's wary of my bonshek dagger.

"You should join the Eskimo club, Aiden. You know, those Cheeseheads who walk into icy lakes with their shirts off.

They're the only ones who'd be impressed with your little display."

"Don't know what that is," he stated flatly. "Killian is waiting."

Hallelujah.

"At the bathhouse? I just came from there. The Red Gym must have eaten the door. It's gone."

"Not the bathhouse, Ms. Hilliard. You've been invited to the Therian Helm."

I read his face trying to spot a tell, to see if he was lying. "Therian Helm? The elemental stronghold? No one goes there."

My mind conjured images of a sprawling fortress teeming with elemental warriors glowing and shining with powers untold. The place was more legend than reality in my mind since I was a small schoolgirl.

Either I had gone mad, or I was dreaming. If it did exist, I would be stepping straight into the maw of the beast, most likely right where the Therian King wanted me. Awake or asleep, I wanted to see the Therian Helm and I wanted to find out who killed Miles. I also wanted to figure out why Killian Tierney was at the murder scene.

Aiden flashed me a grin. "Consider yourself lucky, Investigator. Very few have ever crossed that threshold."

Funny, I don't feel lucky.

He was lucky he was young and dumb.

Chapter 11

WE DROVE FOR AN hour in near total silence, punctuated only by Aiden's grunts and the whistling of the wind as we approached Devil's Lake State Park.

The quiet drive had done little to soothe my growing anxiety. The landscape grew rugged and wild, with towering, snow-covered bluffs casting menacing shadows across the winding roads.

As Aiden swerved onto a narrow dirt path, a gray structure came into view in the headlights, perched precariously on the edge of a cliff overlooking the icy expanse of Devil's Lake. It looked more like an abandoned lodge than the seat of a powerful elemental clan.

"This is it?" I muttered under my breath. "The Therian Helm?" The name promised more than decaying wood and chipped paint.

"Patience, Investigator," Aiden said.

He drove through the rusted gate. The scene rippled like a heat haze as we must have breached an enchanted veil. Fae lanterns glowing an eerie green winked into existence, bathing the lodge in an otherworldly light.

The gray walls shimmered and shifted, shedding their disguise to reveal the real Therian Helm—a breathtaking fortress woven into the landscape. Towering spires of obsidian stone pierced the sky, each crowned with a blaze of elemental fire that danced like specters against the twilight sky. The walls, carved from the very bedrock, seemed natural extensions of the earth. The fortress melded ancient design with the raw, untamed energy of the landscape, making it seem as if it had been drawn out from the ground and sculpted by ancient gods.

Lush ivy, glowing faintly, clung to the stonework. The main gate was wooden and adorned with carvings of mythical beasts and elemental symbols.

The air was charged with tension that caused static on my skin, filled with whispers of ancient magic and the untapped energy of the elemental beings that dwelled within.

The old Toyota Camry sputtered to a stop. Aiden got out and opened the door for me. The arched fortress windows were all dark, except for one brightly lit up in the central tower.

I swallowed. What I felt was awe and I didn't like it. I needed a clear head, not wide-eyed wonder.

Easier said than done. The Therian Helm wasn't just a place; it was a monument to elemental splendor, a fortress so steeped in magic and history that it overwhelmed the senses. More than a stronghold, it held the weight of an empire, a declaration of unmatched power.

Aiden threw back his head and let out a long, high-pitched

cry, his hands glowing with smoldering energy. A chorus of howls and shrieks answered him as flames erupted from a row of windows.

The earth shook under my feet with a primal force. If this was meant to intimidate, damn, it worked spectacularly.

Now would be an excellent time to flee, but my only escape route led straight back into the wilderness.

When the fiery exhibition apparently came to an end, Aiden gestured toward the fortress. "This way, Investigator."

"You guys really like your pyrotechnics, huh?" I quipped. "This place must be impressive on the Fourth of July."

Aiden didn't enjoy my musings one bit. *His loss.*

I followed him up the marble steps to the main gate. The immense door swung open, and Aiden led me through to an inner courtyard, awash in the kaleidoscopic glow of Fae lanterns.

To my right, a spire rose into the evening sky, carved with the image of a red dragon coiling around the tower's length. The beast's mouth gaped open, lit from within by an inferno that caused the stones to smolder.

I tore my gaze away from the hypnotic dragon-wrapped spire. We crossed the courtyard, and the prickling sensation of unseen eyes watching me, studying me and assessing me made my skin crawl. Every corner seemed to hide an elemental warrior waiting for a single misstep, and I was armed with nothing but my wits and an overriding fear.

The primordial power humming through these ancient stones raised the fine hairs on my neck. I was entering Killian's domain, and whatever game the Therian King played, I had no choice but to meet it head on.

I trailed behind Aiden through an archway into a large rotunda crowned with a vaulted ceiling and iron torch sconces on the walls. We ascended a spiraling stone staircase, emerging into a wide hallway. The onslaught of ancient enchantments and centuries-old wards made my head spin, the elemental power resonating through me like a dull ache.

Staying upright took monumental effort. I knew it had all been orchestrated, down to every calculated detail. Killian Tierney wanted me cowed and off-balance before I even laid eyes on him.

Fat chance, dragon king.

The heavy wooden door at the end of the hall creaked open as the wards subsided. I stepped into a grand chamber bathed in a haunting violet light.

Elemental warriors lounged about on plush furniture casually dressed—some honed their swords, others sparred or lifted weights. These men and women were descendants of the Primals, their lineage as ancient as the Titans.

A blue fire crackled in a large medieval brazier near an arched window. The concentrated magic hit me like a physical blow, a tsunami of primordial power. *Too much.* I couldn't decipher individual prints and the combined energy overload staggered me.

Across the chamber, a ramp led up to an elevated dais where a massive throne sat beneath looming stone arches. And there, draped casually over the throne in a studied display of nonchalance, was Killian Tierney himself.

The Therian King stretched like a cat luxuriating after a feast. His movement highlighted the sinewy muscles beneath his form-fitting black t-shirt. His expression was of bored indifference.

He flashed a grin when he caught sight of me. "Ah, our hallowed guest has arrived at last." His rich baritone carried an edge of mockery.

I bowed low, keeping a stoic expression—or so I hoped. "Your Graces."

The gathered warriors turned as one, their eyes sizing me up with undisguised curiosity before erupting into loud laughter that rolled through the chamber like a pack of howling hounds.

Killian didn't so much as crack a smile, his gaze locked on mine. He blinked and the door slammed shut behind me with the clang of a death knell.

He leaned forward, the slightest smirk on his lips. "So, Investigator, how was your scenic drive through our Wisconsin wilderness?"

"Riveting," I deadpanned. "Aiden has all the conversational skills of a particularly uninspired turnip. I would have thought you folks favored quicker means of commuting—portals, enchanted tunnels, ley lines, that sort of thing. Anything to escape the monotony of a long drive."

He chuckled with a low rumble that sent a tremor through me. "I prefer to engage with the world we inhabit, Investigator. It keeps things... grounded. Wouldn't you agree?"

"Please, call me Tess. Or Detective Hilliard if you insist on formalities. Now, can we jump to why I'm here?"

He rose with a fluid motion, every muscle sculpted to perfection. "Come," he said. "We need to talk."

Killian ushered me through a side door into a cozy study lined with bookshelves and the smell of centuries old leather. He settled into the chair behind the desk, gesturing for me to sit opposite.

"What did you discover at the morgue?" he inquired.

"How did you know... ah, I get it," I said, the pieces clicking into place. "You had Aiden tail me despite giving me your word. I will not be spied upon, Killian. I told you, that's a dealbreaker."

His gray eyes flared with an orange spark. I'd hit a nerve. "He wasn't spying on you, Tess," he said. I could have sworn I heard a low purring in his voice. "He was protecting you."

"Oh, sure. Big difference. Nice loophole."

Killian leaned back. "There is a difference. It's a mystery to me how you can't see that."

Such crap.

"That sounds about like the kind of protector I'd get, a kid I overpowered with a butter knife. My one-man secret service."

"Trust me, Tess, you have nothing to fear. We're on the same side."

"Are we? Because last I checked, I'm after justice for Miles and I'd bet all forty bucks in my bank account that's not on your agenda."

His grin might have been charming if we weren't bickering

over murder and deceit. "Perhaps you're right, but what I want is irrelevant. I'll get you that justice without your cooperation, though I'd rather have you on my team."

I wasn't naïve—I knew which side was safer. I planted my elbows on the desk, meeting his gaze dead-on. "No more shadowing, Killian. That's my line in the sand. Take it or leave it."

A flicker of annoyance crossed his face before it smoothed back to indifference. "Fine. Now what do you have for me?"

"You called this meeting," I reminded him. "Don't you have an earth-shattering revelation for me?"

"Indeed, I do have something of interest. But let's hear yours first. I promise, it'll be worth your while."

I remembered my predicament with painful clarity. I was in no position to negotiate. "Okay," I said with a sigh. "I went to the morgue, as you so astutely observed, and saw the body."

"And?"

"Agent Donovan was brutalized." The stark image of Miles's body flashed through my mind again. "But here's the kicker... he didn't defend himself—not at all. That's not Miles. He would have fought to the end."

He stroked his chin thoughtfully. "Curious."

Playing dumb, how tedious. As if you haven't pieced that together already.

"The attacker would have to be something else," I went on. "Faster than a vampire, stronger than a combat mage, and skilled enough to evade every elemental assault Miles unleashed."

Killian's eyes narrowed. "Pet vampires are lethal in the hands of the necromancers who helped turn them."

"You think that vampires did it?"

"It's a logical assumption, wouldn't you say?"

"Funny you should say that. I had a little chat with a necromancer at the Bureau. They sang the very same song you're singing, convinced their kind is being set up."

"Rae Van Zelst?" He scoffed. "Of course she'd say that."

"You think she's lying?"

He raised an eyebrow, his tone dripping with condescension. "If her lips were moving, she was lying. You weigh the word of a necromancer against the Therian King?"

"I don't know, Killian. Your two factions have been at each other's throats for centuries. It would be easy for either camp to find value in pinning the murder on the other. And Raven wasn't at the murder scene—you were."

The amusement vanished from his face, replaced by a surge of raw, undiluted fury that electrified the room like a live wire. He wrestled with that primal instinct for a moment, jaw clenched, before getting it under control. His eyes, which had blazed fiery orange, dimmed back to a cool gray. He seemed perfectly composed again, but that brief surge of rage left me shaken.

"Don't stress it," I said. "Just tell me what you were doing there."

"I don't owe you an explanation, Investigator," he said, detached.

Ah, back to investigator. I realized he used my job title as a subtle jab, a way to defy me and put me in my place.

"I thought we were allies who share everything. Cooperation. Teamwork. Full disclosure. Working for the common good."

Okay, I'm not telling you you're my number one suspect. Not yet.

He arched an eyebrow. "And you share everything, I suppose? You've laid all your cards on the table?"

"Well, yeah…" I faltered, realizing he had a point. "Alright, fine, you got me there. I went to the morgue, and trust me, it was no picnic getting in. I wouldn't have gotten past the front door if Raven hadn't swooped in to make it happen. Saw the body, read the report. Not much on it, except for some unknown signature detected at the scene and that Miles was killed near Picnic Point between ten and eleven pm on Tuesday night. Then, I went there. The scene was too clean, but the leaf pattern on the ground was all wrong. I figured there was more than one attacker and Miles knew at least one of them. It wouldn't be a stretch to conclude he was lured there under false pretenses. And that's my everything."

Except for the marks on Miles's arm… and the illusion veil… and the illusion mage… and the fact that I am a signature detector… oh, screw it.

Killian flared his nostrils slightly, his expression tightening. "And what makes you think I was there?"

I tried to inject a casual shrug into my voice. "Well, I smelled you."

"You smelled me?"

"Yeah, I did, in the wind. I'm a wind mage, not a very good

one, but... the wind tells me things. It's my special skill."

Nice save, Tess, now let's hope he buys it.

"So, you're like a hound," he mused, finally easing his stern demeanor.

I smiled. "Only in the nose department."

He mulled over my words for a moment, as if tasting each syllable. "I appreciate your candor and I'll reciprocate, but you must promise me not to share what I'm about to reveal with anyone, especially not with your new necromancer best friend."

I rolled my eyes. "I'm a professional paranormal detective, Killian. I solve mysteries for a living. I'm not running around town with a megaphone, broadcasting secrets to the world."

"Okay, truce," he teased. "Your detective code is good enough for me."

Why was it that every time he opened his mouth, I was caught between the urge to smack him and the urge to run for cover?

I offered a failed grin. "I'm sorry, it's been a long couple of days."

"We're good," he said smoothly. "The truth is, I've suspected something wasn't right with Donovan. I've been keeping tabs on him."

You son of a bitch.

Anger burnt through me like a lit fuse. "If you knew he was in danger, why didn't you protect him? Why didn't your people protect him?"

"I never said I thought he was in danger. I suspected he

was the danger. He had been compromised. My people aren't babysitters. We didn't track his every move. I'm sure you understand that, given your line of work."

The gears in my head grinded. "Compromised? What do you mean?"

"What do you think I mean?" he shot back.

"I don't know, it sounds like total nonsense."

He leaned back in his chair, eyeing me like a cat would a canary bird. "To see clearly, you must be free of projection. You're not ready for the truth. You're not ready to see what's right in front of you."

"I see that you knew he was involved in something dark, and you did nothing to stop what happened. You were there, Killian. You're not just strong, you're an elemental warrior, a fucking dragon in human form. You could have saved him. All you did was take a photo of his ruined body. Is that your thing? You watch people die, do nothing, and then take your *photo op* to snap a sick fucking picture?"

He licked his lips, clearly annoyed. "If you think I personally stalked Donovan like I had nothing better to do, then you're letting your emotions blind you and turn you into a fool."

His elemental nature buzzed as he wrestled with his temper. I could almost see the dragon scales beneath his skin, the raw power he held at bay with every breath—power that could have easily turned the tide the night Miles was attacked.

I tried to calm the storm brewing inside me. "Tell me then."

"My people kept eyes on Donovan after the Bureau briefing, but he managed to shake them as he often did. By the time they picked up his trail again, he was already gone. I went to the scene to investigate."

That's all so convenient.

"Am I hearing this right? You always knew what happened?" I clenched my fists to keep from screaming. "Why the fuck did you drag me into this? To test me or laugh at me like your cronies did before? Do you enjoy being so cruel? Do you even have an endgame, dragon boy?"

Dragon boy? Okay, I may have a death wish.

His gaze fixed on me, sharp and calculating, like a chess master. "Because, Tess, I needed a fresh set of eyes—sometimes that's necessary to uncover what's hidden in plain sight. You're here because you're not just any detective. You knew Agent Donovan intimately, and you have a knack for sniffing out truths that others miss, even if they're staring right at them. And you're not an elemental warrior or a necro or a vamp. You are free of factional prejudice. Yours are the eyes I need right now. But you need to set your emotions aside and you need to check your vengeance at the door. Or you're useless."

I closed my eyes as the realization sank in. "You *were* testing me."

His eyes held a challenge that pushed the knot in my stomach up into my throat. "I trust you can forgive a little caution, just as I'm willing to forgive your eagerness to cast me the villain in your little murder mystery."

Uh oh, my turn to use caution and tiptoe through the minefield ahead.

"I didn't—"

"Please, spare me the denial act, Detective. You had me pegged as your number one suspect from the moment you laid eyes on me. I get it. It's your job to suspect everyone and trust no one. But let me clue you in: we need each other if we want to untangle this mess. Who killed Donovan, why they killed him, and why the whole damn multiverse is on the brink of implosion—it's all connected, I'd bet my life on it."

"Is this why you were lurking around Sun Prairie library? Keeping tabs on the portal? Or was it Miles you were tailing?"

"Multitasking."

"I don't buy it. You don't need me. You need the Bureau."

He slammed his hand on the desk. I shuddered. "The Bureau will slow play it, assuming they're not in on it, afraid of scandal. They have always viewed their agents as expendable. Their arrogance blinds them. Before too long, it will be too late. I feel it in my scales."

"Why should I believe one word that comes from your mouth?"

He perked up, as if he was five and I had just offered him candy.

"It's time I delivered on my promise," he said. He rose from his chair, a fresh gleam in his eyes. "I hope you have the stomach for it."

Chapter 12

KILLIAN LED ME OUT of the study through a door hidden behind a bookshelf and down a narrow passage, his broad shoulders nearly brushing the rough stone walls. His long strides forced me into an undignified trot to keep up. We stopped before a door guarded by a lone warrior who looked like he could bench-press a car. With a nod from Killian, the guard stepped aside.

The room was furnished with a plain rectangular table and four hard chairs. Seated at the table was a woman in her late forties or early fifties. Her wide face was open and honest, exuding kindness. She wore her light brown hair in a sleek bob and her eyes glowed with a beautiful violet color.

She looked up as we entered, a curious tilt to her chin. "This is her?" she said, her gaze moving to Killian.

Kilian shrugged, the gesture almost apologetic, as if presenting a stray cat he'd found underneath a dumpster.

Hello, I'm right here! Hold off on the eyerolls until I've left the room.

The woman's attention returned to me. "Rest your fanny, dear," she said, her voice a velvety contralto. "What you're about to see might cause a shock, and I don't want you to topple over, faint or, heaven forbid, have a meltdown."

A meltdown? I shot Killian a glare.

He pursed his lips together, suppressing a grin.

Brilliant.

I slid into the chair across from her, my back straight. Killian leaned against the wall, arms crossed over his chest—muscles bulging, veins popping, a total distraction.

"I'm not prone to meltdowns or fainting spells," I informed them, my voice dry as sandpaper. "And I'm getting quite used to shock."

"My heart goes out to you, dear. I'm Clara. I handle the administrative side of things here at the Therian Helm." She studied me for a moment, an unnerving hint of sympathy creeping onto her face.

What in the nine hells had Killian told her about me?

"Are Therian administrators always so sympathetic?" I said, unable to resist the jab.

"Wouldn't know, dear. I'm not an elemental."

I tuned my inner radar, scanning her core for the telltale hum of magic—primal signatures, energy auras, elemental fever prints. Nothing. Nada. Zilch. She registered as entirely human.

"I thought only elementals were permitted in the inner sanctum?" I pointed out. "Yet you command a certain level of respect here, Clara."

"She's family," Killian interjected. "Now, can we get on with it?"

"Of course," Clara said, turning back to me.

Family? Whose family? Killian's? I filed that juicy tidbit away for later use.

Clara pushed a thick manila folder across the table. "This is what we managed to retrieve from the body before the Bureau crew arrived."

I eyed the folder incredulously. "You removed evidence from an active crime scene?"

"Let's just say, we're disinclined to trust the Bureau with evidence that directly implicates one of their own top agents," she said.

Killian was disinterested, content to yield the floor to Clara for now.

I tapped the folder with a single, hesitant finger. "You don't trust the Bureau, but you're comfortable handing *me* sensitive information?"

"Honestly, if it were my call, I wouldn't trust you with my family's gingerbread recipes, but Killian has made up his mind."

"To trust me?"

"To... work alongside you."

I took a breath, staring at the manila folder as if it might spontaneously combust. Finally, I pulled out two transparent plastic A4 sleeves. I carefully unfolded the glossy contents of the first one onto the table—a large map of the sprawling chaos of the Netherworld dimension.

I didn't know much about the Nether Realms beyond them being the farthest, most unexplored corners in the multiverse, filled with unknown and often malevolent entities. The kind of place where reality resembled a bad fever dream. Why would Miles be lugging around a map of that inhospitable dimension?

"The second sleeve," Killian said, his voice laced with impatience.

The way he said it immediately set me on edge. I reached for the second sleeve. A single sheet of paper slipped out, its edges ragged and torn—the missing Codex page!

I shook my head. "No way you found this on Miles."

Clara's expression turned icy. "You think the Therian King deals in lies?"

"I'm saying, it's too convenient. Whoever offed Miles wouldn't leave this behind unless they wanted it found. Once again, this reeks of a setup."

Killian peeled himself off the wall, stalking toward me with lazy grace. "Don't let your hormones fog your judgement, Tess."

His tone might have been neutral, but the insinuation wasn't. *Jackass.*

My face heated up. "Speaking from experience, Your Grace? Lucky for me, I manage just fine without the handicap of a testosterone-addled brain."

Clara grinned, but the severity in her violet eyes didn't waver. "Make no mistake, this isn't a game. What's in that folder could mean life or death on a mass scale."

I glanced at Killian, then back to Clara. "What are you suggesting?"

Killian tapped the Codex page, then pointed at the map. "Do you not see the connection here?"

The Codex page contained a dense constellation of glyphs—the access codes for the portal sequence to Nyx, one of the smaller, largely unexplored Nether Realms.

"We believe that Agent Donovan and his accomplices cut off access to Nyx," Clara said, "then swiped the map from the Bureau archive vault. It looks like a contingency plan, a failsafe to find their way to Nyx without relying on the Codex."

The picture she painted wasn't pretty. "Not buying it. Miles goes to this secret meeting, they kill him, and then they just leave the map and the Codex page behind?"

"We're still piecing that part together," Clara said. "That's why we're asking you to join forces with us. A united front, if you will."

My head swam. If what they wanted me to believe was true, it meant Miles had played me like a cheap fiddle from the start, leading me down a path of lies and deceit. But if that was the case, if he was caught up in a dangerous, treacherous game, why would he drag me into the thick of it?

I rubbed my throbbing temples, squeezing my eyes shut. None of this tracked. Pretty much par for the course with this whole investigation.

"She's not convinced," Clara muttered under her breath.

"Of course she's not," Killian said. "Detective Hilliard has a challenging relationship with trust."

"Just an FYI, I can hear you," I snapped, my eyes flashing open. "In case you weren't aware. I also noticed your eye rolls before."

"Take her to our guest," Killian said, already walking out. "I'll catch up."

"What guest?" I echoed after him, but he was long gone.

"This way, love," Clara said, rising from her seat. She led me back out through the narrow passage, up a staircase and into a wider corridor. She dug a set of keys from her pocket and unlocked a wooden door. The room we entered mirrored the one we'd just left except for the stainless-steel sink and toilet in one corner.

I shuddered. "Is this a holding cell?"

"Nothing so dramatic, dear. We're not the Bureau. Does it look like we've been holding someone captive here?"

Well, not presently. The room was empty and spotless, but that didn't prove anything about the past or the future for that matter.

"Listen," she said, her tone softer. "I know this is a lot to absorb—the Helm, the Therians, everything we've thrust upon you. I wish there was an easier way."

"I can handle the truth," I said. "But I find in my line of work the truth is a burrowing creature that likes to keep hidden and avoid the light."

"Perhaps to many, but not to Killian. He hardly ever misses the mark. In all the years I've known him, since he was a child, I cannot recall a single instance when his instincts steered him astray."

Since he was a child? Who is this lady?

Clara moved around the room lighting the wall-mounted torches. The flames illuminated the worry lines around her eyes and the deeper wrinkles across her forehead.

"What is your relation to Killian?" I said, watching her carefully.

"His mother and I are third cousins. Her bloodline grew only stronger over the generations while mine became increasingly diluted by common blood until we lost all connections to our elemental roots."

"Must be fascinating, living among Therians."

She smiled. "They're a formidable lot, to be sure, especially those with warrior lineages."

"Not all Therians are elemental warriors then?"

"Heavens no, dear, not every transformation is suited for combat. But those that are..." Her voice trailed off as she gave me a slight shake of her head. "They are zealous, ferocious powerhouses, especially the Reivers among them, and Killian is the deadliest Reiver."

I nodded. "Yeah, I figured as much."

Her violet eyes drilled into mine with disturbing intensity. "He is stronger than you can fathom, Tess, a force unto himself, capable of making the most difficult choices when necessary. He burns like the Sun gone supernova and explodes like an erupting volcano. Don't get any fanciful ideas into your head."

Oh, the audacity of the woman.

I circled a finger around my face. "I assure you that no fanciful ideas of any kind ever enter this head."

She continued staring, clearly unconvinced. "Proceed with caution in all things around him. I've witnessed firsthand the effect he can have on women, and you... you clearly know how to push his buttons, and that makes you undeniably intriguing to him."

This conversation is veering wildly off track.

I shifted uncomfortably under her scrutinizing gaze. "If by *intriguing* you mean competent, then you both have it right. I've seen good-looking men before, Clara. There's a dead body, a stolen Codex page, and multiple portal breaches. I'm singularly minded on this. I want to uncover the truth."

Clara exhaled and smiled, weakly, then jerked her chin toward the door. "Of course, we all do, Tess. I believe it's time you met our guest. Brace yourself, dear, this part comes with a real shock."

Chapter 13

A MAN APPEARED IN the doorway, shrouded in the darkness of the hallway behind him. Every hair on my body stood on end, and every molecule of air simultaneously emptied my lungs as he stepped into the torchlight. He was a walking, breathing illustration ripped from the pages of Gray's Anatomy, every muscle, blood vessel, nerve fiber and tendon grotesquely laid bare. The only concession to modesty was a kilt-like fabric wrapped around his waist—clearly for my benefit.

"Ladiesss," he rasped with a voice so gravelly it'd make nails on a chalkboard sound pleasant.

I swallowed hard, trying not to gawk, but how do you look away from someone whose skin isn't just transparent but literally nonexistent? He was all layers of exposed, raw flesh from the tips of his toes up to the sharp angles of his skull, all seemingly held together by gelatinous membranes.

Damn. How is this possible? It must be mirrors and lights.

For a moment, everything else was dwarfed by this surreal spectacle.

Clara pulled up a chair to the table. "Sit, dear," she said. "If you can still hear me, that is."

My ears worked well enough, but my legs were frozen in place.

The flayed man-creature offered a sarcastic approximation of a two-finger salute. "Chaaarmed," he drawled in his thick accent, turning every consonant and vowel into a grind.

I opened my mouth, then closed it with a snap. I thought nothing could render me speechless anymore, but I was clearly wrong.

"This is Zzrask," Clara said. "A visitor from Nyx."

Holy shit, a Nyktian visitor, here, in the flesh—literally and horrifically. I tried to process that bombshell and came up short.

Zzrask's bulbous, bloodshot eyes roamed over me. "Youououu... nice skin. Shaaame... to cover uuup."

OMG. I hurried into the chair Clara had offered, crossing my arms protectively over my chest.

"Your dimension... nice for senseeesss," Zzrask hissed, that guttural voice scraping against my nerves.

Before I could muster a response, Killian materialized in the doorway.

"I think that's enough, Commander Zzrask," he said. "You're making the detective uncomfortable."

His tone wasn't exactly scolding, not really. If anything, he looked quite pleased with himself, a predator relishing the kill. Killian had stayed behind on purpose, I realized, letting me face the visceral presence of a Nyktae without any buffer, ensuring the shock would hit me with all its force.

Zzrask dipped his head to offer an awkward bow. "Apologiesss, deteeective."

"Noted," I managed to choke out.

"Perhaps we should all be seated?" Killian suggested, already reaching for a chair beside me.

Like hell. Don't even think about offering that chair to Mister See-Through with the wandering eyes and the harassing comments!

Thankfully, Zzrask slid into the seat directly across from me, his disturbing eyes glued to mine as he settled into the creaking chair. Clara sat to my left and Killian took the place to my right.

"Nice chairrr," Zzrask said, his lipless mouth stretching in a ghastly smile. "Squishyyy..."

Great, now we are flirting with the furniture.

I figured *nice* must be his go-to word in the English language. "It's, ah, nice to meet you, Commander," I said, putting a bit more emphasis on *nice* than strictly necessary. "I'm Tess Hilliard, paranormal investigator. I trust the Therians have expended you all the comforts you require?"

A hollow rattle resonated from the depths of his exposed chest cavity, a sound that might have been laughter in some alternate universe. "Sheee... izzz... funneee," he wheezed between those gurgling chuckles.

"She doesn't know the meaning of the word," Killian said dryly. "She confuses rudeness and snark for wit."

My first instinct was to kick him under the table, but then common sense intervened. The last time I touched the Therian King, I'd gotten a taste of his crushing power, and I didn't want to imagine what a full-blown kick would do.

Zzrask kept his unnerving gaze fixed on me. "Sheee... learn-nnn."

Yeah, right. And maybe sprout wings while I'm at it.

"How does your presence here relate to the case we're investigating, Commander?" I asked Zzrask, keeping it cool and professional.

"I see thingssss..."

Killian slid a photo across the table toward Zzrask—the image of a very much alive Miles Donovan staring back at us. "Have you seen this man before?" he prodded.

Those monstrously protruding eyes seemed to drink in every detail of the image. "Yessss... twice..."

"And where was that?"

"Nyxxxx."

I scooted my chair forward. "You're saying you've seen agent Donovan in the Netherworld?"

"Yessss... Nyxxxx."

Taking a classified Netherworld map out of the archive vault was grounds for immediate suspension, but actually opening a Nether portal to get to the damn place without authorization? That crossed squarely into treason.

"I'll need more than just your word on that," I said.

The Nyktian commander didn't so much as twitch. "My... orrrrb..." he rasped out slowly.

Clara rolled a sphere the size of a cue ball into Zzrask's waiting, skinless hands. Its mirrored surface swirled with iridescent marble-like patterns. Zzrask wrapped his gelatinous fingers around it, covering it completely.

A series of runes lit up across the sphere's surface as Zzrask closed his eyes, transferring his memories to the orb. A holographic projection sputtered into existence, filling our vision with a glimpse of the Nyx realm.

Every last torch and lamp sizzled and died, turning the room unnaturally dark as if some insidious force had inhaled all the light, leaving only the ghostly glow of the hovering projection.

Morbid fascination battled with a rising tide of unease as I watched a holographic Miles stride confidently across a desolate landscape beneath the swirling black Nyx sky, flanked by two skinless Nyktae. Whether one of them was Zzrask himself, I couldn't tell.

The trio reached a rocky outcrop and came to a halt. Miles leaned in close, his body language tense, and engaged in a conversation with one of the Nyktae. They gestured sharply. Their voices were muted in the projection. A third Nyktian figure slid through the hologram's backdrop.

"That...izzzz... Zzrask." The Nyktae across from me pronounced his own name as if there were at least thirty 'z's in it.

"What were they discussing?" I said, leaning forward. "What was the topic of this meeting?"

Zzrask tilted his head, the movement strangely birdlike. "Not... knowww."

This was getting us nowhere fast. Every second we spent

floundering in the dark, both literally and figuratively, only deepened the mystery.

"Do you have any idea why Miles would meet with Nyktians in the first place?" I said.

Clara flicked on the table lamp, chasing the projection back into the orb.

Zzrask's shoulders twitched slightly. "Deaaal... forrrr... powerrrr..."

"What makes you think that?" Killian said.

"That... what... aaall human... waaant..."

I glanced at Killian, who seemed to be pondering the same thing as me: what kind of power could entice a seasoned Bureau Agent, a man with a proven track record and sworn to safeguard our world, to strike deals in the dark heart of Nyx in order to get it?

"Power for what?" I asked. "What power do the Nyktae have?"

"Change... dimensssion... orrrrder..." he rasped, the words barely audible.

Change the order of parallel dimensions? That wasn't just power—that was the potential to reshape our world. I sank back into my chair. If what the Nyktian Commander insinuated was true, then Miles wasn't just playing with fire; he was juggling infernos.

"If Agent Donovan was looking to change the multiverse order," Killian said, his voice sterner than I'd ever heard it, "then he must have had a specific target in mind. Do you have any idea what world he was planning to alter?"

Zzrask shook his head slowly. "Can't... sayyy..."

Son of a bitch. He knew way more than he was letting on.

Clara's expression hardened. "What would Agent Donovan offer Nyx in return, Commander Zzrask? What price would the Nyktae demand for their assistance?"

Zzrask's eyes flickered with a strange light. "Can't... sayyy..."

Of course. Another dead end.

Killian and I exchanged a troubled look. This wasn't just about a murdered agent or a stolen map anymore. The stakes had just been raised to an apocalyptic level.

Miles Donovan was neck-deep into something terrible. And the only way to get to the bottom of whatever fresh hell he'd set in motion, the only way to stop whatever madness was brewing, was to follow in his fatal footsteps. We had to find a way to Nyx.

"Commander Zzrask, thank you for your assistance. Your insights have been enlightening," Killian said, rising.

The Nyktian bowed his head, then turned to me. "Nice skinnn, Deteeective..."

"Right back at you," I said and immediately wanted to yank the entire sentence back and shove it into the shredder.

Maybe I should just keep my mouth shut from now on. For everyone's sake.

I didn't dare glance at Killian, but I was certain he was either fuming or trying hard not to grin. Probably both.

Clara rose gracefully to her feet. "Commander, allow me to show you back to your quarters."

As soon as they were gone, Killian burst into a fit of laughter. "You just complimented the skin of a skinless man who commands a skinless army," he said, barely controlling his glee. "You have no sense of self-preservation."

"What did you expect from someone who confuses rudeness and snark for wit?" I shot back, imitating his voice. "He creeps me the fuck out, Killian. And how the hell is he even here, at the Therian Helm of all places? You have an open portal to Nyx?"

His laughter cut off abruptly. "No, we don't have a Nyx portal. Zzrask is stranded here. He lost his way back to Nyx but managed to send a distress signal to his legion. They're planning a retrieval operation."

"Wonderful. Just what Madison needs—a rogue Nyktian retrieval party tearing through the Public Library portals in the middle of the night."

"The Nyktae don't do library portals. They have their own methods of dimension hopping—mainly wormholes that can turn incredibly unstable or vanish altogether."

"And you know all this how?"

"It's a long, boring story."

"Try me."

Killian sighed. "The short version is that I've had dealings with Zzrask before. Helped him out of a bind a few years back when he was persona non grata in Nyx. He's since been reinstated as commander."

"So, he's a regular visitor here?"

He shrugged. "He has a fondness for skin, so he tends to visit dimensions where there's plenty of it."

"Please, don't tell me he collects skin souvenirs."

He looked at me as if I'd lost my mind. "He's not a teddy bear, I'll grant you that, but he's not the enemy either, Tess. Let's just say he appreciates the art of survival as much as anyone. He's fascinated with human resilience—thinks it's a riot how we manage to stay mostly intact."

"If that's the case, we should squeeze him harder for answers."

"You can squeeze all you want. The Nyktae are notorious for being tight-lipped. He's already said more to you than he ever did to me. All I got from him before tonight was confirmation that Donovan had been to Nyx. Nothing about power deals and dimension-changing schemes." He paused, giving me an inscrutable look. "I think he likes you."

And... cue the obligatory eyeroll.

"Who wouldn't? Who could resist my winning charm?" I countered, dripping as much sarcasm as I could into my voice. "But in all seriousness, do you trust the creepy Commander from Nyx, Killian?"

The Therian King rubbed his chin, clearly not used to having to explain himself. "Zzrask owes me. And the mindscape orb doesn't lie. I've seen it in action several times; it pulls real memories."

Mindscape orb. It didn't sound like something you'd want lying around. "Is it a Nyktian device?"

"More like scattered across all the Netherworld realms."

"Which begs the question... Ever been to the Netherworld yourself?"

He shook his head firmly. "No. And, under normal circumstances, I would have no desire to change that."

"Well, that ship has already sailed, Your Grace. Like it or not, the Netherworld is where we're headed. I mean, I'm going either way, but I'd much rather have a Therian army watching my back than go it alone. I'm not wild about my chances making it back otherwise, especially if library portals aren't a thing in Nyx."

"There are portals in Nyx," he said. "They're few and far between, but they do exist. I've known for some time now I would likely have to visit the Netherworld myself, but I can't do it alone." He paused, holding my gaze. "Therian energy is very resistant to portal frequencies, almost antagonistic, and multi-portal jumps, the kind we'd need to reach Nyx, would be like having our molecular structures ripped apart. By the time we crawled out the other side, our energy reserves would be depleted. It could take days to fully recover—weeks maybe."

It began to dawn on me. "So, what you're saying is…"

"I need a highly skilled portal walker, someone who can act as a shield, insulating my warriors from the worst of the interdimensional strain. Without that buffer, we'd be going in crippled from the start—a risk I can't take."

Ah, there it is. The real reason for his sudden interest in me. Finally, it all clicks in a manipulative kind of way.

"In other words, you need *me*," I said with a triumphant smile on my face. "A lot more than I need you."

"I need a portal walker, yes, and you're the only one I know who's not bound to the Bureau. Go ahead and soothe your ego with delusions of indispensability if it helps."

I circled him with slow, deliberate steps, studying him from head to toe. "How about you ask nicely? Try... *Please, Tess, with a cherry on top*. It might just sweeten the deal."

He bared his teeth in a mocking semblance of a smile, then growled.

Bad dragon. Time to turn up the heat.

"Here's the thing, Killian—you've been lying to me this entire time. Since you had your flunky drag me to your bathhouse, no, wait, since the Sun Prairie library. You knew Miles had been in Nyx, you knew he was murdered, and you knew he had stolen the Codex page, and you kept your royal yap shut! You just let me flail around in the dark, tripping over every maddening detail. So, the way I see it, if you don't ask me like you mean it, I'm out of here."

I wasn't exactly Miss Transparency myself, but life's not fair.

He cleared his throat. "I may have omitted certain particulars, Detective," he said at last, his voice low and dangerous, "but I've uttered no lies."

I feigned a yawn. "Waiting with bated breath, Killian."

He stalked closer and fixed me with those striking storm-tossed eyes. "I need you, Tess." He said the words like he was forced to recite a dull poem. "Will you please consider helping me? With sugar and strawberries on top."

Was this me pushing his buttons like Clara said?

More like smashing them with a sledgehammer, Tess.

I exhaled a sharp breath. "There, that wasn't that hard. A dash of humility goes a long way. And, yes, I'll help you. But this is a two-way street. You keep things from me, you try to manipulate me ever again, and I swear on every flickering library portal in existence, I'll let you disintegrate down to atoms on the way back from Nyx."

Flames ignited in his irises as a vein pulsed in his temple. I was pushing him close to the edge. "Threatening the Therian King in his own home is a deadly strategy, to say the least."

I met his fiery gaze head-on. "Looks like someone has a fire lit under their tail. Tell me, do you actually breathe fire, or are you all hot air and smoke?"

I didn't see it coming. One second, I was daring a disgruntled dragon—the next, a hand clamped around my throat while another pinned me against the wall. His face was inches from mine, his eyes burning not just with anger but with something both wild and thrilling. The immense power he usually held so tightly in check radiated from his body like a storm about to break.

He leaned in closer, his voice a guttural rasp against my ear. "I will enjoy teaching you a lesson in respect. It will be a glorious day."

My hand shot out, fingers scrambling to latch onto his neck to siphon whatever sliver of energy I could from him in case I'd have to fight my way out of this impromptu lesson in manners.

Before my fingers could find their target, the pressure on my throat eased. Iis hands straightened the crumpled lapels of my jacket, then smoothed my messy hair with a meticulousness bordering on the absurd.

"But it won't be today," he said, taking a step back.

Fucking hothead asshole. If looks were daggers, he'd be an ex-king sprawled on the floor right now. The adrenaline cocktail of fear and anger had my heart doing sprints. "Touch me again and you'll lose more than the hand," I hissed, my dagger flashing at the ready.

The threat was hollow. He'd snatch the blade in a heartbeat, his reflexes lightning fast, and even if I did manage to scrape him with bonshek, it wouldn't make a difference. He didn't need his magic to snap me like a twig with his bare hands.

"I'm sure you'd try," he said. "I'll have a room prepared for you. You look like you could use some beauty rest."

Prick.

I did though. It was three in the morning, and my energy was scraping the bottom of the barrel. The weekend couldn't start soon enough.

Trying my hardest to stay composed, I shook my head. "Thanks, but no thanks. The thought of sleeping surrounded by elemental warriors who could squash me in their sleep doesn't exactly promise a peaceful night."

"As you wish. Aiden will drive you to Madison."

Sweet relief flooded my senses as he walked to the door.

Pausing with his hand on the handle, he looked back over his shoulder. "Oh, and Tess, I would refrain from calling the Therian King *dragon boy* to his face. It can prove a very unhealthy choice."

Shit, he did catch that. "Really? I blame exhaustion. My apologies. I'll just call you an overgrown fire lizard and we'll be cool, yeah? Or is that too on the nose?"

An uncertain laughter escaped his mouth. "Sleep well tonight. A long journey awaits," he said while walking out the door.

I already knew that when I woke up tomorrow, I would remember this all as a dream. If only I had a souvenir, some undeniable proof.

Chapter 14

THE NIGHT FELT GLOOMIER, wilder and deadlier on the way back to Madison. The Therian Helm had vanished from sight the moment Aiden pulled out of the gate, swallowed by an intense, supernatural fog. The snow had stopped falling, but the sky remained a heavy blanket of overcast clouds—no moon, no stars, just the thrumming of the engine.

Aiden squeezed the steering wheel, his lips pursed. Something was bothering him but coaxing it out of him was not on my agenda right now. I had my own set of worries—the secrets I was holding back from Killian, the scars on Miles, and the illusion magic used to conceal them.

I rehashed the list of suspects in my mind: the illusion mage, the Bureau, vampires, and now the addition of the Nyktae, but Killian was conspicuously absent from the list. Despite his unique ability to drive me up a wall, I could no longer believe he had anything to do with the murder.

Why was I so hell-bent on antagonizing him? A therapist would have a field day with me, chalking it up to a defense mechanism masking the inconvenient truth that I was drawn to him. And I mean, yes, he was objectively, blatantly eye-catching—not with the perfect features or polished charm of Miles, but his raw magnetism was undeniable. But his looks weren't the reason I loved ruffling his royal feathers. No, there was something else, a deeper pull, a sense of familiarity I couldn't quite put my finger on. Whatever the reason, I had to dial back the provocations. He'd tolerate me while he needed me, but what happened when he no longer did?

Added to the mix of unease and doubts was the dread of portal jumping all the way to Nyx. I'd faced down werewolves, rogue mages, and even a demon or two at the Academy, but nothing had ever prepared me for crossing into the Netherworld.

Becoming a portal walker wasn't just about stepping through mystical doorways into parallel worlds. It was about learning to survive the feeling of being crushed as reality shifted around you, threatening to tear you apart. It took years of practice, training, and a natural resilience that few among the supernaturals outside of the order of portal mages possessed.

The mental and physical toll of the training was immense, but it was the only way to navigate the labyrinth of portals without losing yourself. Miles was a master of it, and so was I, but my skill remained a closely guarded secret, always wanting to stay under the radar and out of the crosshairs of those who might want to exploit me. Killian had figured it out somehow.

"Something on your mind, Aiden?" I finally asked, breaking the silence to get out of my own head.

He glanced at me, then back at the road. "He should have bound you. With a blood oath."

"You don't approve of me?"

He shrugged. "It's not that. It's about strategy. About our code. Killian respects strength, but besides that fancy dagger of yours, I'm not sure you have any, Investigator."

"Aiden, I swear, if you call me investigator one more time—"

"What should I call you?"

For fuck's sake.

"How about my name? Ever crossed your mind?"

"What, like Hilliard?"

"Like Tess, Aiden," I said, exasperated. "And for your information, I can handle myself just fine. I got skills."

"Against a spell conjurer, maybe. But going up against the things that tore Agent Donovan apart? No way."

"What do you suggest I do? Beg Killian to make me his blood slave?"

"I don't have opinions. It's unusual and triggers my nerves. That's all."

"Well, if you don't have opinions, I guess we're all good here."

Maybe look opinion *up in a dictionary, Aiden.*

The road stretched on, the shadows deepening. I watched the dark landscape blur past, fighting to keep my eyes open.

Did I know Miles at all? Seems I did not, at least not the new version that snuck into the Netherworld and ripped out pages from the *Codex Portallis. That* Miles was a stranger to me. I still had no leads on what the marks on his body meant, or how he received them.

Had Miles learned something about me that had propelled him to seek me out and drag me into his world of deception after two years apart?

Aiden cursed under his breath right as my eyelids began to close, snapping me back into alert mode. Two figures stood squarely in the middle of the road ahead, their eyes glowing red in the headlights.

"Vampires," I said, my hand reaching for my dagger.

The figures were quick, unnaturally so. They leapt onto the hood, and their weight dented the metal, nails scraping against the windshield.

Holy hell!

Aiden stepped on the gas. The engine roared as the car lurched forward. The vampires clung on, their snarls so deafening they made my ears ring.

"Hold on!" Aiden yelled, swerving violently to the left.

One of the vampires lost its grip, tumbling off and rolling into a ditch. The other held fast, its claws puncturing the windshield, causing cracks to spread out like a spiderweb.

I pulled my dagger free, rolling down the window to slice at the vampire's hand. The beast howled, recoiling. Aiden took another sharp turn, sending the vampire flying off into the darkness at the side of the road.

"It's not over," I said, my heartbeat manic. "It's just beginning."

"With you on that," Aiden growled.

The vampires were back on their feet, one of them sprinting towards us with inhuman speed in the rearview mirror, the other darting into the trees.

"They're tailing us," I said, turning back to track the one behind us. "He's gaining on us!"

Aiden pushed the car to its limits, the tires squealing as he navigated the winding road. The vampire leaped forward, landing on the trunk with a thud.

Poor Camry. You deserved a better ending.

"Get rid of it, Tess!" Aiden barked.

"*Me?* I'm not the one who turns into a fucking human torch."

"You're the one with a free hand," he snapped back.

I twisted and leaned out of the window as far as I could and hurled the dagger at the vampire. The blade sliced through its shoulder. Aiden swerved violently, and the vampire tumbled off the car and under the wheels.

Thunk! The car spun out after running over the vamp, veering off the asphalt, the tires skidding across dirt before flying into a ditch. My head snapped forward, smacking against the headrest on its way back.

Aiden reached for something beneath his seat, then burst from the car, moving with the assurance of someone who had done this before. He didn't look like a carefree teenager anymore.

I followed, backup dagger at the ready, my neck throbbing from whiplash, eyes scanning the darkness for any sign of the second vampire. The air was thick with a sticky bitterness.

Necromancy.

"You alright?" Aiden said, a long sword gleaming in his hand.

"I'll live," I managed, my breath coming in icy gasps. "Where's the other bloodsucker?"

Aiden's eyes narrowed, studying the tree line. "He'll be back and he'll bring friends. We need to move."

"Like... on foot?"

"Can you fly?"

"We'll never make it past the next mile marker on foot," I pleaded. "You need to shift, Aiden."

"That takes time. I'm not ready. I can't harness the energy."

I rallied all my desperation. "Try!"

Aiden exhaled and let his eyelids drop, his face a mask of concentration. His body began to flicker with an eerie light, the faint outline of embers dancing beneath his skin. He shivered and the glow fizzled out.

"I told you," he growled.

He was a neophyte still. The pressure was getting to him. This wasn't going to work.

The vampire emerged from the woods, flanked by two larger vamps. The shadows all around us stirred. More beasts surfaced from the darkness.

Thanks, Killian. You gave me an elemental bodyguard still learning his ABCs.

The vampires charged. Aiden swung his sword with an ember-blazing hand, parrying the first attack, but the sheer number of toothy killers was overwhelming. I slashed at one with my dagger, but it was like fighting a storm—unrelenting chaos attacking from every direction.

A smaller vampire hissed at me, baring fangs that dripped with sticky saliva. I slammed my hand against the ground, focusing all my will into an earth incantation.

"From the earth, a fortress rise!" I cried out, not entirely sure I remembered the words correctly.

The ground rumbled as a wall of packed earth erupted between me and the vampire, the impact hurling it backward.

Two more bloodsuckers were already lunging at me. I slashed with my dagger, catching one across the chest, while the other's claws raked my arm, shredding the sleeve of my leather jacket but barely scratching the skin underneath.

Hey! I loved that jacket!

I reached deep inside, pulling on the small amount of wind energy I could command. "Winds of the north, heed my call! Bind them in your icy grasp!"

A blast of frigid air shot from my outstretched hand, encasing several vampires in a thick layer of frost. They shrieked as their advance was slowed to a crawl.

My fight wouldn't last long. There were too many and my bag of tricks emptied fast, my wind magic and my core energy completely drained.

These weren't just vampires—they were thralls, compelled to serve a necromancer's will. The kind of ghastly, ugly motherfuckers who would rip into a human jugular within fractions of a second if released from their masters' control. Spells alone wouldn't hold back these starving killers.

Aiden struggled to keep up with the attacks, his elemental form flickering but never fully igniting, his sword a blur of motion.

The vampires, sensing victory, moved in for the kill.

We're not dying here tonight.

I reached out blindly, my illusion radar probing the night for the necromancer driving the attack.

Wherever there's a thrall vampire, a necromancer won't be far behind.

Everything in me told me that this was a colossal mistake that would come back to bite me, but first I needed to stay alive to pay that price.

There—a creepy pulse within the woods, the twisted necromantic thread connecting the undead to the dark sorcerer. I focused on that pulse, dragging it to me, feeling the connection trying to snap into place.

The dark magic hit me like a punch. My core shuddered. I dropped to my knees, coughing, the pressure mounting inside my head. My mouth was stripped of saliva. My lungs were emptied and wheezing for air.

I wasn't ready. Refining and redirecting dark magic was a skill I hadn't mastered, and my only option was to inhale it all in one massive snort.

Latching onto the necromancer's core, I pulled the dark magic to me in ribbons, feeling it resist, a writhing, sentient thing fighting against my control. Tapping into it felt like pushing a boulder uphill only to realize the boulder was winning and you were about to go down.

I reached deeper, grasping at the threads of control the necromancer held over the vampires, using his own magic against him. I severed those threads, pulling the control away from the necromancer and into my own grasp.

The vampires faltered, their movements becoming sluggish and disoriented by the shift in command as I bent their will to mine.

Aiden grunted, swinging his sword wildly in a wide arc, managing to take down the last vampire lunging at him. I focused harder, the strain of controlling multiple vampires at once pressing against my mind like a vise. Their thoughts, their energies, their insatiable bloodlust flooded my impulses. It was worse than watching a horror show—it was like becoming the horror, being Freddy Krueger.

"Come on," I muttered, sweat beading on my forehead despite the cold.

The vampires stood frozen now, their eyes vacant. I had them under my control, but it was tenuous, a house of cards waiting to collapse.

"What's going on?" Aiden spit out.

"Don't know, but let's not jinx it. Let's get the fuck out of here!" I said, holding back the stunned necromancer in the woods furiously trying to wrestle back control.

"Step back and stay there," I ordered the vampires under my breath, attempting to shield us without giving the game away.

Aiden pulled at my arm. "Time to run!"

We sprinted down the road. The vampires vacantly walked back into the tree line behind us like shadows disappearing.

There was blood on my torn jacket sleeve from the vampire wound—finally, a souvenir from the night.

Chapter 15

By the time I made it back to Jenifer Street, dawn was breaking. I limped up the creaky stairs to my apartment, aching and frozen everywhere. The adrenaline that had kept me on my feet was almost gone. I just wanted to make it to my couch before collapsing and not move again for a week.

My muscles screamed in protest as I peeled off my damp, tattered clothes and wrapped myself in a blanket. A quick inventory revealed that I had many souvenirs from the battle with the undead: multiple cuts and bruises on my face resembling rough terrain, arms and legs that looked like they'd been beaten like piñatas, and a lovely purple bloom spreading across my ribs.

The gash on my arm had stopped bleeding. *I've had worse.* It might leave a small scar. *Cool, I collect them.* I winced as I settled on the couch, too tired to shower or clean my wounds. Mentally and physically, I was spent.

My frozen body thawed into a puddle of regret.

Tapping into necromancy was a bad mistake. Like *summon-*

ing a bus full of killer clowns bad. It should not be done, even out of desperation. Once you tasted the vast depths of dark magic, it lingered. A residual connection to the necromancer was there, in the back of my mind, scaring the shit out of me.

The necro had left their imprint, as surely as if they'd used a branding rod. I felt the darkness latching onto my magic core, a seductive whisper promising power beyond measure. And, gods, it was tempting to let all that power flood me again, feel the intoxicating rush of fullness, the ability to command the undead like so many creepy marionettes.

No wonder necromancers aren't repulsed by their grim trade. Dark magic is addictive, an all-consuming high.

At least, it was Saturday. Two days free from Pankowski's exasperated sighs and Gideon's condescending stares. Two days to lick my wounds and hopefully shake off the taint of necromancy from my system.

I remembered coming across a bottle of ibuprofen last week. I was halfway through fishing it out of the utility drawer when a fist pounded on the front door downstairs.

Another blow, this one even more insistent, like whoever was on the other side was trying to break through the door.

I threw on a pair of sweatpants and a t-shirt and shuffled my feet out to the stairwell. I didn't know who it was, but I knew it was likely *my* bad luck and not my neighbors'. They had lives that made sense.

Leaning over the railing, I was surprised and somewhat amused to see Killian trying to figure out which apartment was mine like a lost puppy.

That was fast. Who the hell buzzed him in instead of calling the cops?

He was dressed in black jeans and a fitted black leather jacket that screamed *'don't mess with me'*. The stubble on his face made him look every bit like an action movie guy, not a lost boy just in from the cold.

Before I could decide what to do, a giggle floated up from the first floor. A door opened a crack, and a blonde head popped out—Marcia or Maggie or something like that, a grad student—followed by an equally curious brunette, her room-mate, both blushing at Killian like he was a strip-o-gram.

They might as well be invisible for all he cared. He breezed past them and bounded up the stairs, two at a time, nimble as a cat despite his long strides.

This is no social call.

I didn't have the energy to fight the inevitable. He raised an eyebrow as he reached the top of the stairs and noticed my state. "Rough night?"

"No, this is just me without my makeup."

"Still trying with the jokes," he said as he stepped past me into the apartment and then stopped cold. "This is where you live? Our holding cells are better."

I thought they didn't have holding cells.

"Not up to your royal standards?"

"It explains a lot."

"Like what?" I squeezed to the door past him to shut it.

"Like why you're so cranky all the time."

Pot meet kettle.

"What's *your* excuse, then?"

He glanced at me *almost* amused.

"Maybe I should build myself a medieval castle. I could spend my days lounging on a velvet throne and barking out orders—*wipe your ass the proper Therian way or get out!*" I said, doing a terrible *Therian King* impression. "No thanks. My life rules. Yours blows."

No sleep. No coffee. No patience. It's math.

He chuckled despite himself. "Always the charmer, Detective."

"Did you grace me with your presence to criticize my home or to highlight my lack of charm with sarcasm, Killian?"

"I came because of the attack on your life last night."

"Maybe they were after the human matchstick."

"Don't be tedious. We both know that's not true."

"Why? Cause your merry band of Therians are beyond reproach and have never made a single enemy? That's funny because they were vampires and vampires hate you guys. And I'm not a virgin, so what would they want with my blood?"

He raised an eyebrow. "That virgin blood thing is not real, they'll take anyone's blood and every last drop of it."

"I know, Killian, I was being tedious."

"Ah, yes you were," he said. "It's not that Therians don't have enemies, it's that no one is stupid enough to challenge me."

"Except me," I said.

"Yes," he said, "except you."

I really don't know what I'm feeling.

"How's Aiden?"

"Healed. Worried." His gaze swept over me, lingering on the bruise on my cheek. "And with good reason. You look one breath away from collapse." He grimaced like he had just tasted bad milk.

I guess I'll hold my breath, then.

"I've had worse. So, Aiden healed already… the healing rumors are true?"

"It's never been a rumor to us."

"Uh huh. And how long do you live?"

He ignored my question, his attention shifting to the coffee table. He picked up my dagger, turning it over in his hands, his fingers brushing against the blade. "Is there bonshek on it?"

I shook my head.

"Last night?"

"Nope."

"Would it have neutralized the uglies if there was?"

"I have no idea. Vamps are different, they don't—"

"Their magic isn't innate," he cut me off. "Sensors don't pick it up. No unique signature or identifying prints. Only necromancy can sustain them."

"Where are you going with this, Killian?"

"What more proof do you need that your necromancers are up to their bony necks in this?" he said, eyes blazing.

My necromancers? Okay, whatever. "All we know is that the vamps didn't want me or Aiden to make it back to Madison."

"And yet, here you stand, against all odds. Did the vampires just let you walk? Decide to call it a night and head home for a nice glass of O-negative margaritas?"

Oh boy. Who knows how Aiden described the fight?

"Maybe they only wanted to scare us."

"Right. You don't believe that any more than I do."

He wasn't wrong. Defending Raven grew more difficult by the second, especially with Killian standing there, circling ever closer to the unsettling truth that I was an illusion mage who had tasted dark magic, and that a part of me started craving after that power for a terrifying instant.

"Alright, fine. You have a point," I said.

"Sorry, what? I couldn't hear over the sound of your ego deflating."

"You. Have. A. Point!" I shouted, cupping my hands around my mouth.

Killian threw back his head and laughed. "I wish I had recorded that. The self-assured Tess Hilliard reduced to a human foghorn."

"Good times. Why don't you use your super brain powers to figure out what happened last night, and how necromancers and vampires fit in," I shot back, "and I'll focus on figuring out how to get us to Nyx, and how to get your delicate ass through the portals in one piece."

"What's the catch?" he said.

"Why does there have to be a catch?"

"It's all too... reasonable. Are you sure you're feeling alright?"

"I am very reasonable."

He snorted. "Even you don't believe that."

Touché. "Look, I'm tired, okay? I can barely string two thoughts together. If we're going to do this whole... unlikely alliance thing, I need at least a few hours of uninterrupted sleep."

"Go ahead," he said, gesturing towards the bedroom. "Catch your Z's. I'll watch over you." He settled onto the couch, making himself at home with a nonchalance that made me want to hurl something at him.

I shot him a glare instead. Was he serious?

"You're so gullible," he said. He pushed himself off the couch, his eyes lingering on mine for a moment. "Relax, Detective. Just messing with you."

But he wasn't. I could see it in his eyes. He would have stayed, planted himself on my lumpy couch while I slept if I'd welcomed it. What game was this, what was he playing at?

"Killian, you could have sent your people to check on me. Why did you come yourself?"

That infuriating grin again. "Because I thought I could see you better in your depleted state, behind the veil of all your facades. I want to know who you really are when our journey begins. And because I wanted to do this."

He closed the distance between us, until he was standing directly before me, his gaze holding mine. My breath hitched in my throat. For one insane moment, I thought he might kiss me.

Instead, he reached out, his hands coming to rest on my shoulders, his touch surprisingly gentle. We just stood there, his warmth seeping into my chilled bones. Then, without a word, he moved me aside, stepping towards the arched window that overlooked the lake.

I watched, mesmerized, as his fingertips lit up, weaving a complex pattern of runes around the windowpane. Wards. Powerful ones. He repeated the process at the door, sealing the apartment in a cocoon of protective magic.

"There," he said, returning his eyes to me. "Nobody gets in without your permission. And even if they had the power to break through the wards, the racket would wake the dead."

He took my hands in his. My whole body shivered with electricity. Energy flowed between us as he keyed the wards to me.

"Thanks," I said, a little breathless. "I'm not very good with wards."

"You're not very good with a lot of things," he said, his eyes on my lips. My heart lost its rhythm entirely. "But what you're good at, you're very, very good at, and that I can trust."

A backhanded compliment, but better than nothing, I guess.

I snapped out of it. "Killian, next time, maybe you could not wake up the entire block? No one just knocks anymore, use your phone, call me when you have something, call me if you come to my door. Now, go."

He grinned, and for a heartbeat I thought he would never go. "Sleep well, Detective," he said instead. "You need your strength, because you're best with your claws out."

I blinked languidly and he was gone.

I stood there for a moment, staring at the empty doorway,

the ward residue of his power tingling my skin.

Claws out, huh? As if our every interaction wasn't a battle of wills more than wit. As if dealing with rogue vamps, meddling Therian Kings, and the seductive lure of dark magic wasn't enough excitement for a lifetime. As if whatever the hell just happened wasn't utterly confounding.

Too tired to think, but there was one last thing I needed to do before sliding under the blankets. If Killian thought I was going to step aside and let him chase the vampire shadows on his own, well, sorry, big guy. I fished out the scrap of paper with Rae Van Zelst's phone number.

Curling up on the edge of the bed, phone in hand, I typed a short, carefully worded text message.

> *Need to talk. It's urgent. Can we meet?*
> *Tess.*

I hit *send* and tossed the phone aside. The moment my head hit the pillow, I went out like a light.

I woke to darkness. The day had been lost, the streetlights painted silver stripes across the ceiling. I fumbled for my phone—8:17 pm. I'd gloriously slept for twelve straight hours, but it wasn't the ridiculous amount of sleep that had me bolt upright in bed.

Raven had replied to my message.

> *Not today. Tomorrow. 4 pm. Olbrich*
> *Botanical Gardens. Thai Pavilion.*

Chapter 16

Showing up at Izzy's door on a Sunday morning felt desperate. I would have been more at ease summoning a demon. I was afraid to call ahead, because I might have chickened out and started spinning some tale instead of sticking to the straight truth. Showing up in person at an empath's house left no room for anything but honesty. Izzy would have seen right through me.

Yazmin opened the door. Her welcoming smile calmed my nerves. I'd met Izzy's partner a few times, always in passing. "Hey there," she greeted me.

"Hey, Yaz, I'm Tess. Is Izzy in?"

"I know who you are, silly, we've met before," she said, pulling me into a hug. "Your timing is perfect. Izzy's wrestling with a pie crust while succumbing to existential dread. She could use a pleasant distraction."

I stepped inside. "Wasn't sure you'd remember me."

"How could I forget? You're one of Izzy's favorite topics of conversation."

Yazmin was a little shorter than me, with sleek black hair, vibrant dark brown eyes, and the kind of effortless warmth that made you feel right at home. Izzy had won the lottery in the life partner department. And vice versa.

She led me through a small, cozy sitting room to a bright kitchen that at that moment resembled a culinary war zone. Cartons, boxes and cans littered the counters. Pots bubbled ominously on the stove, filling the room with aromas of cinnamon, nutmeg and something distinctly… sour? The island counter was buried under a mountain of cookbooks, scattered flour, and a turkey baster that looked like it might have been used in battle.

Izzy stood in the middle of this culinary apocalypse with her back to us, a cloud of flour hovering around her like a halo. She spun as we entered, eyes wide with surprise, not because of my injuries—I'd covered all that up with an extra thick illusion veil. Izzy was shocked simply because I was standing right there in her house.

"Look what the cat dragged in," Yazmin said.

"Hey, Iz," I said with a grin.

Izzy wiped her hands with a dish towel, then rubbed her face, leaving a white streak across her cheek. "Tess? It's Sunday, hon," she said. "Thanksgiving isn't until Thursday."

"I know Thanksgiving is a Thursday," I said. "Sheesh."

"Okay, well, are you okay?" Izzy said. She gestured towards her flour splattered apron. "I'd give you a hug, but this thing might be a biohazard."

"As long as it's not strychnine, you're good," I said.

She chuckled, then pulled me into a hug that smelled faintly of vanilla and pumpkin spice. It felt good, this easy affection. No hidden agendas, no tests of loyalty, no veiled threats. Just a hug.

"Maybe we should move this to the living room," Yazmin suggested. "It's a mess here. Let me take that apron."

"Actually," I said, fixing my gaze on Izzy, "this is not exactly a social call. I need some professional advice, Izzy."

Yazmin's eyebrows shot up, but she just smiled. "I'll be in the bedroom, imposing order on the sock drawer. If such a thing is possible."

As soon as Yazmin disappeared down the hallway, Izzy turned to me, pulling off her apron and tossing it onto the counter with a sigh.

"So, what's all this?" I said. "Are you throwing a party tonight?"

"Um, no. I've never cooked a Thanksgiving meal from scratch before, so this is... a practice run?" She winced. "It's not going well."

"Wow, that's ambitious even for you. What are you going to do with all this experimental food?"

"Share with friends, donate to shelters. Grab anything you fancy."

I reached for a tray of biscuits on the counter and bit into one. It was surprisingly crunchy. And dry. Very, very dry.

"What do you think?" Izzy said.

"Mmm, very... interesting texture," I managed, trying to swallow the mouthful of sawdust without choking.

"You hate it, don't you?"

"No, love it, Iz," I said, taking another bite for good measure. "Yummy."

Izzy rolled her eyes. "That was a blatant lie. What's going on, Tess? Why the surprise visit?"

"I need your expertise, both as a researcher and an empath."

Her smile faded. "Is this for a case?"

"You could say that. But it's not a Shadow Chasers case."

"The Bureau then?"

"Sort of?"

Izzy leaned back against the counter. "Alright, Tess. Out with it. What's got you so spooked you'd brave a visit to my home for the first time ever?"

"It's... complicated."

"Isn't it always? Hit me. What do you need?"

"The Netherworld," I blurted out. "Specifically, Nyx."

The coffee mug Izzy had just picked up clattered back onto the counter. "Nyx? You know what they say about Nyx, Tess. Even demons don't leave a forwarding address when they flee Nyx."

"Yeah, yeah, one of the darkest Nether Realms, I know." I pushed a stray crumb across the counter. "I need your research genius."

"Researching the Nether Realms is like trying to herd cats. Blindfolded. While riding a unicycle on a tightrope. Over a pit of lava."

I bit back a laugh. "I know, that's why I need you."

"This isn't for a research paper, is it? I smell danger, Tess.

Not the fun *send a fuzzy creature back to its realm* kind, but real danger."

"I need to determine the safest portal sequence to Nyx. And figure out how to get someone else there. Someone who can't do it on their own."

Izzy frowned. "This better be a bad joke, because I want no part in getting you killed or imprisoned. You no doubt have access to maps for every dimension tucked away in some secret Bureau vault."

I sensed a tiny bit of resentment in her voice. Damn her empathic senses. She knew I was holding back, hiding things from her.

"My resources are limited just now," I said, avoiding her eyes. "And time is an immutable factor."

I couldn't risk going anywhere near the Bureau's archives. And Izzy, bless her bookish heart, had privileged access to the Runestone Academy's library as a junior researcher, a treasure trove of arcane knowledge that even the Bureau envied.

"You're considering going to Nyx yourself, aren't you?" she said.

"Ah, that's... fluid. It's all speculative." I tried to remain as vague as possible. Lying to Izzy was like tap-dancing on a minefield: risky and guaranteed to blow up in my face. "That brings me to my second ask. I need your help figuring out... something... about someone."

"If you're not specific, how can I be, Tess?"

I took a deep breath. "I need to know if someone is lying to me."

Her face hardened. "Empathy isn't a parlor trick. Prying into someone's mind without their permission is forbidden. I don't do that."

"You do it at the office, all the time."

"People there know I'm an empath. They can choose to shield their thoughts or avoid me entirely."

Shit. There was no workaround. I had to cough up the truth. A version of the truth, anyway. "This isn't an official case, but it does involve the Bureau. And I must be getting close to something big, because last night, I was attacked, as in ambushed."

The color drained from Izzy's face, leaving her as pale as the flour dusting the countertops. "Attacked? By whom? What happened?"

"Vampires."

"My god, Tess, are you hurt?"

"I'm fine," I said. I was beginning to doubt the wisdom of covering up my injuries, but it was too late for that. "I wouldn't have walked away in one piece if it hadn't been for Aiden, a fledgling elemental warrior. He's the only reason I'm standing in your kitchen right now talking to you."

Another carefully crafted partial truth.

"What have you gotten yourself into?" she muttered, likely picking up on the dissonance between my words and my body language. "Wait, the person you want me to read... is a necromancer?"

Even when not using her empath skills, she'd always been a great reader of body language and voice tone and the confessions of the human face.

I nodded. "Maybe let's forget the whole thing—"

Izzy held up a hand, silencing me. "Who is this necromancer?"

"Rae Van Zelst, she works with the Bureau."

"Tess, there's a limit to what I can do, even for you. I can't just read anyone's mind. Elemental warriors, vampires—their magic is a fortress. It's like trying to pick a lock with a noodle."

"Raven's not a vampire."

"No, but she's fully *bonded* to one. Their auras are intertwined. Her mind's off limits, even for me."

I chewed on that. Did it mean Rae Van Zelst was *involved* with a vamp she helped create? *Holy shit.* "How do you know any of that?"

"Believe it or not, Gideon revealed that. Let's just say, it came up at the Bureau during one of his visits."

Gideon Crawford? What the hell was he doing, poking around in the Bureau's dirty laundry?

Part of me wished I'd never dragged Izzy into this mess. I never wanted her to touch the darkness I'd touched. The path of least resistance would be to bring her to the meeting with Raven under false pretenses, then piggyback on Izzy's empathic skill to pry into Raven's mind myself, but if Izzy couldn't pierce the vampire's shield, I stood no chance.

Unlike Gideon's persuasion magic, which was a battering ram, a force that projected his will outwards, Izzy's empathic power was a finely tuned antenna, receiving and amplifying emotions and intentions. Even on a good day, the emotional overload was too much for me to handle, which was why I was never tempted to tap into Izzy's magic.

"Why didn't you go to the Bureau with this?" Izzy went on. "They have the resources and connections to handle this kind of stuff."

I stared down at my hands. "The Bureau is crawling with secrets and, possibly, double agents. Raven could be playing both sides for all I know. I have no idea who's on whose side. You're the only one I can trust, Iz."

She sighed, running a hand through her hair. "Look, the research part I can do. I'll hit the library and see what I can dig up about Nyx, but—"

"That's great, but I really need to know if Raven sent her vampires to kill me, or if she knows who did it, and if they killed Miles Donovan."

"Miles Donovan? The Bureau coordinator? They said he died in his sleep."

"He was murdered. And the scene... was brutal."

"You're serious? This is big, Tess. Bureau-level big. Bigger than you can handle alone. It's *fucking deadly*."

The fact that Izzy, who rarely cursed, swore with such conviction proved how deep I was going and how careful I had to be.

I made up my mind. "It's personal. I was close to Miles... long ago."

Understanding dawned in her eyes. "You dated him."

"Back at the Academy. We kept it quiet at the time, because of the whole teacher-student thing, but he meant a lot to me." I reached out, taking her hand in mine. "Here," I said, channeling a thread of her magic into the touch, letting her feel the truth of my words.

Her fingers tightened around mine. "I'm so sorry, Tess."

She left the last part unsaid. *I'm sorry everyone dies on you.*

"I need to find his killer," I said, "before there's another victim."

Izzy rubbed her temples. "If it comes down to Raven's involvement with a vampire, it complicates things. Their bonds are deep, intertwined with magic that even I can't breach without unseen consequences. The vampire will shield her and when I try to force my way in, that vamp will get frisky."

"What if we separate them? Not for long, just for the time you need."

Izzy studied me, weighing her options. "We can try. But the moment things go sideways, we pull out. No heroics."

"Understood." I meant it, for a moment, mostly.

"You have to promise me one more thing."

"Anything."

"Next time, just call first, yeah? And maybe bring coffee. Bradbury's, the good stuff. I love Yaz but her coffee tastes like it was brewed inside those socks she's organizing."

I laughed. "Deal."

"And Tess?"

"Yeah, Iz?"

"Be careful. This rabbit hole you're descending... it's deep and dark. And there's nothing good to find at the bottom."

I shrugged. "Who knows? Maybe I'll run into the Easter Bunny."

Oh, shit, I am tedious.

THE BITING WIND NIPPED at our faces as Izzy and I trudged along the snow-powdered paths of the Olbrich Botanical Gardens. We crossed the arched bridge to the Thai Garden, and the golden pavilion came into view, a stunning splash of color against a white winter wonderland accented by desolate trees and striking frost-glazed branches.

"The Thai Pavilion in absolute silence," Izzy said, her breath misting. "Either Raven's hopelessly romantic, or she's angling for creepy isolation."

"Those are the same thing to her," I said, my senses on high alert.

The air felt different here. Denser, charged with a malign energy that prickled my skin like static electricity. I could sense them out there, lurking behind trees and thickets—vampires.

Raven leaned against a pillar under the pavilion's red ceiling, which was decorated with gilded lotus blossoms. Her long, dark hair hung loose, framing a face that was beautiful in a sharp, haunting way. Her blue eyes were fixed on the frozen pond in front of the pavilion. She projected a profound sadness. I imagined her tears were made of sapphire. Dressed in a long, black coat, she had the dark sorcerer look down to a T. Her pale as porcelain skin seemed almost luminescent in the dim light filtering through the winter clouds.

Even from a distance, I could feel the necromantic power thrumming around her, triggering an unwanted memory—the intoxicating surge of dark magic flooding my own core. But it was the chilling lack of emotion in the immaculate, chiseled features of the man standing behind her that truly unsettled me. He was someone who had walked in the shadows for so long that he seemed entirely made of long shafts of gloom and shades of gray.

I glanced at Izzy, who gave a small nod, her expression tense.

"Raven," I said as we drew closer to the pavilion. "I'm sorry we're late."

Raven's pale eyes met mine, a flicker of curiosity passing through them. "Tess," she replied smoothly. "I see you've brought a friend."

"I see the same," I countered, my gaze shifting to the silent vampire at her back. "Seems like you have a whole squad here."

"Hey, I'm Iz," Izzy said, waving a friendly hand.

Raven's gaze shifted to her and intensified. "Pleasure."

The hidden vampires pressed closer, like a cold hand on my spine. I forced myself to stay collected if not calm. I now knew they fed on fear and hesitation, and I wasn't going to offer them a platter.

"The Pavilion is breathtaking in winter," I said, breaking the ice.

Raven's lips curved into a smile. "An elegance within the wild."

Two vamps shot out of the trees, taking up positions on

opposite sides of the pavilion—a male and a female.

The male vampire was tall and lean with gleaming amber eyes and a scruffy appeal. The female vampire was petite and graceful, with skin so white you could see the faint blue veins in her neck, yet with eyes as black as coal.

Raven's energy had shifted now that she had vampires at her side. The casual, approachable façade she'd worn at the morgue had vanished, replaced by someone far more guarded, someone who was as comfortable commanding the forces of darkness as she was choosing apples at the grocery store.

The most arresting thing, though, was that Raven's vampires looked startlingly human—not just that, they were beautiful. I'd heard plenty of tales of pet vampires, cherished companions to their necromancer creators who retained their humanity, their bloodlust kept in check by a careful balance of dark magic and willpower. But seeing that bond firsthand was something unexpected. These were no vampiric beasts, nothing like the bony, feral monstrosities that had attacked Aiden and me.

Raven was clearly bound to them, using her magic resources to shield them from the sunlight, feeding them with... well, I didn't want to delve too deep into their private affairs, but whatever the logistics, it was working.

Turning a human into a vampire involved much more than a big bite with big fangs. It required a dark ritual, a necromancer's unique touch to weave the forces that twisted life into undeath. This created a bond between the newly turned vampire and the necromancer, a link that was often harmonious, but at times fraught with tension and resentment. By ancient rite, a vampire could only be made with the full consent of someone on the brink of death, but in rogue corners of the supernatural world, necromancers routinely ignored the rules.

For many necromancers, these bonds were disposable. The fortunate vampires, the ones brought immediately under a necromancer's protection after turning, were spared the savage frenzy of a blood-sucking rampage that could drown the rational part of their mind. These controlled undead often stayed close to their makers, though some rejected the bond eventually and roamed free, their elegance masking their darker nature.

When vampires were bonded after going feral and losing themselves to the beast within, they became thralls, vampiric beasts bound to their master with an unbreakable, eternal leash that made them attack dogs.

The vampire at Raven's back was something else. Tall, powerfully built, with dark skin and eyes like twin pools of molasses. An aura of quiet strength clung to him, his gaze never straying from Raven, every muscle coiled with a readiness that bordered on obsession. This was the fully bonded one. The one whose life was inextricably linked to hers, making her a closed book that even the most skilled empath couldn't crack open.

I had made a colossal mistake bringing Izzy. If Raven decided to set her vampires on us, I could not hijack her power fast enough to stop them.

"Vampires," I said as I glanced at the silent predator behind

Raven. "Not exactly my cup of tea. No offense."

"They are not wired to be offended," Raven said.

I know how they're wired.

"Couldn't they, you know, go on a bathroom break?"

"They're here because right now trust is a luxury I can't afford."

"Hey, you told me to come to you for help."

"That was before I heard about the company you keep."

She obviously didn't mean Izzy.

Raven let out a slow, measured breath. "Word is the Therian King has taken a shine to you, and you don't seem to shy away from the attention."

Izzy pinched my arm, hard. *Ouch.* I shot her a bewildered look. She met it with a silent question in her widened eyes. *Seriously, Tess? Playing footsie with a warrior king and I'm the last to know?*

Clearly, my secret maneuvers had quickly become public knowledge.

Total fucking mess.

"What are you suggesting, Raven? You think I'm sleeping with Killian Tierney?" I said in a pissy tone. "I'm not. How rude."

"Don't insult my intelligence, Tess. You think I don't have sources?"

"You need better sources," I said. "I ran into Killian while investigating a library portal malfunction. After Miles died, he became interested in the case because, like you, he thinks his kind are being framed. That's it. Nothing more to it, other than you are both equally pushy and rude. I'm in no way working with him against you behind your back. That's not my job. I don't take sides."

"Killian and his elemental warriors could slaughter my vampires before we had time to blink. You should understand my concern."

"Good for you that I am here instead of him to face your false accusations then!" I snapped back. I looked down to my feet, trying to tamp down the irritation I felt. "Unlike your entourage, Izzy and I are not killing machines. We are unarmed, deficient in combat magic, and we're here to talk, not brawl."

Raven snapped her fingers. The female vampire appeared before Izzy and me in a blur of motion. She craned her neck, sniffing the air around us like a hellhound. *Oh shit.* If vampires could sniff out magic signatures hidden under illusion veils, we were screwed.

The vampire finally stepped back, seemingly satisfied with whatever she smelled. "They're clean," she said, her voice surprisingly soft.

"Thank you, Amara," Raven said. "Give us some privacy."

The vampires retreated to the stark winter tree line, keeping their unnerving glances locked on us.

I couldn't help myself. I waved goodbye. *Yeah, yeah, go find someone else's throat to rip while I discuss grown up stuff with your mistress.*

The moment they were gone, the tension in Raven's shoulders eased, her face relaxing into her trademark blasé expression.

"Sorry about the theatrics," she said. "I have to keep them sharp."

She descended the pavilion steps, casually, to stand with us like three girls in the school yard. *Multiple personalities much?*

"Really, because that sucked. Power plays are useless directed at powerless people like us," I said, making no effort to hide my annoyance. "You could have just *asked* about Killian."

"Human social graces are not my strong suit," she said. "And I confess to have both enjoyed and found answers in the look of terror on your face. In my own way, I do like to have a bit of fun."

This crazy bitch!

"I was most certainly *not* terrified."

"Both of you were a little freaked." She considered Izzy, who was doing a commendable job of staying low key despite fangs flaring around us.

"Well, yeah. Vampires are scary," Izzy said.

Raven's eyes narrowed. "What's *your* reason for bringing company, Tess? Her soul is too gentle for this business. She is not adequate backup."

"Izzy works with me at my agency. I trust her with my life, and she thinks I need a babysitter, and, well, she was dead on."

I had no idea if Raven believed a word, but she seemed satisfied.

"What do you have on your mind, Tess?" Raven said as if the last ten minutes never happened. "Anything you're willing to share?"

"I have nothing new except that on Friday night I was viciously attacked by vampires hoping to ingest me."

Her eyebrows shot up. "Attacked? By vampires, multiple vampires... and you survived without a scratch?"

For the second time today, I realized hiding my vampire injuries with illusion magic wasn't the best move.

"You sound disappointed," I said.

Raven tilted her head. "Of course I'm relieved you're in one piece, but vampires against a low-level wind mage? The math doesn't add up."

"I wasn't alone," I conceded. "The specifics of how I got away aren't important. What matters is who controls those beasts."

"You don't think they were mine?"

I shook my head to dispel that notion as fast as possible. "No, I am not so quick to accuse as others. Those were feral, mindless beasts, fueled by bloodlust, tethered to the will of a necromancer like puppets on strings."

For the first time, Raven looked unnerved. "Were they thralls?"

"I'm no expert, but, yeah, they might have been."

"A black day," Raven said under her breath. "Only an arch necromancer can command thralls effectively."

Peachy. Not only was I attacked by rogue vampires, but they belonged to a notoriously sadistic type of dark sorcerer. "So, I'm basically screwed?"

"Yeah, you are, but not just you."

What else is new? "Any ideas on the arch douche's identity?"

"It's better you don't know," Raven said. "Going after an

arch necro leads to one possible outcome—your death."

"I'm not going after anyone." *Izzy's lie detector must be going haywire.* "But I'd like to know who I need to avoid."

"If I could help, I would, but I'm persona non grata among my fellow dark arts practitioners thanks to my affiliation with the Bureau. They would sooner share secrets with a drunk at a bar than with me."

"Right," I said, "I get that, however, any hunch that crosses your mind or old scraps of intel you come across would be more than I have."

"For the record, I aggressively think this is a terrible idea," Raven said, "but I'll run it around the block and see if there's anything out of place."

"Appreciate that, Raven, I really do."

She raised her chin and looked down her nose at me. "For one as powerless as you claim to be, you sure attract a lot of heavy hitters."

"That's her one special power," Izzy chimed in. "Butting her cute little nose in to where it most certainly does not belong."

I glared at her. She shrugged, unrepentant.

"Raven, one last thing. The missing Codex page at the Corinth library."

She crossed her arms. "How did you hear about that?"

"Miles mentioned it. What was on that page?"

Raven rubbed her neck, a glaring nervous tell. "A Nether-world portal nexus," she said. "And you didn't hear that from me."

"Do we trust Raven?" I asked Izzy as we walked to the parking lot.

"About as far as I could throw a mountain."

We climbed into Izzy's beat-up Subaru. I peeled my gloves off and rubbed my numb fingers together to regain some feeling. Izzy started the car and flicked on the defroster. The windshield cleared slowly, revealing the snow-dusted gardens we were leaving behind.

"Were you able to read her?" I pressed.

"Yeah," Izzy said flatly, pulling the car out into the street.

"Don't keep me in suspense," I said, watching as headlights from the oncoming traffic sliced through the gathering dusk.

"She's sincere to the extent that she believes what she's saying is true," Izzy said, swerving to merge onto Atwood Avenue. "There wasn't any obvious deception, but that doesn't mean much with necromancers."

I chewed on my lip, my anxiety hitting new highs. "So, not exactly *welcome to the coven* material?"

"Rae Van Zelst is dangerous, Tess. She creeped the hell out of me, and that's with a capital C. There's a deep well of power in her, and she's fiercely protective of those vamps. But beneath it all, there's a flicker of... fear. Maybe for herself, maybe for someone else. That doesn't matter. That fear is her north star and the only thing she will remain true to. She wants something from you. FROM YOU. Not for you. So, no, not trustworthy. Not even close."

I replayed the scene in my head. Raven's bonded vamp made me shiver just thinking of him—a big, flashing warning sign wrapped in a menacing, hyper fit, somewhat enchanting package.

"Thanks for the reality check," I said. "I'm glad you're on my team."

She snorted. "You're lucky is what you are, Tess Hilliard. Having a walking lie detector as your work bestie has its perks."

Bestie... even work bestie, I'll take it.

I liked having someone to trust. I never had that. I even liked Izzy's bluntness and her stern lectures. It felt... real. Grounded.

"And Tess? About Nyx... You're not fucking doing that."

When I said blunt, I meant it. *Sheesh.*

Chapter 17

MONDAY MORNINGS WERE USUALLY a madhouse at Shadow Chasers Agency, but this was Thanksgiving week, traditionally the slowest stretch on the calendar. While cases tended to spike around holidays, whether they involved genuine paranormal phenomena or just overactive imaginations fueled by holiday stress, Thanksgiving proved to be the exception to the rule.

I leaned back in my office chair, booted feet propped up on the desk against a stack of cold case files. I twirled a pen between my fingers, staring at the blurred photographs of alleged cryptids plastered on the off-white wall across the room.

Half the staff was out for the week, getting ready to dig into stuffing and pumpkin pie with their families, including Pankowski and Gideon. My request for vacation time had been denied with a resounding *not-a-chance*—penance, I supposed, for my increasing number of unexcused *personal days* lately.

The old phone on my desk rang. *Anonymous caller*, the blinking display informed me. I snatched up the receiver with a jaw-cracking yawn.

"Shadow Chasers, Investigator Hilliard speaking, how may I help you?"

"What did your necro pal want?" Killian's low growl was unmistakable.

Fucking hell. Was my life broadcast to everyone? Was I unwittingly cast as a baby in the sequel to *The Truman Show*?

"I'm at work," I hissed quietly between clenched teeth. "I'm busy here. I don't have time for this right now."

"Why did you—"

I hung up on him. I counted to three. Sure enough, the phone shrieked again, somehow shriller than usual. I picked it up then slammed it back down with enough force to make the stapler jump. The bastard had me shadowed. Again. After I explicitly demanded him to stop. Twice now. *Ugh.* The man had no concept of taking no for an answer.

The main door banged open. Izzy blustered in, her wild fiery curls escaping her messy ponytail and her cheeks flushed, a thick tome tucked under her arm. She made a beeline for my cubicle.

"You're late," I said, quirking an eyebrow.

"I was at the Runestone Library," she said, panting. She shrugged off her oversized peacoat. "Mapping out the safest route to Nyx."

I perked up at that. "Really? Iz! You rock, tell me!"

She dropped the book onto my desk with a thud. "The fastest way I could chart involves navigating eight different portal nexuses, two of them in the Netherworld. Even with the best-case scenario, we're talking about two days of travel, one and a half if we're lucky, assuming no dimensional turbulence or unforeseen detours."

Eight portals... Getting Killian and his entourage through that gauntlet would be a monumental undertaking, to say the least. I smothered a groan.

"But that's not even the interesting part," Izzy said. "I dug up some pretty fascinating information in those old tomes."

I got my feet off the desk to lean forward. "Oh? You are a beautiful dangerous genius."

"Guess who's mastered the art of teleporting others through portals?"

She paused for dramatic effect. I shrugged, playing along.

"Vampires, that's who," she proclaimed triumphantly. "More specifically, pet vampires with strong necromantic bonds. They've been escorting necromancers through portals for centuries."

I chewed on that, considering the possibilities. "Meaning..."

"Meaning, if you can borrow one of Raven's vamps, your problems are solved. They could ferry your mystery person through all those nexuses with no issue. *All gas, no brakes* as they say."

That was an ingenious idea, apart from relying on a vampire and being completely dependent on Raven's unpredictable moods. Yet, it was infinitely better than my current non-plan of stumbling blindly from one portal to the next, hoping no one noticed.

"How many non-walkers do you think a single vampire can usher through a portal at the same time?"

Izzy furrowed her brow, her excitement extinguished. "What in the world are you planning, Tess? Marching an army through to Nyx?"

"Not quite an army..."

Izzy threw up her hands with an exasperated huff, smacking her palms on her thighs. "Nope. I'm done. No more involvement with your suicide schemes until you level with me. We're doing this my way—complete transparency, no dodging. Who is it you are so determined to drag to the darkest corner of the Netherworld?"

"I don't want you involved any further, Iz, but you deserve to know what's going on. I'll tell you everything, but not here."

"Lunch?"

"Yeah, sure. Let's do that Cuban restaurant on State Street and—"

Killian burst through the main door, his eyes blazing with hellfire.

You've got to be kidding me. How did he get here so fast? And why did he look so damn good with his chestnut hair blown back? Worn leather jacket, black biker boots, smoldering eyes. Did he ride a motorcycle or a ley line here?

Stop it, Tess. Just stop!

He stalked across the floor, weaving around desks, shoving past a stunned Delgado, our gruff ex-military tracker, sending the burly man staggering. The terrified look on Delgado's weathered face told me he recognized the infamous Killian Tierney. Few people radiated that much raw power and contained fury—not even in our line of business.

The Therian King planted himself directly in front of my desk, towering over Izzy, his presence looming over the entire agency floor.

"You have some nerve," I ground out.

"No, what I have is authority. And you, Investigator, are going to tell me exactly what I need to know."

Shoving away from my chair, I rose to my feet and braced my hands on the desk. "This is what's going to happen, *dragon boy*. You're going to turn around and march that smug face of yours right out of my cubicle area."

Izzy went completely pale. She shot me an incredulous look that pretty much screamed, *what the hell are you doing?*

A low, rumbling growl reverberated from Killian's chest.

"Oh, am I supposed to be impressed by that?" I scoffed. "I'm sorry, let me put on my *dazed with terror* face."

His hand whipped out, but I'd seen that *deadly grip* move before. I leaned back just in time, his fingertips grazing the side of my neck, leaving a trail of goosebumps in their wake.

"You had me followed!" I shouted, my anger exploding. "How many times did I tell you that was a dealbreaker?"

The effort it took him to stay composed, to rein in his fury, was visible in the tightening of his jaw, the flare of his nostrils. "I didn't break my promise. You told me not to have you followed. I never did. I followed you myself."

Oh. My. God. The sheer audacity of this self-serving, arrogant prick!

"The fact that you think there's a difference just proves everything. You are a giant, egotistical child."

I slammed my palm on the desk for emphasis.

Izzy had turned into a statue, caught between intervening and making herself scarce.

"Izzy," I said, turning to my wide-eyed friend, "give us a moment."

She hesitated, her gaze darting between Killian and me. "I can stay if you need backup," she offered.

"Nah, he's mostly bark." *Or whatever the hell dragons do.*

She remained uncertain but gave a reluctant nod, gathering her peacoat and her book. She shot me one final worried look before slipping away.

The moment we were alone, Killian caught my arm in a gentle but firm grip. "Let's move to more private grounds."

"Oh, Tess, why don't you just drop everything you're doing and come stroke my ego," I said in my best mocking voice, yanking my arm away from his grasp.

He scouted the office floor, his gaze lingering on the empty chairs and abandoned coffee mugs. "What are you doing exactly? Guarding the chairs?"

"What I do is none of your business."

The Therian King sighed. "If the mule won't go to the field to graze," he muttered under his breath.

Did he call me a mule?

He made a circle with his hand in the air. The circle shimmered faintly, like heat ripples, then expanded all around us—a dome of swirling energy that cloaked us in a shielding veil.

"There, now we can speak privately right here. Though I must admit, I still consider these chairs riveting adversaries."

Cute. He thinks he's charming.

"You've been stalking me," I said, the realization dawning. "Shadowing my every movement."

"And you demanded honesty and transparency," he countered, eyes locked on mine. "That was supposed to be a reciprocal arrangement."

"Obviously. I wasn't planning on hiding that I met with Raven, or the details she shared. But unlike you, I can't just drop in at your palace whenever I want to update you. Hell, I don't even have your number."

He exhaled, nodded and brushed back his hair. "You might have a point there. I can see how that makes communication... difficult."

Understatement of the year.

"What was that, oh mighty King? Sorry, I couldn't hear over the sound of your ego deflating," I teased, throwing his own words back at him.

He nipped a grin in the bud. "I'm here now, so enlighten me. What unreliable manipulations did the *lovely* Rae Van Zelst try to pass off as secrets?"

"Nuh-uh," I said, crossing my arms, enjoying this rare moment of holding all the cards. "First, exactly how long have you been stalking me? And why are you not busy... oh, I don't know... vanquishing our enemies? Saving the world? Performing the kingly duties we agreed on?"

He didn't appreciate my tone, but he reined in whatever retort was on the tip of his tongue. "The wards alerted me when you left your house. I wanted to make sure you were not set upon again by assassins."

The wards. Of course. There was an ancillary reason behind his generosity and concern. Why is there such a fine line between chivalry and opportunity?

"You really are insufferable, manipulative—" I struggled to find more appropriate descriptors, my vocabulary failing in the face of such audacity.

"Concerned?" he offered, helpfully. "Protective? Effective?"

I glared at him, my heart surging in my chest. "Don't push your luck. Stalking might be tolerated in Dragonland, but in Madison, Wisconsin, it's called being a creep. If you insist on pulling this chauvinist schtick, you need to give me a heads up, so I know you're lurking, got it?"

He exhaled sharply through his nostrils, then brought one hand up to rub the tense muscles at the back of his neck.

"What, no witty comeback?" I prodded.

"I have listened to your proposal..." He met my gaze evenly. "I agree to tell you when I am lurking, but you are essential and must be protected."

"That's what we call an understanding. Not so hard."

He said the words, but... he'd acquiesced a little too easily.

"You have your victory," he said, sternly. "Now detail this impromptu meeting with Van Zelst."

"Couldn't you hear us? I thought dragons had incredible hearing."

"She chose the open location for a reason," Killian said. "I couldn't get close enough to make out most of it. If I had, we might be eating broiled vamp burgers right now."

I cringed. "That's gross, you sociopath. And incinerating potential allies is a terrible strategy. Raven is not responsible for the vampire attack."

"Because she talks girl talk with you?"

"Girl talk? What? No, you weirdo, because I had an empath with me."

"Ah, the redhead?"

"Her name's Izzy."

"And you trust her judgment?"

"More than I will ever trust yours. Raven revealed that the Codex page that went missing in Corinth was another portal nexus to the Netherworld."

He nodded, slowly. "It all tracks. Anything else of importance?"

"Just that I've mapped a potential route to Nyx. And I believe I've landed upon a method that could Express Pass us all the way through."

"Excellent work," he said, turning to go. "I'll make haste to arrange the preparations on my end."

"Wait, hold on! What about you? Have you made any progress or discoveries from... *your end*?"

He paused, his shoulders rising and falling in an indifferent shrug. "Why bother when you clearly enjoy doing it all yourself? *You* are my discovery."

Was he sulking? And trying to share the credit like a spoiled child?

"I'm just doing my job."

Fast as lightning, Killian snatched the Twix bar off my desk, unwrapped it and took a big bite.

"See you tonight, then," he said, mouth full, going for the door.

"Tonight?" I echoed. "Where?"

"Haven't decided yet," he threw over his shoulder. "But I'll let you know when I know, *sweetheart.*"

The privacy veil shimmered and vanished leaving me standing there, speechless, staring at the empty space he'd occupied a moment before.

Unbelievable.

I grabbed my jacket and marched over to Izzy's desk. "Come on, we're going out for lunch. Sorry about all that."

Izzy glanced up at me. "It's not even ten yet."

"Don't care, we're doing lunch. I'm hungry!"

She held up her hands in surrender. "Alright, lunch it is then."

I spun on my heel and pushed through the front door, needing to escape the office. Izzy hurried to catch up as I scurried toward the lake shore.

"Tell me if I am out of line," she said, "but the way you talked to Killian Tierney... do you think it wise? How do you know him that way?"

I shot her a sidelong glance. "It's the only way to talk to a man like that. It's necessary to penetrate his thick, arrogant skull."

"Tess, I don't understand. He's the leader of an elemental warrior clan. He's notorious, and not for his kindness. He wields ancient powers and he's a direct descendant of the Primals, used to commanding others, and you're treating him like a... a disobedient mutt. But you knew that already. You know exactly who and what he is."

"From your eyes I look reckless, I get it, but it didn't start that way. That man makes me behave this way."

She pinned me with a knowing look. "You chew him out with no fear. Raven might be right about this. Have you slept with him?"

"You two gossip girls. No, there's no secret sexcapades going on, Iz."

"Yeah, not now, but if that was any indication, they're in your future. The sexual tension back there, you'd need a chainsaw to cut through it."

For crying out loud. Sexual tension. Ha! "Half the time he's probably fantasizing about ripping out my spine," I said.

"Such thoughts could be his kink, you don't know. And the other half of the time what's he thinking? Because damn, Tess... he may be a Therian predator, but he's also fit like a gladiator. I'm a happily committed woman, but if I was single? My goodness, I'd happily fall right on his sword."

That image... what the hell, Iz!

"Wait... You're bi? And nasty?"

Izzy shook her head. "Listening is not your power. I've mentioned it before, Tess. But that's beside the point. What I'm saying is, watch your step. Defying an elemental warrior of his stature at every turn is a recipe for disaster. Don't make yourself such an obvious challenge."

"It's him. He's the one going to Nyx," I blurted out. "And with luck, maybe he'll stay there."

Izzy stopped walking. She frowned. "That last thing you said, you were not sincere. I felt it. You're so deep in denial, buried in it. I also sense you are hiding, from everyone, but mostly from yourself. This habit runs deep, it makes you vulnerable. Your enemy might be you."

Iz, now you decide to see me? For the first time? We're trying to have a fun lunch. My goodness. Broken women need to eat, too.

Chapter 18

Confiding in Izzy about Miles, Killian, the Codex pages and the whole Nyx business had felt like the right call at lunchtime. I mean, it wouldn't have been fair to ask for her help without looping her into all the gritty details, right?

Wrong!

By dinner, second thoughts picked at me like gremlins. I'd broken rule number one and flung the doors open to my dangerous games, all for the fleeting comfort of Izzy's steadfast loyalty. Now, the only decent thing left to do was to slam those doors shut again to protect her from the inevitable fallout, no matter how much we both suffered in the process.

I plopped down on the couch, a bowl of vanilla ice cream in one hand, remote control in the other, flipping through channels until an old rerun of *Everybody Loves Raymond* caught my eye. Two more days of the usual grind at the office, then a four-day weekend, which, if everything went as planned, could involve a trip to Nyx.

Freaking bonkers.

My phone buzzed, cutting through the TV's canned laughter. *Blocked caller ID.* Dragon King, back for round two? I braced myself, half-expecting him to announce he was camped out on my fire escape, binoculars in hand, taking his stalking game to a whole new level of slimy.

I forced some calm into my voice. "Hello."

The clipped voice on the other end was familiar though unexpected. "Detective Hilliard? This is Director Harris. I need to speak with you. In person."

I almost choked on my ice cream, bolting upright so fast I feared I'd swallow the spoon. "Director Harris? Of course, whatever you need."

"How soon can you get to the Bureau?"

"What? Right now?"

"Yes."

"Um… I can be there in half an hour."

"Good. My assistant will be waiting for you in the lobby." *Click.*

What's happening right now? I stared at my phone, stupefied. 8:12 in the evening. What was so urgent that it couldn't wait until morning?

It's a setup, Tess, my inner voice hissed. *Don't go. Not alone.*

I knew the voice was right. Director Harris summoning me after dark was suspicious as hell. We barely knew each other, and, well, let's just say I wasn't someone she respected. Then again, since my secrets hardly remained secret these days, she might want to grill me about Killian. Or Raven. Or both.

Only one way to find out. Imani Harris may not have been

my biggest fan, but she was still the Bureau's top dog—when she called, you answered.

I threw on some clothes, snatched my trusty dagger and slid it inside my boot sheath, then tucked a tiny vial of my last remaining supply of bonshek, the magic-eater as Killian had put it, securely into an inner pocket.

A girl needs to be prepared.

The Bureau's main lobby was a ghost town at this hour. The Director's assistant, the tall spell conjurer I remembered from my last visit, greeted me with a frown. She looked like she'd rather be cleaning goblin vomit than escorting me to her boss's fourth floor office.

Director Harris was hunched over her desk, her face illuminated by the glow of the computer screen. She looked tired. There was a deep weariness etched into the lines of her face.

"Director Harris," I said quietly, trying not to startle her.

"Thanks for coming on short notice, Detective. Please take a seat."

Well, the civility took a step up from our last encounter.

"Thank you, Reece, that will be all," she said.

The assistant closed the door behind her, leaving us alone.

"I'm not going to beat about the bush," Director Harris said. "We found an item among Agent Donovan's personal effects—something I hope you will shed light on."

That caught me completely off guard. Everything felt wrong.

She turned her monitor around, the screen facing me. A video file popped up, the image a bit grainy: Miles, sitting in a windowless room, a single bare bulb overhead—a basement most likely. He looked different, haunted... his usual easy charm replaced by a chilling intensity.

Director Harris pressed play. Miles's deep, velvety voice filled the office, a ghost from the past whispering secrets in the present.

"If you're watching this, Tess, I'm either dead or trapped in the Netherworld, likely blind to whatever fucking chain of events landed me into this... unpleasant situation." His gaze was fixed on the camera, making me squirm in my seat. "An apocalyptic danger hovers over our world, a threat unlike any monster we've faced before. Take my warning seriously. This is an end days level threat."

He paused, gathering strength. "They need to be stopped at any cost, Tess, and fast, before they can get a whiff that you're onto their game. Listen to me, you can't be the one who takes them on directly. There are more answers out there... in the prickling of needles on young skin... in a library of ashes burned to the fucking ground."

He winked, then reached forward. The video ended. The screen went black, leaving me staring at my own reflection, my eyes wide with a mixture of shock and sadness. *Miles knew*. He knew my past. He knew who and what I was. He knew *everything*. And now, Imani Harris with her unnerving perception would be expecting me to fill in the pieces.

"Care to enlighten me?" she said. "Any idea what any of that means?"

I knew her telepathic senses would probe for cracks in my

mental defenses as I spoke. I slammed them shut, layering my illusion veils with a fresh wave of misdirection. I met her gaze full-on. "None whatsoever. That crushed me actually. He sounded like a man on the verge of a nervous breakdown, frightened or paranoid or delusional. Just days ago, he was so alive, so... *Miles*. I wish I could unsee that video."

She tapped her fingers on the desk. "Why mention *you* specifically by name? What about the rest of us? What about the rest of the world?"

"I don't know. Miles and I were close once, but we lost touch years ago. Aside from that Sun Prairie portal investigation and the pomdor, we only spoke twice before he died. He never mentioned any cosmic doom. If you want answers, find his killers, make them talk."

She leaned back, studying my face like a map. "His killers?"

I guess we're playing this game. "We both know Miles didn't choke on his own spit or any other such absurd cover story."

"Sounds like you've been on the job. Any leads on said killers?"

"That's your job, not mine. Are you asking me to join the team?"

A breath of amusement shaped her lips. "And if I ask, you'll express bewilderment regarding the Netherworld reference, I suspect. Nor will you escort me to this library of ashes of which he spoke. Am I correct?"

I shrugged. "Would if I could."

Sustaining an illusion shield against a telepath of Imani Harris' caliber was like trying to hold back the tide with your hands. I could literally feel her mental probes brushing past my clenched defenses.

"I believe Agent Donovan to have been speaking in code," she said. "A cryptic message that he believed, or at least hoped, you could decipher."

"Miles thought everyone's mind worked like his, but he was one of a kind. His belief in me was a blind spot. He gave my intelligence far too much credit."

She didn't smile this time. "Detective Hilliard, I understand we got off on the wrong foot. You don't trust me, but this message could be the key, the one and only key, to cracking the case wide open—who killed Miles, what threat he was so desperate to communicate. Help me make sense of it."

The weight of my lies pressed down on me. "A lot of that was straight forward. There's an apocalyptic threat, and I shouldn't be the one to take it on. I will take heed of that, but all the rest, the parts about needles and skin and a library fire... None of that pertains to me. Maybe he sensed what was to come. Maybe he only knew bits and pieces and hoped we could discover what those words meant if he never did. I don't want to remember him like that."

"Agent Donovan was among our finest, a dedicated agent. He wouldn't have left such an ominous message unless he was certain it would reach the right person. The one person he deemed essential."

"I'm afraid he was mistaken about me being that person."

Tapping into her telepathy again to peek into her mind was tempting, but I wasn't about to repeat that mistake. A single occurrence she might write off as a false alarm, but twice? It would only solidify her suspicions.

"And you don't think the message might be connected to your recent associations?"

I stiffened, my hand going for my dagger, but I quelled my temper. "That doesn't fit the timeline. You could check with them, though. They may shed more light on such cryptic messaging than I ever could. Now, it's been a long day, Director. I'd like to go home."

"This isn't a matter of personal choices, Detective," she said, her voice hardening. "The Bureau has a vested interest in maintaining a neutral stance in the supernatural world. Your association with Tierney puts that neutrality at risk. If he starts throwing his weight around, we'll all be in trouble."

"I don't work for Tierney and, frankly, I don't work for you either," I reminded her. "My actions do not affect the Bureau or its neutrality, and I would never do anything to jeopardize your investigation."

"See that it stays that way. For your sake, and ours." She held my gaze for a long moment, then she nodded slowly. "If you remember anything relevant, you bring it straight to me, is that clear?"

"Crystal."

I PULLED MY COAT tighter around me as I paced the rain-slicked sidewalk outside the Bureau, waiting for my Uber ride, my head a hurricane of swirling thoughts and emotions. The words Miles spoke echoed in a haunting loop... *There is an apocalyptic danger... They need to be stopped... You can't be the one... In a library of ashes...*

What the hell did he know? And how did he know it? When had he figured out my secret? The only other person who knew was the illusion mage himself.

A sickening thought cut through my frustration, an outlandish possibility I would have never considered only a moment ago. What if Miles *was* the illusion mage? What if he was the monster who had murdered my parents with a casual flick of his wrist, who had robbed me of anything resembling a normal life, leaving me with nothing but a solitary thirst for vengeance?

Another dark thought that will never leave me.

When new seeds of doubt took root, sprouting their way into my heart, choking the last vestiges of my faith, my humanity died for a time. I became my vengeance. Nothing else. I worked hard to reestablish a faint connection to the world, to people, but when a new doubt took root, I gave up. I didn't want to change the way I thought about Miles. I respected him.

Had he been playing me all those years? Had every stolen kiss, every whispered promise been a lie? Had he made love to me knowing he was the villain who had slaughtered my family and shattered my world? The thought was repulsive, a violation that went deeper than skin. I wanted to scrub myself raw, to erase any trace of him.

I fought back a wave of nausea. What proof did I have? They were both tall, yes, dark-haired, dark-eyed, but those were generic similarities. I strained to remember more. My mind latched onto the sensory details—the acrid smell of burning books, blood turning cold on the floorboards—but the finer points eluded me. The mage wore a mask and the trauma of that night had fractured my memories. Could I really trust them?

No. Miles wouldn't. He just couldn't. Kind, gentle, dependable Miles who had been my mentor, my friend, my lover—the only person who had truly believed in me, even when I was a clumsy first-year student at the academy. He wasn't capable of such gratuitous evil. He couldn't be the monster who had haunted my dreams for all these years.

Then again, he had stolen Codex pages, he had secret dealings in Nyx, and he had sent me on a wild goose chase, starting with the Sun Prairie portal.

The Uber let me out in front of 5310 Card Street in the quiet suburb of McFarland—the house I grew up in.

I took a deep breath as I stepped out onto the curb. The house stood utterly still, heartbreakingly sad with its dark windows staring at me like empty eyes. The front yard had been abandoned to the elements—shrubberies grown wild, decaying leaves and branches littering the walkway.

I reached for the key in my pocket, unsure if I was doing the right thing. It had been over a year since the last time I'd set foot in the house, but Mrs. Winslow, my parents' dear friend and neighbor across the street, had kept a watchful eye on it, airing out the rooms, dusting, sweeping, and chasing away the ghosts once a month—all for a modest fee.

I stood in the dark hallway, memories crashing into me like spectral apparitions, spinning before my eyes with worried faces. So many years had passed, yet the essence of my childhood still clung to these walls along with the echoes of laughter and sting of loss.

I switched on the lights and headed straight for the library, my hand trembling as I reached for the door handle. I hadn't been inside this room since the attack, having instructed Mrs. Winslow to leave it undisturbed save for some light cleaning.

As if the dead can be disturbed...

The library had been my mother's sanctuary, her most prized design, an extension of her very being. Everything she was, everything she had been, her aura, her essence—it was all still here, lingering on shelves, worn armchairs and aged paper like a persistent spirit.

My heart fluttered as I entered and flipped the switch. The sudden, harsh light illuminated the room, casting distorted shadows. The burned patches on the carpet where the illusion mage had incinerated stacks of invaluable tomes seemed larger than I remembered.

A library of ashes...

Whatever answers Miles wanted me to discover were hidden in here.

But where? I tried to think like him—where would he hide the clues?

The obvious answer was among the remaining books. I

quickly scanned the shelves, then did a closer inspection. One book stood out, perched at an odd angle on the very edge of a shelf, as if purposefully left slightly askew, and supported only by the weight of the thick volumes flanking it.

I squinted to read the faded title on the worn spine: *Misplaced Codex Cryptograms and How to Retrieve Them.*

When I gently pulled the book free, a metallic glint sparked in the dim light at the back of the shelf where the book used to sit—a flash drive.

I raced out of the library and up to my father's small study on the second floor. With shaky fingers, I jammed his old laptop into a power outlet and booted it up. For a few heart-stopping moments, the machine just sat there, but then it whirred to life with a groan, the screen flickering, the image of my mother smiling back at me from the desktop background.

My heart clenched in my chest. I swallowed the lump in my throat, blinking back the sting of tears. My mother's beautiful smile, frozen in time, her vibrant life stolen, her happiness shattered by unspeakable violence.

Focus, Tess. Focus.

I inserted the flash drive into the lone USB port. A new folder popped up on the desktop, labeled *For T.* Like I was his special little project. I double-clicked the folder, revealing a newer video file, dated November 13th. That was the day before the Bureau called asking me to consult on a case, the day before Miles waltzed back into my life, drawing me back to his world.

He planned this. He was setting all this in motion.

My hand hovered over the small trackpad. What fresh hell was this? A love letter? A confession? Or another warning from beyond the grave?

Screw it. I clicked play.

The video opened to a scene I knew too well—our old bench at Picnic Point, where we'd train in the dark until we dropped and then made out like a couple of teenagers. And there was Miles, facing the camera with the lake at his back. Only this wasn't the strong, steadfast Miles I knew. This Miles looked pale, haunted, a shadow of the cocky Bureau agent who had won my heart.

"Well, well, Tess," he began, his voice strained. "It's been a while, hasn't it? Figured I'd pay a visit to our old stomping ground. Tomorrow, I'm going to ask you to consult on a case for the Bureau, but let's be honest, that's just the tip of the iceberg."

He paused, his dark eyes locking right on the camera, as if he could see me through the screen and sitting in my father's study right now.

"Let's hope you never have to watch this, because if you are, well... it will be past my expiration date. No more margaritas on the beach for this guy. Anyway, on with it. There's some dark shit on the rise. A year ago, I stumbled onto a secret society. They call themselves the Cult of Erasure. Yeah, I know, the name screams *Saturday morning cartoon villains*, but trust me, these guys are the real deal." He raked a hand through his hair, a nervous gesture completely out of character for the unflappable Miles Donovan. "Their power is staggering.

Their methods are ruthless. They have their sticky fingers in the Codex, in the portals... messing with forces I can't begin to unpack. The endgame here is to rewrite reality itself, to wipe out worlds and realms entirely, every tiny piece of grass, starting with swaths of the Netherworld."

My jaw hung open. The Cult of Erasure? Rewriting reality? It sounded like frivolous nonsense, stoned imaginings, at best a bad B-movie, but there was Miles, the most pragmatic, whiskey-loving, hard-ass cynic I knew, spewing off about a cosmic conspiracy.

He sucked in the lake air, his chest rising and falling rapidly. "There's a lot you don't know about me, Tess, sides of me you've never seen. Darkness. Ambition. A ruthlessness I was reluctant to acknowledge for too damn long. So yeah, at my lowest I made a deal with the devil. I joined their ranks in exchange for—"

He left the sentence unfinished like a noose ready to be pulled tight.

"The Erasers are itching to get their claws on you, Tess. They'll be sniffing around at that portal in Sun Prairie tomorrow. They want to gauge how resilient you are, how much that portal bends to your will. They are convinced you are a limitless dynamo, a walking nuclear reactor, the key to erasing entire worlds from the archives and the Codex, sealing them off forever.

"I never meant to throw you to the wolves. When I brought you in, I planned to safeguard the whole operation, make sure you walked away unscathed. If you'd been handed to any other handler, they wouldn't have lifted a finger to protect you. But I underestimated them. They're not just toying with the Netherworld; they've got it on a leash. I'm in way too deep to back out now, so consider this your life insurance policy."

He leaned closer, his voice urgent.

"This is life-or-death, Tess, so listen up. The power is in the marks that we share. We have the same blood conduit abilities." He rolled up his sleeve to expose the twisting scars on his forearm, the very ones I'd seen on him at the morgue. "But my ability to channel power is a candle to your wildfire. You haven't scratched the surface of your potential, but even at full force you can't stop the Erasers. That level of power is beyond us."

He hesitated, his gaze intensifying. "If I end up in a body bag, don't think about pursuing this further." His voice hardened, and his eyes held the weight of a final plea. "Get out of Madison, quick, create a new identity off the grid, go full ghost. Don't let them find you. If they find you, they will use you."

He took a step closer, his handsome face filling the frame.

"Forget about the Codex pages. Steer clear of portals, and for god's sake, never set foot in the Netherworld under any circumstances—not a single toe over that line, you hear? Your life depends on it, Tess Hilliard, but more than that—the fate of our world hangs in the balance. You can't let them modify you into a nuclear weapon. Whatever you do, avoid the Nether Realms. Stay the hell away from that place, forget it exists."

His piercing eyes were filled with terror. "In exchange for

power, Tess. That was their promise to me. The kind of power that could reshape the world. Or shatter it into a million pieces."

The video cut to black. The silence that followed was deafening, broken only by the echo of his words still ringing in my ears.

Never set foot in the Netherworld.

I stared at the blank screen, utterly dumbfounded.

Life insurance policy, my ass. You double-crossing, backstabbing son of a bitch, you sold me to the highest bidder to get your hands on some cosmic power.

I'd given that man two years of my life, two years of blind trust, and the whole time I had no idea I was his product. Was he insane? Delusional? Or was it all true? Was he really in bed with a group of world-erasing cultists?

I mean the crazy things he had said couldn't be true—blood conduits, erasure cults, my supposed *limitless* power. What the hell was he on about? I was hardly the first illusion mage to walk the Earth. My magic wasn't common, but it sure as hell couldn't erase a single, goddamn parking ticket, let alone entire realms.

And how the hell could he have predicted his own death? Or my journey to the Netherworld? It was as if someone had been pulling the strings all along, orchestrating my every move.

Fuck. This. Shit.

I was done. Done with my crazy ex-boyfriend ranting from beyond the grave, done with the suffocating weight of his secrets.

I was drowning in a sea of crazy, and my dad's old office was the last place I should be.

Air, I needed some goddamn oxygen for my sanity.

The little nagging voice slithered into my mind again. *The Mustang, Tess, dad's baby covered in dust in the garage.*

Like everything else that belonged to my parents I hadn't wanted to touch it, but Mrs. Winslow dutifully took it for a spin every month, a short drive to the grocery store and back, to keep the engine tuned.

I pushed away from the desk and shot downstairs, out the side door and into the garage. I flicked on the overhead light. The car sat under a tarp in the corner—a midnight blue 2014 Ford Mustang.

I yanked the tarp off, flung open the driver's door and slid behind the wheel. I closed my eyes, taking a deep breath. The phantom touch of my mother's hand, the echo of my father's laughter... The memories had me by the throat and wouldn't let go.

After a few turns of the key, the engine roared to life with a satisfying growl. I waited for the garage door to open, then slammed the car into reverse, backed out of the garage, and peeled off into the night.

Killian was waiting for me on the porch of the American Foursquare on Jenifer Street. I parked down the block so I could walk a while and take in the crisp winter air before brushing past him without a word, unlocking the door and holding it open for him.

Chapter 19

KILLIAN STALKED INSIDE THE apartment like a predator on the prowl, his face drawn taut, his storm-cloud eyes determined. The scar that bisected his left cheek seemed deeper, more pronounced, reflecting the violence that simmered beneath his carefully controlled exterior.

I was so tired, so fucking sick of it all—the secrets, the lies, the endless parade of threats. I wanted to rip the mask off my face, to shed the illusion veils and expose my own scars. I wanted him to see them, to trace the jagged edges with his fingertips, to know the darkness inside me that mirrored his own. Maybe then someone would finally understand.

Instead, I turned away with a huff. "Took you long enough."

"I didn't follow you," he said. "I don't know where you went, but I know something's wrong. I smell trouble."

"That's touching, but unnecessary."

"What happened?"

The question lacked the usual bite. Wonders never ceased with this man.

I held his gaze for a beat, then lowered my eyes. "It's personal."

"Personal," he repeated. "Like those vampires who tried to rip your throat out *personal*? Or like the necromancer who's playing you for a fool *personal*? Or maybe *personal* as in, dead dude still messing with your head?"

Ah, there he is. The Killian I've come to know, the sarcasm King of Therians.

"Do you ever get tired of that attitude? Like ever?"

He pondered the question, or pretended to, until his lips curved into a crooked smile. "I'd love to say yes, but honestly? No. Not really. Feels right."

I pounced for the door, intent on ending all this talking, but he was faster. His hands clamped on my shoulders, spinning me back to face him.

"Don't," he warned, his voice raspy. "Don't shut me out, Tess."

"You were right about Miles, okay? You were right about everything. He wasn't just compromised; he was in the shit up to his neck. He used me, he lied to me, he manipulated me. There, happy?"

"It doesn't make me happy, Detective. What did he do now?"

"He's dead, Killian," I spat. "What more could he possibly do?"

"Not sure, but he got to you somehow."

I stared at him, my heart pounding. I was done with men knowing everything before I did. "How could you—?"

He cut me off with a wave of his hand. "It doesn't matter. Tell me everything that happened."

"Well, for starters, I know who killed Miles. A secret society, called the Cult of Erasure. Ever heard of them?"

Killian's eyebrows shot up. "That's a new one."

"They're a cabal of power-hungry lunatics with a world-ending plan that involves…" My voice trailed off. I bit my lip, choosing my next words. "Director Harris hauled me into the Bureau tonight. She shoved a recording in my face that Miles made right before he died. It was a warning, filled with cryptic references that meant nothing to Harris, but—"

"But you cracked the code."

"Yeah. I told Harris I couldn't make heads or tails of it."

"You don't trust the esteemed Director?" It wasn't a real question.

"The jury's still out on that."

He leaned closer. "And do you trust me?"

"Harris made one thing explicitly clear—I'm not to loop you in on the recording or anything else. She's not a fan."

His irises flared orange sparks. "And your stance on that directive?"

I shrugged. "Reivers are the elite of elemental warriors, fierce and deadly, and you're their alpha dog, the very top of the food chain, in the flesh. If what Miles said about these Erasers is true, I know who I need at my back, and it's not a by-the-book suit-wearing Bureau agent."

The wolfish grin that spread across his face was all sharp teeth and menacing charm. "Detective, I may have vastly underestimated you. You have whipped me into a frenzy. Please, do tell what the too stubborn to stay dead Agent Donovan had to say about this... *Clan of Eraserheads?*"

"Cult of Erasure," I corrected him.

"Ah, big miss. They could have called themselves *The Dukes of Delete.* That would have been cool."

I glared at him. "What are you talking about? Wait, what's that smell?"

"What smell?" Killian said, sheepishly.

"Have you been smoking pot?"

"Can't say for sure. I arrived an hour ago. Two dudes across the street invited me in from the cold to wait. When they offered to share their smoke, I did not want to be rude. It was quite odorous."

Where to begin with this? "You're a King, Killian."

"And I've never felt more like a King than now," he said. "It reassures me that you have kind neighbors. They now consider me their dude."

"You have no idea what you smoked," I said. "I should be having you followed—you're completely reckless, and possibly now a crackhead."

He clutched his chest. "Lesson learned, now lay it on me. What apocalyptic scheme is this self-important secret society cooking up?"

"Concentrate, please. According to Miles, the Erasers want to hit the multiversal reset button, erase entire dimensions, starting with the Netherworld, and rule over what's left."

Killian processed, hopefully trying to shake off his high.

"Oh, shit. And I thought they were just a pretentious campus poetry club."

"I can't talk to you like this."

"No, no, I'm good. Really."

"Just be serious for a moment. Miles's details were sketchy at best, but one thing he made clear: he'd thrown in with those psychos."

"He was one of them?"

"It seems that way, yeah."

He clucked his tongue. "Shocker."

"Actually, yeah, Killian, it fucking is. Do you have a problem with that?"

"No, Detective, not at all. I blame whatever I smoked."

"Well, that's convenient. We need a plan, and we need it fast. There's not going to be an *undo* button with these psychos. Once a world's gone, it will be gone forever."

"Right, right. But let me get this straight... you really thought the Bureau's golden boy was so squeaky clean he could never get his hands dirty? Are we talking about the same guy?"

He had a point, but he still managed to irk me.

"I knew Miles wasn't the ultimate paragon of virtue, but I didn't think he was stupid enough to hand a lit match to a bunch of arsonists. Entire worlds were at stake. Then again, maybe I'm just that naive when it comes to the men I let into my life."

His demeanor changed. He was himself again. "Tell me more about the Eraser plan."

"Apparently, they need human... batteries, I guess? No, human *conduits*. Don't ask me what that means, but that whole situation with the Sun Prairie portal was some kind of a stress test to—"

"To see if you were their little magic Energizer Bunny?" he offered, a dangerous glint in his eyes.

Careful, Tess. Dude takes a mile if you give him an inch.

"Their conduit, yeah."

"Why you?"

"I don't know... because Miles offered me, because he could easily push my buttons to get me to the spot? I was a low-hanging fruit and, apparently, because I'm the world's most gullible, clueless idiot? Go ahead, say it."

He studied me for a long, weighted moment. "Nope, no one thinks you're clueless. Miles didn't offer you, they set him up to get to you. I felt it at the portal, a current of energy probing your energy core, trying to crack it open but bouncing right off—just like my sensors bounced right off you when I tried to assess what the hell was going on. You are a locked vault, Detective. It's why I tore open the portal's pulling web. It was the only way to break you free from that unrelenting hyper vacuum."

It all clicked into place. The sudden shift in the strange energy, the way the portal's persistent draw had lessened. Deep down, I'd known all along that Killian had intervened, that he had helped pull me back from the brink. What I didn't know was that Miles had led me there on purpose, to be taken.

Killian raised an eyebrow. "What exactly are you, Detective Hilliard? A Lamia? A Fury? A Gorgon?"

Fury? He wasn't wrong about that part. And damn, the man knew his Greek mythology. A little too well maybe.

"Chimera?" he went on. "Sphinx? Maybe a Kraken?"

With a weary sigh, I brushed past him and sank onto the sofa. "Why do I keep letting you bait me with all this pointless banter?"

"Because you want to break from your grumpy detective routine. It is obvious you crave my scintillating wit."

I played up my exhaustion, so he wouldn't notice the teeny tiny part in me that was inclined to agree.

"Tess..." He settled beside me, his voice softening just enough to let a hint of concern shine through. "What now?"

"There's only one thing to do. If Miles didn't want me anywhere near the Netherworld, then that's where I'm going."

A slow, predatory smile spread across his handsome face. "Now you're speaking my language."

"Huh, it must be a very primitive language, full of grunts and chest-pounding and fire-breathing."

Killian laughed. "My dudes across the street get me. I noticed your sense of humor improving, but let's get one thing straight. Our multi-dimensional joyride was my idea, my plan, my game. Once we breach Nyx, you don't take a single step out of my sight, understood? Ideally, I'd send you straight back to our realm, but I need your portal navigation skills to guide us safely out of that hellscape. So, you stick by my side like glue. No running off to do your own thing, no Joan of Arc heroics.

I don't want your pretty little head decorating a Netherworld spike because you refuse to follow someone else's plan. There's no beginner's luck in battle."

He doesn't know me like that. No one does.

"That was not exactly a vote of confidence. I'm not completely helpless, you know." I ticked off my points on my fingers. "Combat training? Check. Wind magic? Check. Offensive and defensive spells? Double check. And let's be clear, I'm not going to Nyx because of you. I'm going because this whole twisted affair ties back to me."

He opened his mouth, eyes blazing, then snapped it shut. He took a deep breath, a muscle in his jaw twitching. "I know you're capable, but we have no idea what lurks in the land of Nyx. You give me your word you'll follow my lead, or this whole operation is grounded."

His tone left no room for argument. Whether it was genuine concern or his inherent need for control, or a toxic cocktail of both, he was dead serious.

"Fine, yeah, General Tierney. I'll be your obedient valet and follow your battle plan like a good little soldier."

The smile on his stupidly handsome face was insufferably smug, like he was the big lottery winner. "Where are we on securing a viable portal path?"

I puffed out a long breath. "This part might get a little... unorthodox."

"Have we hit a wall already?"

"No, not quite a wall. It's just... Remember that whole *potential route to Nyx* I told you about? The one where I implied

I'd found a reliable way for us to travel between realms?"

He nodded, suspicion bubbling up in his eyes.

"Well, I may have neglected to mention that our mode of travel… could involve some people with whom you wouldn't share an elevator."

He looked at me like I'd sprouted a second head. "Vampires? What kind of tour guide from hell are you? We're not riding with vein drainers on this or any other job. Are you outside of your feeble mind?"

That went better than expected. Jeez.

"I know it sounds bad—"

"Really, because it sounds like you know nothing."

"Killian, hear me out. These are the pets. They've been in the business of escorting necromancers through portals for centuries. It's the fastest, most reliable option we have. And the only vamps I can think of who might be marginally willing to help—"

"Don't say it. Don't fucking say Van Zelst's brood," he said.

I said nothing. That was how he knew.

He stretched like the room couldn't contain him anymore, joints cracking, his muscular thigh brushing against mine. A shiver jolted through me, tingling my skin, an instinctive reaction to the sheer, brutal power coiling inside him that made my hair stand on end. His magic crackled like a live wire, shocking every nerve as it flooded into me through every pore.

I scrambled off the couch, a split second too late.

His hand shot out, gripping my wrist. He fixed me with a smoldering glare, his breathing heavy. "You felt it, didn't you?"

he said. "You felt my magic spiraling wildly out of control, on the verge of exploding."

Refusing to be cowed, I raised my chin. "All I felt was your monumental temper tantrum." The edge to my voice was shakier than I would have liked.

With visible effort, he released his hold on me, his hand dropping to his side, his fingers curling into a fist. "Tess, what you're asking of me..." He fought to keep from transforming. "It's madness. Do you know anything about pet vampires? They aren't pups or misunderstood wolves. They're leeches, draining life for sustenance. They don't have a moral compass, they don't have a code, and they are without scruples, because they're not alive, Tess!"

"They may not, but Raven does."

Would I bet my life on it? Hell, no, but this was the only way.

"Necros are about as trustworthy as scorned lovers," he growled. He surged to his feet, towering over me, his eyes sparking orange. By now, I knew that meant he was either pissed off or alerted. Or both. "At first you trusted no one and now you trust everyone, Detective. Do you have a death wish?"

"You told me I had trust issues," I shot back. "Here I am, taking your advice and spilling my guts to you, laying everything on the line, and you're giving me a lecture on trust? You of all people?"

"Trusting me is the sanest choice you've ever made. We all have to pick a side, and you've picked the right one."

"I'm not one for sides. I'm a detective, not a cheerleader. But I know when to compromise." I jabbed a finger at his chest. "And I've bent over backwards to accommodate you like a bloody circus contortionist. I'll stick to your masterplan, play by your rules—whatever you want to call it—but we need Raven and her bloodsuckers, and we have to offer them protection. Raven will be sticking her neck out by allying with us, and her brood gives us the best shot at making it through the portal death maze in one piece."

He paced the room like a caged tiger, fingers drumming against his thigh, a low, thunderous grumble in his throat.

Finally, he halted, nostrils flaring. "Fine, but on one non-negotiable condition. I'm there when you speak to the Necro bitch."

"Watch your mouth," I said. "We won't be having any of that kind of disrespect on this operation."

"Fine, but I'm there at that meeting. Period."

"If you can behave, you can be there. I mean it, no one gets hurt, Killian, or we're through. Raven will be positively thrilled to have the world's grumpiest Reiver chaperoning our meeting."

His lips twitched into a half-smile. "I'm counting on it."

Chapter 20

PICNIC POINT RESEMBLED A frozen wasteland under the eerily pale moonlight. The night sky was clear, but the wind howled off Lake Mendota, biting through my layers of clothing as if they were tissue paper.

I checked my phone—five minutes to three. I was beginning to regret agreeing to meet Raven in the small hours of the morning. Late November in Madison always turned harsh, but this year, it turned mean. Even my thermal socks felt like they were woven from ice crystals.

"This was a stupid idea," I muttered, shuffling from foot to foot. "We could be sipping hot cocoa by a roaring fire right now, plotting our Netherworld excursion. Instead, we're freezing our asses off, waiting for our friendly neighborhood vampire trainer who might decide to make me a midnight snack for her pets when she sees who I brought to the party."

Killian stood unfazed, his broad shoulders hunched against the wind, his gray eyes scanning the shadows of the wooded path that led back to the city. He wore his usual black jeans and jacket ensemble as if freezing temperatures were inconsequential. Maybe for a Therian King with dragon blood coursing through his veins, they were.

"Your incessant yapping is the unbearable part," he said. "The way I remember it, we're here due to your insistence on this little tête-à-tête with Rae Van Zelst."

"Yeah, but not at the North Pole! *We* should have been the ones to show up late. Let *them* freeze their stupid fangs off. It's their frigid rendezvous. Why not a nice log cabin or a museum basement or anything with central heating? I'll be an ice sculpture soon, a cautionary tale for those stupid enough to trust a necromancer."

He chuckled, a low, warm sound that was surprisingly agreeable. "Always the optimist, I see. It's to protect *you*, Detective. Vampires tend to be less volatile when they're nicely chilled. Less chance of you becoming a snack."

Oh. Well, okay, but it's still fucking cold.

I glared at him, my teeth chattering. "You could have told me that earlier before I said all that."

"I waited until you stopped talking," he said. "That took a while."

"When I shiver, I talk nervously hoping to get warm," I said. "Or maybe to take my mind off the cold."

Killian turned his face, his gaze sweeping over me, taking in my shivering form, my gloved hands clutched tightly inside my pockets.

"You're on a fast track to hypothermia," he stated, as if it were a complete revelation to him.

"I've been saying that, Sherlock."

He took a step closer, warmth radiating off him like a summer camp bonfire—an unsettling reminder that he was not entirely human. He reached out, his hand cupping mine, forcing a jolt of heat through my frozen fingers.

"What are you doing?" I demanded.

"Hush, remain still."

"I don't think I will."

He ignored my protest, his grip firm but gentle as he peeled off my glove. The moment his skin touched mine, a wave of heat spiraled up my arm.

I really needed him to stop touching me. Every time he did, a tiny pulse of his magic bled into mine, inviting my illusion sensors to breach his elemental shields and absorb the signature of his chaotic power, unraveling the secrets woven into his essence. The possibility scared and fascinated me in equal measure—a push and pull between curiosity and fear and I wasn't sure which would prevail.

His thumb traced the back of my hand ever so slowly. The warmth of his touch spread out, flowing through me like liquid fire, chasing away the creeping cold, thawing every cell of my body.

I hung my head, confused. Killian Tierney was more than a warrior, more than a king, more than a Therian primal, and more than a man. He was an elemental dragon through and through.

It was a dangerous game, this sensory connection. One false move, and my carefully formed illusion veils would shatter, revealing... all of me.

I pulled back a little, trying to break contact. "You're showing off on purpose, aren't you?"

He licked his lips like he was ready to feast. "I'm helping," he said. "If frozen your cognitive functions will lag."

Despite myself, I leaned into the warmth, letting it seep into my bones, feeling an unreasonable sense of security in his presence.

"Don't try to intimidate Raven," I warned. "Or her vampires. We need them on our side. A synchronized team."

His grip tightened. "Do you know about Reivers, Tess?"

"Supercharged elemental warriors on adrenaline overload?"

He gave me an odd look, somewhere in between amusement and exasperation. "Vaguely accurate. We're an anomaly, we carry a rogue gene, a genetic mutation that amplifies our transformation abilities, our strength, our instincts. We are evolution on fast-forward."

"You can still choose not to intimidate, can't you?"

He shrugged. "I am telling you that if control is lost, our elemental form takes over, we become feral, consumed by the elemental beast within, turned into a fountain of pure, destructive power."

"So, don't lose control. The vampires have the same challenge."

He shot me an irritated glance. "We're not like vampires. We follow no one, answer to no one, bend to no will. We are free. We're in control. But it's a double-edged sword. A constant battle."

I resisted pointing out that his elemental warriors most definitely followed *him*. They'd likely bend to his will too, seeing how they looked at him.

"How do you mean?" I asked.

"The more we master the elemental forces, the more our magic dims. Indulge them too much, chase after their full potential, and the risk of complete surrender spirals. You can't let it go too far either way. It's a very fine line, finding that balance, keeping ourselves intact."

"Is this why Aiden can't fully shift?"

"He hasn't found that balance yet, can't trust himself to let go. He's caught in the liminal space between, but he's a fast learner."

"I couldn't do it," I said. "I'm always teetering."

Good and evil. Light and darkness. Control and chaos. Will the center ever hold? Or do we all fall down?

A subtle shift in Killian's posture snapped my attention back to our surroundings. His hand tensed around mine before letting go and sliding back into his hard-edged Therian self.

Leaves rustled in the wind, branches cracked under a sudden gust, and the moon vanished behind a veil of churning clouds. An owl hooted, a mournful sound echoing through the stillness.

"We have company," Killian murmured, slipping the glove back onto my hand. The casual intimacy of the gesture contrasted with the coiling tension in every line of his body.

My fingers clenched into fists. My senses, already heightened by Killian's nearness, went on overdrive. I picked up the faintest whisper of movement in the shadows, the crunch of leaves underfoot.

Raven wanted a dramatic entrance. At least, I *hoped* it was Raven.

The air around Killian buzzed, energy rippling outward, distorting the moonlight. His human form blurred, his edges flickered, as if nature itself was struggling to contain the power surging within him.

He spun inside a whirlwind of energy. His clothes flew off in every direction as his body exploded into something enormous and terrifying.

His skin stretched, scales erupted like crimson diamonds and spread across his flesh—a shimmering, impenetrable armor. Massive silver wings ripped free from his back with a thunderous snap—their span blotted out the moon above. Two rows of black spikes ran down his back and two silver horns burst forth on his forehead, curving backwards. A silver star, the archaic mark of the Therian King, blazed on his chest.

His eyes, no longer gray but a shining, molten silver, burned with a ferocious intensity that made my breath catch in my throat.

The transformation was violent, explosive, lightning fast, a primal force unleashed in a heartbeat. Just like that, the red and silver dragon stood before me in all his magnificent glory.

I staggered back, shielding my face from the searing heat that rolled off him in waves. I stared up at the towering fire goliath standing at fifteen feet tall and twice as long tail included, no longer an infuriating man but a creature of legends, a primal predator whose power could level mountains.

His claws, lethal and gleaming, dug into the earth, carving deep furrows. His heat melted the frost and charred the leaves on the ground into a wide circle around us.

How had he managed such a swift transformation? I wasn't going to pretend I understood how any of it worked, but elemental shifting was a complicated affair that required a deep cellular focus and meticulous control of power, time, and dimension. Clearly, he came prepared.

Shame on me for trusting him. Again.

He lowered his massive head, his silver eyes finding mine. My heart attempted frantic cartwheels. Killian, in his full draconic form, mesmerized and stole my breath. He unfurled his immense wings with a sudden snap that sent a gust of wind blasting into me, cutting off the oxygen supply to my lungs.

He immediately abandoned the plan!

Was *that* his idea of not being intimidating? I just couldn't with this dragon jackass anymore.

Worst. Partner. Ever.

Everything quieted. Mist snaked out of the trees, coiling around us. The stench of necromancy hit me square in the face, stirring an unwelcome distress inside me. The dark magic and the vampires gliding through trees were not my main concern.

It was Killian.

Assuming that fifteen-foot fire-breathing beast is still Killian Tierney.

"Don't even think about going feral," I muttered.

Four silhouettes dressed in long black cloaks emerged from the mist on the trail, their steps silent—Raven, flanked by her vampires.

They stopped in their tracks at the sight of the dragon behind me. The always composed Rae Van Zelst raised an eyebrow.

The vampires watched me with predatory focus like I was a walking juice box at a thirst convention.

Killian breathed out a cloud of smoke. I fought the urge to get behind him.

The vampires fanned out around Raven and snapped into defensive stances—backs hunched, fangs bared, hisses snarled.

A low rumble vibrated in Killian's throat a second before twin jets of flame burst from his nostrils. The heat seared past my face, close enough that I thought my eyebrows would crisp down to the Lord Voldemort special, but, thankfully, the flames quickly died out.

The Dragon was toying with us, I realized. Killian really wasn't trying to incinerate anyone. Just offering the possibility of his draconic wrath.

Thoughtful dragon.

"Anyone bring marshmallows?" I quipped, the joke missing by a mile.

Raven's eyes, blue and hard like gemstones, narrowed. I don't think the *near-death-by-dragon-snort* experience had done much for her mood.

I took a step forward, about to position myself as a mediator between the opposing forces, when Killian stomped his massive foot—or was it a paw? I had never taken Dragon Anatomy 101. The ground shook with the impact, nearly knocking me down.

Dude, come on. I shot him a perplexed look.

"He's offering you protection," Raven explained. "That scorched-earth circle around you... that's his fire-retardant ward. Anything within its bounds will be safe from his searing breath."

I glared up at the great scaly lizard. "Thanks, but I'm good, big guy. I don't need protection. Stop overreacting." I swiveled back to Raven. "I don't even know if he understands me."

"Oh, he does," she said, her eyes never leaving the dragon. "And he's relishing every second of this."

There was something in the way she regarded Killian—it wasn't quite fear and it didn't feel like hate, more like... bad blood? Ancient history?

"Why's he here?" she said. "I thought we had an understanding."

I opened my mouth, then closed it again. My diplomacy skills were not well developed. I'd brought a dragon to a vampire soiree when Raven had specifically expressed her distaste for elemental warriors.

Killian had gone still—only the occasional twitch of his tail and the embers glowing in his throat reminding us he hadn't turned into a stone gargoyle. His silver eyes flicked between Raven and me, and I got the impression he was waiting for a signal. What was I supposed to do?

"Look, Raven," I said, "I didn't ask him to go full Smaug on us. But since he has, let's all take a deep breath—" I paused, reconsidering. "Actually, scratch that. Let's all just try not to roast, maim, or exsanguinate each other for five minutes. Think we can manage that?"

The handsome dark vampire who was fully bonded to Raven hissed, a sound like silk tearing. Killian's wings twitched, and I swear I could feel the temperature rise a few degrees.

Fantastic. I brought a powder keg to a match factory in the shape of a flame-shooting parade float.

"We have a favor to ask," I said, because why not pile impossibility on top of insanity? "It would involve all three—" The female vampire flashed me her fangs. "—all six of us working together."

Tact was a survival skill in this debacle.

Raven's lips curled into not quite a smile. "That was the last thing I expected to hear. You are a haughty little thing, aren't you?"

I sighed, already nostalgic for the simplicity of hypothermia. "Trust me, I know how that sounded. I say it because it's what must happen."

Raven tilted her head, eyes raking over Killian's massive form. "I thought you'd be bigger."

Oh, for the love of—

The dragon reared up, unfurling to his full height. His wings snapped open as a bone-rattling roar tore from his throat. The sound reverberated through the trees, setting my teeth on edge. They probably heard that all the way to Milwaukee.

"Bad dragon!" I snapped, because apparently, I'd lost my mind. "Sit!"

Nobody moved. The vampires were coiled to spring, Raven's eyes glittered with a dangerous challenge, and Killian... well, Killian looked like he was seriously considering scorching the Earth and all of us with it.

If this is it, I've wasted my life.

Slowly, he lowered himself back down. His wings folded in, and he fixed me with a look that clearly said: *You fucking gnats are barely worth saving, end this or I will.*

I'm not going to be intimidated, but I will be careful.

"If you two are quite finished measuring wingspans," I said, glaring at Raven, "maybe we can talk."

Could the dragon talk? I had no clue. Maybe in his draconic form, Killian could only communicate with smoke signals.

Raven's stance shifted as her shoulders relaxed a little. "I was about to reach out, but you beat me to it. I've gathered intel you'll want to hear."

I inched forward, careful not to leave the ward circle. "What is it?"

"The Codex," she said, "more pages gone missing. The tome's vanishing right before our eyes."

"Vanishing?" I echoed. "As in—*poof*? Gone? The Bureau's taken no additional security measures? How many pages are we talking about?"

"I don't have an exact number, a few, but enough that we

know it's an ongoing and fast-moving attack."

Behind me, Killian let out another low rumble. Whether it was a question or a stomach growl, I couldn't tell, but Raven seemed to take it as the former.

"I don't know what the Bureau's doing," she said. "They're more tight-lipped as the days pass. But... I've been able to confirm that one of the five Wisconsin arch necromancers has gone off the grid."

"It's like there's no resistance," I said. "We can't rely on the Bureau. Something has to be done, even if we have to do it together."

Raven's gaze flicked to the vampires flanking her, then back to me. "The thralls that attacked you, Tess... Rumor in necromantic circles is that thralls from a parallel dimension have breached multiple portals to enter our world."

For a moment, all I could hear was the blood rushing in my ears. Thralls from a parallel dimension were gunning for me. Because clearly, my life wasn't complicated enough. I needed some otherworldly horrors added to the mix, just to spice up my nightmares.

I turned back to Killian, half-expecting him to have transformed back into his human form so he could say, *just get this over with*. But he was still every bit a dragon, his silver eyes sparkling with orange flames.

"Okay," I said, dragging a hand through my hair. "We know exactly where those thralls are coming from. And this is where I bring up that favor."

Raven sighed. "Let's hear it."

"We believe the thralls are spilling over from Nyx. There's evidence Miles Donovan was there and, worse, that he was working with rogue individuals determined to alter the multiverse as we know it."

"Rogue individuals? Like the arch necromancer?"

"It's a strong possibility."

"A full-blown interdimensional conspiracy… that's interesting."

"If by *interesting* you mean going to Nyx to face off against skinless armies and rabid thralls, then yeah," I said. "It's a real thrill ride."

She blinked, her composure slipping. "You can't be serious."

"Unfortunately, I am. Deadly serious. Unless you can think of another way to get answers and stave off entire realms disappearing."

"Nyx, huh?" She let out a short, humorless laugh. "Nyx is no place for the faint of heart or those with hero complexes. It will chew you up before you can take two steps. Add an arch necromancer to the equation and you're pushing the boundaries of sanity."

I shrugged. "Thralls are chasing me and I'm fresh out of options."

"And how do you propose to get Tierney and his merry band of elemental gremlins into the heart of the Netherworld? Charter a magic school bus? Book a group tour? Oh, wait, let me not guess—you need my vampires to hold your hand and help you across every crosswalk in hell. Is that your ask?"

"Raven, there's no other way. We need your vampires to

keep us from becoming interdimensional roadkill."

She shook her head in a sharp, cutting motion. "I will not risk my vampires on a suicide mission, no matter how noble the cause. I'm not the multiverse taxi service."

"It's not a noble cause, it's the last cause!" My voice spiked with frustration. "Consider it pragmatism. What future do your precious vamps have if we don't stop this, if we let the Codex keep unraveling, if we let some creepy-ass arch necromancer keep playing cosmic puppeteer with an army of thralls?" I paused to collect my thoughts. "I know it's a lot to ask, but the stakes are the highest possible. Endgame high. We need to seal the rift that's allowing those thralls to crawl through before things spiral and the veils between worlds begin to fray."

She held up a hand. "I know the stakes. Better than most." She looked at Killian. "And you think *he* is the answer? An elemental warrior with access to more magic than any of us could comprehend? He'll burn everything to the ground, Tess. He'll start a war that will consume us all."

I spied Killian, his scales gleaming like rubies in the moonlight. I looked at Raven, pale and deadly. I studied the vampires, still eyeing the dragon like they were trying to decide which part to bite first.

"He's not looking for a fight," I insisted, even though I wasn't entirely convinced. "It's the last thing he wants. But if he doesn't step in to stop what's set in motion, then who will? The Bureau? Do you honestly think they'll get off their bureaucratic asses before it's too late? How many committee meetings and subcommittee meetings and subcommittee-of-the-subcommittee meetings will it take before they clear a plan of action? Killian wants to safeguard our dimension and keep the veils intact, just like we all do."

Wow, that last bit came out fangirlish. Major cringe.

"He wants to *control* the situation, Tess. He wants to rule, just like his father and his grandfather did before him. And dragons... dragons don't play well with others. They take what they want, burn everything else. And he's not just any dragon. He has a wyvern form. Those gnarly bastards are as rare as they are destructive. You're a fool if you think he'll break that chain."

Okay, that was zero fangirl vibes.

A growl rolled through the night, the draconic equivalent of clearing one's throat. A wave of heat swept over us, the air sizzling with energy. Killian was shifting back. The dragon shimmered, blurred, then imploded, collapsing inward, scales dissolving, wings vanishing in a rush of fire and smoke.

Embers whirled in a vortex around him, obscuring his form for a few heartbeats. When the smoke cleared, Killian stood before us, naked as the day he was born and unconcerned about it, like that night at his bathhouse.

His battle-scarred skin glistened in an otherworldly light with a sheen of sweat—or perhaps it was condensation from the rapid transformation—his chest heaving, his gray eyes blazing with a primal vitality that made my pulse quicken. A thin trail of smoke curled from his nostrils with each exhale.

It took every ounce of willpower not to openly gape. I mean, it wasn't the first time I'd seen him naked, but... this dragon daddy wasn't just smoking, he was smoking hot.

Should I... offer him my coat? Gather his scattered clothes? Pretend this wasn't one of the most awkward moments of my life?

Before I could act, Killian raised his hand, his fingers flexing, and his clothes flew toward him, swirling around him like a mini cyclone. I watched him dress with effortless grace, his movements as fluid as a slow dance.

He was a force of nature, this man. King. Warrior. Dragon. *Wyvern?* Why was I still staring? Because I was in over my head.

Killian turned to Raven, his gaze meeting hers, a silent challenge bubbling between them. He bowed his head, a gesture that seemed wholly out of character. "You know I don't do anything halfway, Rae."

He spoke to her with an easy familiarity that caught me off guard. Like he knew her, *really* knew her, on a personal level that had nothing to do with the centuries-old blood feud between their factions.

Calm and composed, as if he hadn't just tried to scare the living daylights out of her with his draconic display of power, he held out a hand, palm up. A small orb of orange flames danced to life. The air around us grew warmer, not uncomfortably so but enough to remind us of the elemental power simmering beneath his skin.

"Whatever happens in Nyx, your vampire guard will be under my protection. You have my word... and, as a peace offering, I will return the flame of Esgoth that was stolen from your House a century ago once our mission is complete."

The fireball in his hand pulsed once, twice, then winked out.

Esgoth? I've never come across it in the Archives.

Raven stared into his eyes for a long time. Finally, she let out a slow, measured breath. "I'll give you one vampire. One. Amara or Tristan. They can decide which of them gets the dubious honor. But that's it. Don't ask for more. And don't expect me to clean up your mess when it all goes to hell."

"One? One's good. One vampire guide is better than no vampire guides," I said. "But the thing is… we need more than just Killian and me waltzing into Nyx. We need to bring back-up."

Raven's gaze narrowed. "How many?"

"A handful? A dozen maybe?" I glanced at Killian, hoping for confirmation or at least a hint of what he was thinking, but he seemed unconcerned.

"A dozen?" Raven's eyebrows shot up. "Do you have any idea the kind of energy it takes to guide a single non-walker through a portal, let alone an entire battalion?"

"A battalion? No. It's more like… a highly motivated security detail." I turned to Killian. The stubborn prick continued watching with an infuriating detachment. "Right?"

"Of course, Detective," Killian drawled. "Just a casual stroll through the Netherworld with our bodyguards."

I shot him a glare. Would it kill him to be a little more helpful?

"How many elemental warriors can a single vampire reasonably usher through the portals into Nyx?" I asked Raven.

"At most? Three. Any more than that and the nexus energy becomes critically unstable."

Three measly warriors? That wouldn't be nearly enough firepower to survive the depths of the Netherworld. But I couldn't push Raven any harder, and I didn't want to reveal I was a portal-walker capable of shielding three more warriors through.

"I can take four," a smooth, deep voice said.

The vampire I assumed was Tristan stepped forward. He was a striking figure with a martial artist's lean physique and finely chiseled features. His eyes, a smoldering amber, held mine with a quiet intensity.

He inclined his head toward Raven. "With your permission."

Raven nodded. "So be it." Her attention shifted to Killian, holding his stare for a long beat before returning to me. "Let me know when Tristan should report for departure. And try to stay out of harm's way on your little field trip. No noble sacrifices. I'm starting to like you."

Tristan's eyes seared into mine one more time before he followed Raven down the trail, melting into the shadows with his brethren.

Creepy.

Chapter 21

"Wʜᴀᴛ ᴛʜᴇ ʜᴇʟʟ ᴡᴇʀᴇ you thinking, turning into a fucking dragon?" I snapped as I stomped up the stairs to my apartment, Killian trailing behind me.

"It worked, didn't it?" His tone was infuriatingly smug. "Those dead bastards will think twice before they ever breathe on you the wrong way."

He shut the door and headed straight for the mini fridge. He cracked open a bottle of water and downed it in one gulp. Seriously, the entire thing was gone in seconds before he immediately reached for another.

Dragons must get serious dry mouth.

"I'm famished," he said, wiping his mouth with the back of his hand. "Got anything edible in here?"

"It's four in the morning. You want a meal right now?"

"Shifting back always depletes nutrients and fluids. I need to refuel."

Resigning myself to the fact that my breakfast plans were going up in smoke, I gestured at the fridge. "There's cheese and a slice of cherry pie."

"Mmm, I love cherries."

My traitorous stomach growled as he inhaled every last crumb.

Bye-bye cherry pie. I hardly knew you.

I put my hands on my hips, my annoyance growing by the second. "And what's with all the roaring and rumbling? Anyone in Madison could have heard you sounding off like a petulant teen, Your Grace. They could have called the cops or—"

"The ward circle contained the sounds," he cut me off, his voice maddeningly matter of fact.

Of course, he had an answer for everything.

He spread his arms wide. "If you stop assuming I'm a babbling idiot who acts randomly, we could avoid these tedious conversations."

I knew he didn't act randomly. He was always calculating. The problem was his calculations always landed on the extreme.

"If everything you do is intentional, what's with the naked thing? We all concede that you are hot, Tierney. Do you really need constant reassurance? I mean, keep it classy, jeez."

He grinned. "I'm hot? Is that a pun or did you enjoy what you saw?"

"Here we go again," I said. "The insecure King who constantly needs his ego stroked. This is why we need more females in charge everywhere."

His expression sobered. "Your vision is stilted by the human societal lens through which you see everything. Humans have been crushed by shame and the feeble ideologies they have built to avoid being afraid of the dark. For Therians, bodies aren't mere shells to propagate instincts—they are expressive in many ways, including as weaponized deterrents. We do not suppress their voices or their might, because they're part of life's delicate balancing act. Our bodies are essential for survival. Madness comes for those who don't achieve balance. Looking *hot* is the least of our concerns."

"And that's why you work out constantly? Not to look good, but to achieve balance? You could meditate instead."

"A system in harmony is a system in control," he said. "The entirety of life is my meditation." He assessed my body from head to frozen toes. "You're no stranger to regular physical conditioning. Does it make you shallow?"

He had me there. I loved my gym. Or used to before my life turned into this never-ending nightmare.

I plopped down on the sofa with a loud exhale. "I'm just tired of you pushing all my buttons. I don't know what to make of you. One moment you're acting all reasonable, the next it's insane asylum season."

He looked at the night sky through the arched window. "The wards here are formidable, but you should stay at the Helm to guarantee your safety."

I kicked off my boots, one loud thunk and then another. "Not this again."

He'd asked me to hole up in his dragon castle twice already during the fifteen-minute drive from Picnic Point, and I'd shot him down each time.

"The world depends on you," he continued.

I dug in my heels. "I'm not leaving my home. I might never return from Nyx, and I want to sleep in my own bed while I can."

His expression soured as he surveyed the clutter of my apartment.

My mind began to churn. *The Cult of Erasure... The Arch necromancer... The Nyktae... Miles and his peculiar illusion scars...* How did it all connect? How did that hodgepodge of characters all piece together? What was the driving force behind them? And Killian... Killian was a fucking colossal distraction. The further apart we were the better.

"Too much free will is not always a good thing, Tess."

I had zero patience for his fortune cookie bullshit right now.

"You need to listen to me when I talk, Killian. I'll have no more of your outbursts. No more grandstanding. I asked you not to intimidate Raven and it was the first thing you did!"

"I heard you fine, Detective. Why do you think I took one of my smallest forms?"

Oh gods. That was his *small* dragon? May I never see the larger one.

I shook my head. "I can't trust what you say. You'll just twist the truth whichever way it benefits you."

"I don't recall committing to a zero-intimidation policy."

"Save it. Moving on, was Raven correct? You are a wyvern?"

"I have many forms, Tess."

"How many?"

"Stay with me at the Helm if you want to find out."

Uh huh. Right. Like that was going to happen.

"What's the deal with you and Raven anyway? It looked like you two couldn't decide if you wanted to kill each other or do the tango. And don't feed me some bullshit story. If there's something going on between the two of you that could compromise the mission, I need to know."

"Are you insane?" He sighed, running a hand through his chestnut hair. "I've crossed paths with Van Zelst at the Bureau, that's the extent of it. But I happen to have in my possession the trinket she desperately wants returned. It has tormented her our entire lives."

"The Esgoth Flame."

He nodded. "An ancient necromantic artifact of great power. It can fully shield the undead from the sun and can enhance their humanity. It can also facilitate faster, more efficient turnings."

"How did it end up in your possession?"

"The Esgoth Flame belonged to the Van Zelst House for centuries. When one of their vampires was accused of killing a Therian infant in 1921, my great-grandfather, a hard ass with a short fuse who wasn't exactly lauded for his diplomatic skills, raided the Van Zelst residence, killed a child in retaliation, imprisoned the House heir in our Helm and stole the Flame."

"And Raven knew that?" The pieces clicked into place. That's what she had wanted all along. Izzy had warned me Raven had an ulterior motive.

"She did," Killian said. "And she knew you and I had met,

and that you would do anything to solve the murder, so she sought you out offering to help. The vampires were her bargaining chip and she hoped they would be worth the price of the Esgoth Flame."

"Why am I surprised? People suck." I was so weary of the deception, the maneuvering, the endless schemes and half-truths. I'd started to like Raven, to feel a kinship with her, a shared sense of purpose. "I'm such an easy mark."

Killian sat beside me on the sofa, the cushions sinking under his weight. "That's all on her, Tess. Forget it. We have her vampire. That's what matters."

"You could have told me this earlier."

"I had to be certain."

"You had to face her to be certain?"

"That wasn't my priority. You were. I was there to make sure you'd come back to me in one piece."

"*Back* to you? I was never *with* you, Killian."

"I can't do this without you. We need each other. For better or worse."

"Such glowing praise. How could a girl resist strolling through the Nine Hells by your side after such sweet talk?"

"You're the one woman I know who doesn't need to be convinced to walk straight through hell. Are you a masochist, Detective? Or are my charms so hard to resist?"

Don't smack him, Tess. Count to three.

I craved the sound of a good slap but resisted. "Speaking of hell, are you fireproof?" I asked him. "I mean, in human form? How does that work?"

Killian's face lit up. "Funny you should ask. I was about to ask the same question. I mean, not about being fireproof, but about you, what secrets are you hiding under all those shielding layers?"

"What you see is what you get," I said. "Stop projecting your delusions onto me. I'm an investigator at the second-rate Shadow Chasers Agency. This is all the square feet I can afford. I am in every way unexceptional. You can ask anyone. Oh, you probably have. I forgot, you're a stalker."

"Tell me... or not," he said. "The truth has a way of finding me."

"Right. Let me not interrupt your ego trip."

He leaned in, grin sharpening. "I see you, little butterfly. There are three types of supernaturals that can detect Therian energy unassisted. Therians, which you clearly aren't. Illusion mages, which would be surprising given the distinct lack of any signs of it in your family tree. And blood demons." He blinked, slowly, like a resting predator. "Are you a blood demon, Hilliard?"

Blood demons wielded a potent mix of blood sorcery and dark magic. They could drain the blood out of your veins from a distance, or just siphon the magic from your blood if you caught them on a less homicidal day, among a hundred other lethal mage tricks.

"Wait, did I really hear that? You studied my family tree?"

"I didn't hear a denial."

I forced a laugh. "Sure, Killian, I'm a blood demon, the scariest one in all the realms. Prepare to lose your dragon mojo along with all those other fancy forms you've been bragging about."

Shit. He was getting too close to the truth. I should swear off sleeping with anyone ever again. Miles had figured out what I was, and now Killian was edging dangerously close just from simple, skin-to-skin touching.

His hand shot out, cupping my face. I tried to jerk away, but he outmuscled me effortlessly, his grip firm but gentle. Our gazes locked in a silent battle of wills. His face dipped toward mine, achingly slow, as his grip loosened just enough to give me a choice. I could spring off the sofa, put some much-needed distance between us, but I stayed in the moment, caught in the gray depths of his eyes.

He kissed me, his tongue sliding against mine like a match to gasoline. I kissed him back with equal fervor because, sometimes, you just have to embrace the crazy and hope you emerge on the other side unbroken.

I surrendered to the kiss, and then, *bam*, the realization hit me. His magic slammed into me, probing the magic in my blood with staggering force. The raw power I felt in him dwarfed anything I'd encountered before in other magic wielders—even *his* previous displays paled in comparison. It was like being in the eye of a magical hurricane, winds of insanity whipping around us.

Instinct took over. I released my illusion sensors, determined to return the favor. His shields snapped into place with lightning speed, blocking my probe. At the same time my own veils hardened and expanded, forcing an impenetrable barrier to snap into place between us.

We were locked in a breathtaking collision of shields, a staggering show of strength. Tongues tangled as our wills clashed, neither accepting defeat. The dual sensation—the physical pleasure of the kiss, the intoxicating rush of our magic duel—overwhelmed me to my core.

Hunger and addiction. Lust and possession. I am shattering in place.

It felt so good I stopped caring about the consequences. Killian kissed the same way he forced his will upon the world—wildly with abandon and a scorching need to dominate. My heart thundered. My legs turned to lead. Every nerve ending lit on fire, as if plunging into rising lava.

I could feel the heat radiating off his skin, smell the faint scent of smoke and night dew that still clung to him. His fingers tangled in my hair, his grip tightening as our duel intensified, his power a relentless tide threatening to pull me under.

A single thought came to the rescue. *This flood of sensations is too fucking dangerous!* Gathering every bit of resistance left in me, I pushed him away, my breath coming in choking gasps.

"What's wrong with you?" I snapped. "What the hell was that?"

He leaned back, smug grin on full display. "Silencing tactic."

I didn't have the energy to glare but tried. My lips still tingled from the electric kiss—a surging buzz raced beneath my skin like a live wire.

Killian casually smoothed back his hair. "I should go, Detective. Bright and early, I am to begin the selection process to find three elemental warriors that will accompany us to the Netherworld."

That snapped me right out of my post-kiss haze. "Make that six."

The corner of his mouth rose. "Six?"

"Don't play dumb, Killian. You know damn well I can escort three other elemental warriors through the portals. It'll give us the best odds."

He studied me for a moment, then nodded. "I am to begin the selection process to find *six* elemental warriors. I'll let you know when we're a *go* for the Netherworld." He strode out the door, whistling.

Way to go, Tess, you tart!

He never even pretended to object to me breaking from the kiss, or ending whatever might have happened next. Killian was already moving on, as if our clash of magic, our tangled limbs, the raw hunger in his kiss, was a typical moment for him that had meant nothing. It was like I was an okay meal he had already forgotten.

The unsettling feeling was more than jilted romance.

Gods. What the hell did I just give away?

Chapter 22

I slipped into Madison Central Library on West Mifflin Street at 3:45 pm sharp, fifteen minutes before they rolled down the shutters. Outside, fat snowflakes pirouetted against the massive glass panels that offered a glimpse into the multi-story building.

My boots squeaked across the polished floors as I navigated the aisles. A few die-hard bookworms still hunched over tucked-away tables, oblivious to the imminent shutdown. I tried to quell the dread that was growing stronger with every step. This wasn't the Netherworld. It was just a library. Sure, a library that housed the first key in the chain leading to Nyx, the dark realm threatening to erase our very existence, but still... Just. A. Library.

I climbed the wide staircase, rising above the endless rows of books in the fiction section below packed with stories of mystery, adventure, love, loss, epic battles and the occasional zombie apocalypse—the real magic of our world, human imagination, archived by the thousands.

But the magic I was hunting today was personal and a hell of a lot more likely to get me killed.

Speaking of personal...

Killian's kiss flashed through my mind with an urgency that had nothing to do with magic and everything to do with the way his hand had gripped my hair, the taste of his mouth, urgent and dangerous. Part of me craved a replay just to feel the exhilarating rush again as his untamed power rampaged through me. Another part wanted to grab a bottle of hydrogen peroxide to wash my mouth clean and forget it ever happened.

Focus on your priorities, Tess.

The second floor was eerily quiet. The rows of bookshelves had been abandoned and the study rooms were dim and empty. I made my way to the Non-Fiction Reference section at the end of a long hallway. A small study room lay behind it, its door slightly ajar.

I pushed the door open, wincing as the hinges protested. The overhead light flickered for a moment, casting wavering shadows on the walls.

A quick glance at the wall clock confirmed that Izzy was running late—probably wrapping up her day at the Agency.

The air crackled, the energy pulsing like a heartbeat, drawing me closer. The first domino. The nexus point. Thankfully, right where it should be.

I ran my fingers along the lone shelf on the wall, feeling for the precise location, the focal point where the energy currents converged. *There.* A tiny indentation in the wood, barely visible unless you knew exactly what you were looking for.

Time to get to work.

I centered myself, drawing on the well of magic in my core. I directed it at the nexus point, a thread of light connecting my energy reserves to that tiny imperfection in the wood.

A low hum vibrated through the floor as the center of the portal cracked open, rapidly expanding. I caught my first glimpse of Nexilis—a realm of swirling mists and floating clumps of bare rock. Nexilis served as a cosmic crossroads, a near-empty world that bridged the gap between countless others. Its emptiness made it the perfect waystation for portal walkers traversing the boundaries between worlds.

One portal down, seven to go.

The door creaked open behind me, shattering my concentration. The emerging portal flickered, its energy signature spiking erratically. My annoyance swung to relief as Izzy rushed in, her cheeks rosy from the cold, a few renegade snowflakes clinging to her hair.

Izzy grinned. "Capitol traffic in the snow. And I stopped for coffee. I'm not facing portal mayhem without industrial-strength caffeine." She held up a cardboard tray with two steaming cups. "Double espresso, extra shot."

"You're a lifesaver, Iz." I took the offered cup, a small comfort in the face of the monumental task ahead. "Ready to tip your toes into another world?"

Her eyes lit up. "You found the nexus? Please tell me you've stabilized it. Because I'm *not* in the mood for a roll of the dice to spit us out into an uncharted dimension."

"You're just in time for the fun part," I said, gesturing toward the ripple of energy. "Care to help me calibrate our gateway to Nexilis?"

Izzy sidled up next to me, cracking her knuckles with a loud pop. "Oh, hon, you had me at *calibrate.*"

"Once we've stabilized the energies, I'll hop through, check the second portal on the far side, and that'll be it as far as safety checks go." My fingers literally itched to reach out into the portal's pull.

"I don't suppose you know anyone who's actually *been* to Nyx? Or any of the other outer nexus points on this little scavenger hunt?" Izzy said with a sigh, her gaze checking the room as if expecting *that someone* to materialize from behind a chair or under a table.

"Even if we could find someone who'd been to Nyx and lived to tell the tale, they wouldn't be the trustworthy sort. Rule number one of portal travel: never trust anyone who's taken an interdimensional vacation in the Nether realms. Especially if they offer you directions."

"Can't argue with that."

A flick of my wrist, a whispered command, and the *Codex Portallis* materialized inside a whirlwind of dust, landing on the shelf with a dull thud.

My hand paused in midair, inches from the Codex, as my mouth opened in a yawn the size of the Grand Canyon.

"Rough night?" Izzy said.

"Trouble sleeping." My adrenaline never came down after Killian had stormed off. The few hours I managed had been restless, riddled with unsettling dreams, none of which I cared to analyze.

"You're going straight home and crashing after this."

"Love that plan," I said, already dreaming of my pillow. "Assuming, of course, we don't trigger Armageddon in the next ten minutes."

I snatched up the Codex. Its familiar weight was comforting, the worn leather cool against my skin.

Please, please, portal sprites, let the pages be intact. Let this whole damn mess not explode in a shower of magical confetti.

Then again, with my recent luck, spontaneous combustion of a priceless magical artifact wouldn't even crack the top ten strangest things to happen to Tess Hilliard this week.

Izzy unfurled a hand-drawn map on the table, a mess of colored markers and coffee stains. "Okay, so, grand tour itinerary: first stop, Nexilis. Then a quick hop over to Solerta for an all systems check. After that?" She shrugged. "We won't know until we snag our undead chaperone, grab Killian and his crew, and pray we don't end up as a happy meal for Nether beasties on the way to the main event."

"Right," I said, my attention on the Codex. My fingers traced the embossed symbols on its cover, each swirl and line imbued with centuries of magic. "But let's get one thing straight—there's no *we* beyond this library. Your involvement ends here, Iz. You've already gone above and beyond."

"I thought maybe I could—"

"Nope. Not happening."

I tapped the portal with a single finger, the jolt tingling up my arm.

Opening a portal to the Netherworld without authorization wasn't just hazardous—it was suicide, and strictly forbidden. I wasn't about to expose Izzy to disciplinary action from the Bureau, or worse.

I began to weave the complex pattern of the stabilization spell, my fingers leaving trails of golden vapor in the air. The portal pulsed, contracting and expanding as my magic took hold.

Izzy let out a dramatic sigh. "You're the best portal walker I know, Tess. Better than half those stuck-up Bureau portal mages. Pankowski should give you the real cases, the ones that matter. You'd blow them out of the water."

I smiled. "What? And risk the wrath of Gideon, Delgado, Nadia, and Marvin? I'd rather face a rabid horde of hellhounds."

Our top agents at Shadow Chasers were territorial and insecure. Adding extra competition to the mix wouldn't be a recipe for workplace harmony.

I opened the Codex. The scent of ancient parchment filled the air. Instead of the familiar table of contents, the book flipped to a yellowed page near the end, covered in swirling glyphs and arcane symbols that shimmered with an ethereal light. I tried to turn the page, but it wouldn't budge.

The doorway to Nexilis vanished, replaced by a blinding white light that flooded the room. I blinked furiously, trying to adjust to the light.

Izzy's hand found mine, squeezing tight. "Tess, I've heard stories about this light. You've been summoned by the Cosmic Library."

I'd heard the stories too. Whispers among academy instructors and students of a power so ancient, so vast that it existed outside the boundaries of the known realms. The Cosmic Library wasn't some hipster book club. It was the highest authority in the multiverse, the ultimate enforcer of order, the cosmic judge, jury, and executioner. You couldn't outrun its reach. And you couldn't get out of it like jury duty when you were summoned.

The white light engulfed us completely as the library lights clicked off.

Closing time.

The energy around the portal intensified. The kaleidoscope gateway pulsed, swirling faster, a vortex of energy tugging at me impatiently.

Izzy and I exchanged worried glances.

I shrugged. "Maybe it's a good sign?"

"Sure it is," Izzy said unconvincingly. "Like *hold my beer while I wrestle an alligator* good?"

I sighed to calm myself. "It's not like I have a choice. If I don't go, they'll send a portal warden to retrieve me, and they won't be nearly as polite."

"Okay, but do you have to go alone?"

"It'll be fine. The Cosmic Library isn't known for kidnapping or torturing those they summon." *That we know of...* "And we both know this was not a coincidence."

Am I trying to convince Izzy or myself?

"Definitely not," she agreed. "That's what has me worried."

"The only thing to it is to do it," I said. "If I don't come back in an hour, go to Raven. And tell her…" I hesitated. "Tell her to get Killian."

Izzy's grip tightened on my wrist. "Raven? Seriously? Of all people?"

"With Raven, I know the game she's playing. Can't say that for the rest."

Overthinking was a luxury I couldn't afford. I stepped into the heart of the portal. The world dissolved into a kaleidoscope of disorienting sensations. My skin tingled as if I'd been dunked in a vat of carbonated fluids. The air was so thick it pressed against my eardrums. For a moment, I was everywhere and nowhere, my body stretched across countless realities.

Then, with a sudden snap, I was whole again. My feet touched solid ground and I blinked, my vision adjusting, my senses recalibrating.

I stood in a vast library that seemed horizonless, built on a scale that defied comprehension. Everything—the floor, the impossibly high ceilings, the towering bookshelves—was a pristine, almost painful white. The only color came from the spines of the books, each one a vibrant hue, painting a rainbow serpent winding its way to infinity.

The silence was absolute, broken only by my heavy breaths.

I ran my fingers along the nearest shelf, half-expecting a jolt of electromancy, a ward snapping to life, or a magical booby-trap.

Instead, the sensation was cool and smooth and utterly ordinary.

I took a step forward and the floor beneath me rippled like the surface waters of a disturbed lake, sending tiny waves of energy outward, disrupting the perfect stillness of the library.

"Hello?" I called out, my voice sounding small, lost in the white vastness.

No response came, but several books on a nearby shelf began to pulse with an inner light. A heavy volume bound in a rich blue leather slid out from its place and hovered before me, pages fluttering like the wings of a bird.

Cheap tricks already? This library has serious customer service issues.

I reached for the book. As my fingers brushed the leather cover, a voice echoed in my mind, carrying the weight of the Universe.

"Detective Tess Hilliard of the Madison Chapter," the voice boomed, each word settling heavily in my ears. **"The Cosmic Library welcomes you. We trust our summons was received without distress?"**

"Um, for sure," I stammered, mentally kicking myself. *Tess Hilliard, the smooth-talking genius.*

"And your portal transit was uneventful?"

"Absolutely."

Unless you count the near collapse of the Nexilis portal, the interdimensional blender ride that felt like being pulled apart by horses, and the general weirdness of... well, *everything* that happened in the last twenty-four hours.

Other than that, totally smooth sailing.

"We are pleased."

Will I seriously be conversing with a talking book the whole time?

Clearly, the Cosmic Library didn't value the overall guest experience.

A faint sound of shuffling feet answered my unspoken question. I turned and found myself facing a man—if *man* was even the right word.

He stood before an ornate white archway a few feet away, dressed in a long, flowing tunic of the same immaculate white as the library covering him from neck to toe. He was tall and regal, with an otherworldly grace. His golden hair was intricately braided on one side, the other side of his head shaved and tattooed with Codex runes that seemed to continually shift shape.

He glided forward, his movements so fluid he seemed to float. His eyes, a startling, almost luminous azure, met mine. They were beautiful, captivating, and utterly devoid of warmth, or anything resembling human intimacy.

"We are pleased to have met you, Detective Hilliard," he said, his voice echoing with the same strange resonance I'd heard in my mind.

"Charmed," I mumbled, cringing inside at my awkward word choices.

He gestured toward two white armchairs that sprouted from thin air. As I took the offered seat, a ridiculous part of me worried it would disappear the moment I sat. My host took the other chair, smoothing the white fabric of his tunic over his legs with unnatural elegance.

"How could you know about me?" I asked, my voice echoing in a void.

"The Library knows all, Detective," he replied, his azure eyes boring into me like icy lasers. **"All that was, all that is, all that will be."**

"Then your Library must know I have no real authority."

He snapped his fingers. A complete tea set materialized atop a white table that appeared between us with a soft whoosh. The white porcelain was as pristine as everything else in this place, rimmed with delicate silver filigree.

"You are here," he said, pouring the steaming tea with royal etiquette, **"to speak of the Cult of Erasure."**

I blinked, momentarily taken aback. No beating around the bush, no cryptic pronouncements, no sip of cosmic tea, straight to the point. *My kind of guy. Or guys? Or entity?* Hard to pinpoint, given his proclivity to refer to himself in the plural.

"News travels fast," I said, sniffing a cup of tea that smelled a lot like jasmine and lemon.

His eyes held mine, and for a fleeting instant, I was staring into the depths of terrifying emptiness. **"Not nearly fast enough,"** he said, his voice shedding most of its resonance. For the first time, it sounded human.

I took a sip of the tea, a delicate blend of sweetness and spice that lingered on my tongue.

Cosmic nectar I'll call it when I tell Iz.

"Alright," I said, setting the cup on its saucer. "Let's speak. What does the Cosmic Library have to share about the Cult of Erasure that warrants summoning a random detective from a backwater dimension?"

"The chosen are rarely exceptional at the outset."

Oh well, thanks for the honesty, I guess.

"What exactly have I been chosen for?"

"For a century, The Cult of Erasure has been a plague, attempting to breach the defenses of the White Library."

The White Library? "I thought it was the Cosmic Library."

"The Library exists in two separate wings," he explained, leaning forward. His eyes softened, taking on the warmer hue of a summer sky. The shift was subtle, but it relaxed the angles of his face, making him seem almost approachable. Almost. **"The White Library..."** He paused, his gaze holding mine, **"and the Green Library."**

"What's the difference?"

"The White Librarian is the guardian of portals. The protector of the pathways between worlds and keeper of balance." He paused again. **"The Green Librarian is creation's avenger."**

Creation's avenger? Now that had a nice ring to it considering the conundrum at hand. A bit on-the-nose, but effective. "So, why not unleash the Green Librarian upon the Erasure cultists and be done with it? Snip. Snip. Problem solved."

The Librarian's expression hardened, the warmth in his eyes extinguished like a snuffed candle. **"That course of action would incur a heavy cost. Innocents would suffer.**

Tens of thousands would perish. The methods of the Green Librarian are uncompromising. For this reason, the avenger has rarely been loosed upon the world. The White Librarian works so that the Green Librarian may enjoy tranquility."

Yeah, I'm with that, let Green rest. Collateral damage on a multiversal scale sounds unhelpful.

"And you think I can thwart their plans?" I asked, incredulous. "When even the White Librarian can't?"

"The Cult seeks to sever the connections between key worlds, to disrupt the flow of magic to the nexus points," he said, his gaze fixed on a distant point beyond the endless shelves. **"This will be done to diminish the Library's awareness, to limit our influence. They mean to create a vulnerability they can exploit."**

"Word on the street," I said, again confused by my word choice. "What I heard was they wanted to literally *erase* dimensions, that they're obsessed with wiping entire realities from existence."

"Deception is their shield and their ward," the Librarian said, his voice cold as a dead star. **"They covet the Library itself. Should they succeed, they would reign over all that exists. Every realm, every dimension. Each breath. Each dream. Eternally."**

Miles had been deceived and used. The sheer scale of their ambition staggered the mind. "My breaths are my own. These culty bastards need to be stopped. How do I help?"

"They consider you the linchpin, the key to achieving

the first stage of their plan—isolating the Netherworld and severing its connection to the rest of the multiverse. If that happens, if the Library loses its link to that entire dimension... the veils will weaken. Our power will wane, while theirs... will surge."

I took another sip of the tea, buying myself time to process. "And are they correct? Do I really have that kind of power?"

"We believe so."

"*What* is this power?" I pressed, my frustration mounting. "How do I wield it if I have seen no signs of it? Because I'm fresh out of cosmic cheat codes, and the fate of humanity is depending on me to figure my shit out."

"That knowledge cannot be revealed to you. Not yet."

This ain't it! Another tight-lipped guardian of cosmic secrets trying to finesse me. I was done with the whole "on-a-need-to-know-basis" routine.

"Are you for real expecting me to save the universe, and you're not going to tell me *how*?"

"For now, you must rely on your intellect and resourcefulness, Detective Hilliard." His voice sounded as precise as a recording. **"Untapped potential exists in all living things. Self-discovery is the real journey. We do not interfere with that unless absolutely necessary. Power that comes too easily destroys too easily."**

I threw my head back and laughed. *What a crock of shit!*

The White Librarian raised an eyebrow, the gesture so startlingly human it stunned me. **"I have amused you?"**

"No," I said, my laughter fading. "You're not funny, but I

learned I'm exceptional after all, and that's the funniest thing ever."

He stood, his white tunic flowing around him. **"Power unearned does not elevate, it pulls you down. The grander impulses turn primal."**

"You're afraid of what I might do?"

"No. Not at this precise juncture."

This gets more ridiculous by the moment.

"Okay, so, huh… what you're saying is, basically, that I am tasked with saving the Cosmic Library and, by extension, the entire multiverse, armed with nothing but my middling detective skills, and my lonely girl sarcasm. Right? Oh, wait, I forgot the kicker. I could become a real liability which would give you no other choice than to unleash your green hitman on me."

"Your powers of deduction are impressive, Detective Hilliard."

Gods, was that a flicker of a smile on his face?

"Right. I've had better offers in my life. Drunk guys at bars have better offers, in retrospect. Maybe you didn't present this better because of the whole *existence hanging in the balance* thing. You knew that part was a winner. Honestly, does it really matter? If everything hinges on me, we're doomed already."

"You underestimate yourself, just as others do."

I took a deep breath, trying to center myself. "Okay. Say I take you at your word, what would you have me do?"

"The wheel is already turning. The Cult presses forward even as we speak. You must depart for Nyx, immediately. Reach the Nether Realms before this oppor-

tunity vanishes. Stop the negotiations currently taking place in Nyx. Safeguard the integrity of the Netherworld portals."

Oh, is that all? No problem. Could you send a spreadsheet? For a moment I thought it might be something difficult.

"That is all," he said, tilting his head, as if he'd heard my thoughts but not quite grasped the sarcasm. **"The White Library is restricted by our mandate. Direct intervention in the affairs of individual dimensions is forbidden. You are not restricted. Seek out your allies. Tip the scales."**

Stopping the Erasers, protecting the multiverse… it all felt so impersonal, so abstract, detached from the grief and anger that churned inside me. "It's not enough," I said. "I want more. I need more. I want to make those assholes pay for all the misery they've caused. For the people they've hurt."

"Revenge is outside our concern. The Library neither condones nor forbids its pursuit. You choose your path."

"I don't need the Library's permission. This is my show now."

He nodded, his expression settling into cold neutrality. He raised his hand, his long fingers tracing a complex pattern of glyphs in the air. A portal shimmered before me, crackling and spitting energy.

"Tess Alexandra Hilliard," he said, his voice resonating with power, amplified until it seemed to fill the endless library, vibrating through my very bones. **"The Cult of Erasure poses an existential threat, one of the most profound the Cosmic Library has yet known. We grant you full**

authority to neutralize the threat by any means neces-sary. May the destinies favor you, Detective. Go home for now. And be safe."

The portal opening tugged me in, making my head spin.

No Thanksgiving dinner with Izzy and Yazmin tomorrow. No more banter with the cherry pie thief, no more falling asleep to Nina Simone. Just a one-way ticket to a nightmarish parallel dimension, a showdown with a cosmic horror, and a desperate fight to survive.

The portal swallowed me whole.

Chapter 23

As far as missions went, this had to rank among the least sensible in the grand circus of human idiocy. Tristan the vampire had insisted we hop into Nexilis at the stroke of midnight. Why? Moonrise, moonset and the moon's meridian moment change every night. Are vampires superstitious? Film buffs? His reasons remained locked behind his creepy thousand-yard stare. I went along with it, because, hey, he was the trolley conductor. No Tristan, no mission.

Killian and his Therian warriors were on their way, a select squad of six Reivers who'd volunteered for this suicide expedition—or maybe they refused to say no to their revered lord. Either way, they'd be arriving soon, ready to plunge into the swirling vortex of doom with *Captain Blood* and yours truly.

I'd obsessed over this journey for days, planned it, anticipated it, *craved* it, ever since learning about Miles's dealings in Nyx. Yet now, with one foot practically inside the portal, doubt crept in, that sinking feeling you get when you realize you're in way over your head.

It reminded me of the day my dad started training me to swim. He'd sat me down, looked me straight in the eye, and said first I must master holding my breath underwater in the bathtub before getting near the pool.

Seven-year-old me had stared at him, bewildered. "But, Dad, that's not normal. Not unless you have gills."

Apt metaphor for my entire life. Head underwater without gills.

Tristan, predictably, wasn't helping. He leaned against the wall, watching my every move with an intensity that made my skin crawl. I tried to stare him down, to meet his gaze with my own brand of crazy, but those amber eyes were unnerving, like windows into the cold expanse of space.

"You should try blinking," I said. "You know, to shake the zombie vibe."

"Your aura is unstable," he said, ignoring my stellar advice.

"Thanks for the riveting observation."

"It has three colors. Why would your aura be tricolor?"

"I don't know, Tristan, maybe I'm feeling patriotic today," I retorted, my annoyance growing. "You seem to be the expert. Enlighten me."

He sneered, his chiseled features twisting into an expression of disdain, his eyebrows drawing together in a dark V. "And you're not formidable."

"Aww, stop it. All this sweet talk will make me blush."

"You have some potential... Physical strength for someone your size... Threads of magic... But you hold it back. You need to... exude it."

What girl doesn't enjoy being dissected by a vampire? At least he had appealing cheekbones, a handsome pouty face and a chic designer trench coat.

"I think we're covered in the brawn department. Reivers are about as subtle as a sledgehammer, and Killian's a one-man army."

Tristan kept watching, trying to discern my signature. Vampires. They had an intense focus, a compulsion that was as hypnotic as it was terrifying.

"Where's your dragon?" he said with a hiss.

"He'll be here. We have twenty minutes till midnight."

Killian loves a dramatic entrance.

It was no time to worry, it was time to freak the fuck out. Where the hell was he? When we'd spoken, he said he'd get here early. This mission was starting to feel jinxed from the start.

But hell would freeze over and serve snow cones before I would share my fears with a vampire. Especially *this* vampire.

I stepped closer to the portal. My senses tingled in anticipation. A deep, guttural roar echoed from the hallway, vibrating through the walls, the floor, my very bones. It wasn't the predatory growl of a dragon. This was different, more chilling, mournful and... *terribly wrong*.

Tristan stiffened, his amber eyes widened, his fangs glinted. "What sound—"

Before I could finish, the portal erupted in a blinding flash of energy, nausea rolled over me, a sense of vertigo swept into me. I stumbled, my hand grasping for an anchor to steady myself.

Tristan's hand clamped onto my arm, his grip like cold iron, but the portal had other ideas. It yanked me in with the force of a black hole, my body contorting, twisting painfully as if being wrung out like a wet rag, bones grinding, muscles screaming. It was a sadistic rollercoaster of pain designed to tear and torture by a furious cosmic force.

This wasn't the typical quick adrenaline rush portal hop. Oh no, this was a cage match against your own physiology, and gravity was fighting dirty.

I slammed onto solid ground, the impact knocking the air from my lungs. The world kept spinning, even if I did not. A dizzying kaleidoscope of distorted shadows, my senses reeling, my stomach churning... I lay there gasping for breath, trying to make it all stop, trying to get my bearings.

A heavy thud beside me, followed by a muffled string of curses.

"Tristan?" I croaked.

"Rough welcome," he grumbled, his voice close but his body still lost in the shadows. "We should not be here. It's all wrong."

I pushed myself up, my vision slowly clearing. We were in a dark place, the air heavy with the scent of damp earth and metal. Rough, uneven terrain stretched out before us, illuminated only by the glow of the portal behind us.

"Where..." I started, but the words died as dread settled over me.

This wasn't Nexilis. This wasn't any place I wanted to be.

The portal flickered, its light pulsing like a dying heartbeat. Tristan grabbed my arm, his grip urgent. "It's destabilizing.

We need to move. *Now.*"

We lurched toward the fading portal, boots slipping on gravel, my vision swimming, only to watch it implode and vanish in a blink.

My legs, still wobbly from express teleportation, betrayed me. I pitched forward, bracing for a faceplant against the jagged ground. A force field slammed into me, halting my fall only inches from a pile of rocks. Tristan's levitation magic.

An inhuman growl echoed from the darkness, raising the hair on the back of my neck.

"Welcome to Nyx," Tristan hissed, yanking me to my feet. "You better hope your dragon finds you before anything else does."

With that, he spun on his heel and took off like a rocket.

Wonderful. Stranded in the Netherworld without backup.

How did we get to Nyx so fast? Izzy mapped a complex sequence of portals spanning several dimensions that would have taken many hours or even days to navigate. What in the multiverse had just happened? Did we get sucked into a secret wormhole backdoor?

And what about Killian? How would he travel the portals without us and how long would it take? How would he know where we went? Assuming, by some miracle, he managed to navigate the nexus maze, would he be able to track me in this forsaken wasteland? Would he even try?

I closed my eyes, taking a deep breath, forcing myself to calm down to assess the situation.

Nights in Nyx were starless, a fact I'd first gleaned from some book at the Runestone Academy's library years ago, and the days weren't much brighter. The realm didn't share its name with the goddess of night for nothing.

My eyes flew open, my vision slowly adjusting to the gloom. Shapes began to form in the darkness—jagged bluffs that clawed at the sky like the teeth of gigantic beasts amidst a rugged landscape of loose rocks and scrub. Clusters of flickering yellow lights shone like fireflies in the distance.

The options were bad and worse. Stay out here and take my chances with the ghastly things that prowled the Nyktian wild, or risk contact with the Nyktae, the realm's infamous skinless inhabitants?

The Nyktae weren't known for rolling out the welcome mat, but they weren't mindless savages either. They had a complex social structure, certain technological advancements, access to earth magic, and could learn to speak foreign languages, as I had learned from my encounter with Commander Zzrask. Mentioning his name might be a ticket to safety, or it might get me killed. I was certain that Zzrask had as many enemies as allies.

Another growl, closer this time, ripped through the silence. Not a sound you could mistake for anything friendly.

That made up my mind. Time to meet the Nyktae. At least with the gelatinous people of Nyx, I had some reference of what to expect. The things lurking in the shadows... I only had the blood curdling growl to go on.

I picked my way through the uneven terrain as carefully as I could, my anger simmering. Tristan had bailed at the first sign of trouble, probably already halfway to a bloody rampage.

Trust a fucking vampire. That should teach me.

At least my fanny pack had survived the portal jump. I chuckled like a crazy person. The energy bar inside might very well prove more useful than my mother's precious relics—moonstones, enchanted pendants, charmed silver and iron shavings, tiny glass runes. Time would tell.

I pushed forward, my feet crunching gravel and snapping twigs, every nerve ending on alert. The silence was unsettling, more so than any growl could be. Every shadow conjured a grisly shape in my mind.

A clicking sound, like claws on stone, stopped me cold.

Six points of light pierced the gloom. Three sets of eyes, too large and too perfectly round to belong to anything even remotely humanlike.

Get ready! Survive... at all costs.

I drew my dagger, my fingers tensed around the hilt, bracing myself for a battle for life. If these things flanked me, I was done.

My heart pounded faster than I thought possible.

As the creatures drew closer, my stomach lurched with a numbing panic. Those weren't three separate beings. They were one. One head. With six eyes!

The creature before me resisted comprehension, a gruesome fusion of insect and reptile. Its body was the size of a buffalo, covered in silver plates that suddenly ignited like backlit mirrors. Six spindly legs supported its bulk, each ending in wickedly curved claws that could easily tear me in half. Its head was triangular, reminiscent of a praying mantis, but with those six glowing eyes arranged across its forehead like a grotesque crown. Mandibles clicked together, dripping with a viscous fluid that sizzled when it hit the ground.

I froze, my instincts screaming at me to run and not stand there like a deer in headlights. But there was nowhere to go in this unknown desolation, nowhere to hide.

Will any of my mother's arcane relics work here?

Magic in the Netherworld was notoriously unpredictable—slippery, volatile, untamed. I couldn't get a firm handle on it. All the tricks I'd learned at the academy—the combative spells, the defensive shields, the protective wards—felt woefully inadequate against this opponent.

I reached inside my waist pack, fingers curling around the smooth surface of my mother's enchanted pendant. *The Radiant Shard.*

The creature let out a guttural growl and crouched low to the ground, its muscles coiling, ready to spring.

I whipped out the Radiant Shard, holding it high in my left hand, my right hand already moving, tracing arcane symbols in the air.

"Fotisma!" I roared, pouring every ounce of will and desperation into the word. *"Bring forth the radiance!"*

A blinding flash of light exploded from the pendant, disorienting the creature. It spun around, snorting, but recovered faster than I had hoped. It roared, shaking the ground, and charged.

I rolled aside, narrowly avoiding its snapping jaws. I scrambled to my feet, my hand already reaching for the vial of enchanted iron and silver shavings. I hurled it at the creature. The vial shattered against its chest, and the metallic powder exploded in a cloud of sparks.

"Displodi!!" I shouted, slamming my will into the spell.

The creature shrieked, clawing at its chest, as if trying to tear away the burning metal. It was now or never. I seized the opportunity, lunging forward with my dagger, the blade glinting against the creature's mirror plates before sinking deep into its exposed underbelly.

The beast staggered, its movements growing sluggish. I pressed on, my dagger flashing as my wind magic swirled around me, forming a fragile shield.

The creature's primal rage fueled one last desperate attack that caught me off guard. One of its claws ripped through my defenses, catching my left hand with a force that sent spikes of pain shooting up my arm.

Adrenaline at an all-time high, I plunged my dagger deeper, twisting the blade. A sickening crunch echoed through the silence as the blade found its mark. The creature let out an agonized roar before it turned and fled, disappearing into the shadows with an uneven trot.

I stood there for a moment, chest heaving, heart pounding. My hand and arm throbbed, a dull ache that pulsed with every beat of my heart. This didn't feel like a victory. More like a short reprieve, the first act in a play that would most likely end with my brutal death by mauling.

I tore a swath of fabric off the bottom of my shirt to wrap

my wounded hand. The lights ahead had multiplied, a constellation of flickering yellow, blue and green. Torch flames? Enchanted lanterns? Phosphorescent crystals? Bioluminescent flora? All or none of the above?

I had to keep moving. I had to find the Nyktae. If the multiverse, or whatever cosmic entity was currently using me as its plaything, decided to throw me a bone, I might even stumble across one of the rare Nyx portals.

The one thing that gave me a sliver of hope was that the creature hadn't used any magic. If that held true for all the creatures in Nyx, I might stand a slim chance to survive a few hours.

Killian had said the Nyktae themselves weren't able to wield combative magic. But there was little known about this Nether realm, so jumping to conclusions was a surefire way to start off in the wrong direction.

I staggered toward the lights, the shadows lengthening around me, the silence closing in, the darkness a suffocating blanket.

The Nyktian town was within reach now and larger than I'd imagined. Thick glass walls reinforced with visibly shimmering wards enclosed a sprawling network of buildings and winding streets. Guards armed with bows and spears patrolled the perimeter.

At the single gate into the town, silhouetted against flickering torchlight, stood a figure I recognized. One of the Nyktians who had accompanied Miles inside Zzrask's mindscape orb—a tall, imposing figure fully dressed in leather armor with eyes that glowed crimson on his skinless face.

He's not here for me. Can't be. Just turn and keep walking.

"Welcome to Esperia," the Nyktian said, his voice echoing through the space between us. "We've been expecting you."

Chapter 24

THE INSIGNIA EMBLAZONED ONTO my Nyktian escort's worn leather armor—three bold golden stripes bisected by a red hexagon, marking him as an officer of rank in the Nyktian army—was the only detail I remembered about him from the holographic projection of Zzrask's mindscape orb.

Esperia unfolded like a living maze. Narrow cobblestone paths snaked between tightly packed buildings, opening into wider streets paved with porous volcanic rocks.

The ink-black night sky was beginning to bleed into a bruised purple.

As we ventured deeper into the town, darkness yielded to an unexpected luminescence. Esperia sprawled around a cluster of crystal formations that glowed at its center, bathing the town in a violet blue light.

The houses were built with a strange organic phosphorescent material. Vines, woven into intricate patterns across the walls, glowed with a mesmerizing emerald bioluminescence. The Nyktae had clearly mastered the art of bio-architecture, a necessity for a world that flickered eternally between night and twilight.

Every so often, a pair of curious eyes would gleam behind a window, vanishing as quickly as they appeared.

The Nyktian officer moved beside me with quiet confidence. His six fingers, a trait common among his kind, flexed rhythmically on the hilt of the curved sword strapped to his hip. He hadn't uttered a word since approaching me at the town gate. His silence only amplified my unease.

We arrived at the largest building in town, a towering structure of polished stone stretching five stories high in the heart of a bustling marketplace. Two guards with horned helmets snapped to attention. The Nyktian officer growled something in his native tongue, a sandpaper sound that grated against my ears. The guards stepped aside.

The heavy wooden doors groaned open. We entered a long, stone corridor lit by oil lanterns that hung precariously from the ceiling. My escort halted in front of an unmarked door that had neither a handle nor a lock. He pressed his hand against the cool stone surface and the door slid open, revealing a chamber bathed in the ethereal glow of bioluminescent flowers blooming in large ornate planters.

I stepped inside, my gaze darting around in search of escape routes. There were no bars on the windows and no guards at the door. A queen-sized bed dominated the space, draped in a lush quilt. Two fluffy pillows sat at the head carefully arranged. A cold fireplace stood against one wall, flanked by a high-backed armchair and a small side table. A writing desk sat near the window with a single feather quill resting on a sheet of paper.

"You may... ressst here," the Nyktae rasped.

"I appreciate the hospitality, but I don't plan to stay," I told him, eyeing the open door.

"He will... sssspeak with you ssssoon," he said, his words unnervingly clear. He'd spent time conversing with humans, his accent softened by practice. *Or maybe they offer conversational English classes in Nyx.* "You can... sssspeak your wordssss... to him."

"My words? Look, this is a big misunderstanding, a mistake. The portal malfunctioned. It broke and I ended up in the wrong dimension. If you could point me to the nearest functioning gateway, I'll get out of your hair fast as a heartbeat."

Awkward word choice. Like all Nyktae, he was as bald as a peeled potato.

"He will decide. Now resssst."

"He? Who's he?"

The escort turned and left, the door shutting behind him.

I paced the room, my mind racing. My injured hand throbbed. Options, I needed options. My search for hints of magic signatures, anything I could exploit, came up empty. That White Librarian entity was right. I would have to rely on myself, my wits, my instincts, my chameleonic ability to blend and adapt. At least my illusion sensors still hummed contentedly, my magic core teeming with a steady stream of energy.

I stepped to the window. The night had faded to a dull twilight. A smallish Nyktae (possibly a child) scurried down the street, clutching a leash attached to a creature that resembled the unholy offspring of a tortoise and a poodle. Its phosphorescent shell pulsed green as the tortoise-poodle pranced along on six graceful furry legs.

The bed with its invitingly soft pillows beckoned me. If I closed my eyes for a moment, I'd drift off into a blissful slumber. Sleep deprivation during the past week had become my hazy companion, but even a quick nap meant letting my guard down.

Time blurred into a monotonous green soup courtesy of the bioluminescent flora. Thirty minutes? Three hours? Who knew? The silence was so profound it felt like a palpable substance, pressing in from all sides. Exhaustion gnawed at the seams of my sanity, threatening to pull me apart.

The door opened, startling me. A Nyktian guard with a grotesquely scarred gelatinous face bowed his head. "Heee... ssseeesss... youuuu... nowww." The mangled syllables oozed out in a thick accent.

I rose to my feet, ready to follow him, but instead of leading the way, he stepped aside, his stance rigid as a board, his crimson eyes fixed on a point above my head.

The signature of the man who stepped into the room slammed into me like a thousand bee stings. The surge of dark magic flooded my senses, momentarily collapsing my illusion veils, sending my core thrumming with chaotic energy. I fought to regain control against the potent cocktail of dark sorcery and forbidden ritualistic proficiency.

The man was about six feet tall, lean, clad in a navy-blue robe studded with silver stars and crescent moons. His long dark hair was streaked with silver, framing a face that was both old and unsettlingly ageless, a result of a life spent diligently avoiding sunlight. His beard was neatly trimmed, lending him an air of scholarly respectability. All he needed was a pointy hat and an owl, and he'd have the full-on Wizard fit.

The arch necromancer Raven warned me about.

He dismissed the guard with a wave. The guard retreated, closing the door quietly behind him.

The necromancer's charcoal eyes narrowed in detached curiosity. "Detective Hilliard, I presume? You must be wondering why you're here."

"I am here due to a portal malfunction and an unexpected detour. If you could direct me back to my dimension... I wouldn't want to impose on your hospitality any longer than necessary."

"Ah, the innocent bystander routine. *Show me the door and I'll be on my way!*" he said. His voice had no mocking tone, but he was clearly amused. "Unfortunately, you're not a convincing actress."

"It's the truth," I said. "What are you implying?"

He ignored the question and walked to the fireplace. A snap of his fingers roared the fire to life. "You broke into Nyx for the purpose of disrupting meticulously laid plans, fighting off villains and playing the savior. A foolish notion, albeit commendable."

"In your hypothetical scenario, there are villains in Nyx."

"The only villains in this story, Detective Hilliard, are the Cosmic Librarians," he said, his voice hardening, eyes blazing with a righteous fury that surprised me. "They perch on their ivory thrones, using their unelected authority to suffocate the multiverse, to stifle innovation and block new realities, to hoard power and knowledge for themselves."

Ha. Unexpected villain monologue. I wasn't prepared for a philosophical treatise from an arch necromancer whose basement was likely full of thralls.

"They claim to be guardians and protectors," he continued, his voice rising, "but they are nothing more than tyrants. They fear change. They fear progress. They fear anything that challenges their dominion."

"Let me guess, the Erasure cultists are misunderstood heroes who are going to liberate all worlds from the oppressive yoke of... librarians? Is that your bedtime story, the one all good little wannabe dictators tell themselves? *Look at me, I'm not power-hungry, I just want to free everyone, then crush them under my iron-fisted rule because only I know what's good for the people.*"

A flicker of surprise flashed across his face, a brief crack in the hardened façade. The fact that both Miles and the White Librarian had specifically mentioned the Cult of Erasure was news to him. I might have overplayed my hand, revealed too much too soon, but the truth was, there was no way he was going to let me walk out of here. I was cooked, no matter what I said or did.

His lips thinned into a harsh line. "We intend to wrestle control from the Librarians and restore it to the individual realms where it belongs."

"Oh, right," I scoffed. "Because a vast multiverse governed by a patchwork of conflicting laws and regulations is *such* a surefire recipe for peace and harmony between realms. No chance of injustices, unrest, or wars with that flawless plan, eh? Read a book. When has that ever worked?"

He brushed aside my comment. "Those are the lies of history. A central power always ruled, even if they pretended the power was spread evenly to all regions. Propaganda spread by the established order. You don't have to understand it, Detective Hilliard. Your role is to help make it happen."

Of course, everyone from Miles to the White Librarian to this narcissistic psycho seemed convinced I would have a role in taking down worlds, though no one was willing to elaborate.

No one tells the pawn anything.

I crossed my arms, ignoring the way my scars tightened under my clothes as if trying to burst out. "I think you might be beyond help, because if you think kidnapping me is going to make the Cosmic Library hand over the keys to the multiverse, you're sadly mistaken."

If he was annoyed, he didn't show it. "I am quite aware the Librarians find you expendable, but that's not what's happening."

"Then why am I here? Wait, I got it. You need to hold someone captive to have a captive audience for your delusional monologues?"

"Eight years ago, a power was bestowed upon you. Your blood was primed for this moment. Embrace it, Detective Hilliard, it is your destiny."

Was it my scars he was referring to? Or my illusion magic? According to Miles's cryptic video, the scars were the thing, but how they triggered a universe-altering power remained a mystery. One more secret in a parade of secrets. Being the last to know pissed me off.

"Specifics would be nice if you're trying to recruit me into your little world-domination scheme. Maybe there's something in it for me?"

He cocked his head to the side, studying me like I was a particularly fascinating lab rat. "The extent of your knowledge is irrelevant. Our immediate objective is to isolate the Netherworld, to sever its connection to the rest of the multiverse for an indefinite period."

"A little quarantine for the Netherworld, huh, *Archie*? And you need my help with this disappearing act? Maybe you want me to handle the farewell party for the departing dimensions? Streamers, confetti, that sort of thing?"

"Such a reliance on ludicrous comments to mask emotion. You even twist my title into a name. Tedious. I am Kyros." His lips twisted into a chilling smile. "Your perspective is limited. Severing the connection is well within our own capabilities. Years of meticulous preparation have ensured that. We don't require your assistance for that mundane task. Your role in the grand design is far more nuanced."

I chewed on that, my unease growing. "Nuanced? Is your

explanation nuanced? Because I don't understand at all. Are you expecting me to keep the Netherworld functioning like I'm some cosmic battery while you jet off to wreak havoc on more worlds?"

"Intrigued, are we?" He made a throat noise, a chuckle perhaps, a low, dry sound that scraped against my nerves. "Excellent. A dash of curiosity makes the inevitable much more *delicious.*"

Kyros settled into the armchair by the fireplace. His gaze lingered on me. I fought the urge to blast his unsuspecting head with a mini tornado.

"Only a very small, very select inner circle is privy to the true nature of your involvement," he confided. "You see, we have stumbled upon a treasure trove—a vast reservoir of untapped, unexplored magic pulsating within the Netherworld's core. A magic so potent it defies all boundaries and transcends comprehension. Power that can turn back time. Imagine the implications. The ability to selectively alter history, to rewind and reshape reality to suit our vision. With a snap we could neutralize nuclear weapons—or *create* them."

His eyes mirrored the predatory glint I'd seen in that six-eyed beast I fought in the wild. "Imagine a power so absolute it could bend every single world to our will. We will unleash this behemoth and claim it all. Sealing off the Netherworld is a necessary precaution, ensuring neither the Cosmic Library nor the Bureaus nor any other Arcane authority can intervene."

It wasn't just Miles who had it wrong. Even the White Librarian had been woefully off the mark. Neither had grasped the full picture, the terrifying, world-shattering scope of the Cult's ambition.

A cold wave of misery washed over me. I'd been played. The Cult of Erasure had manipulated my every step, from that damned library portal in Sun Prairie to this godforsaken Nyx town.

"I was right all along," I said, my voice flat, tired. "Absolute power is the real endgame. The rest—the liberation, the new world, equality, peace—it's all a bullshit spin."

He chuckled. "That's our little secret, Detective. We don't want the rank and file to... get wind of our long-term intentions. Not yet."

"But you're fine with your virtuous inner circle knowing, a bunch of psychos who lie and betray in every direction and crave ultimate control?"

His gaze turned sharp, assessing me. "Savian had you pegged. An annoying delight with a hit or miss cynical insight."

"Savian? Who the fuck's Savian?" The name meant nothing, but the way he said it triggered a slow panic.

"Let's not labor the finer points. The outcome is set. The launch of a new world order. We can accomplish this. Together. We all have our roles to play."

"Enough nonsense. What's my role?" I asked, my voice tight. "I don't care if it's as a human sacrifice or whatever. Just spit it out, Kyros!"

"Oh no, young Tess." He smiled, all teeth. "You underestimate yourself. You're much more than a mere sacrifice. You're the safeguard that makes the impossible possible. To harness this power, to siphon it from its source, we need a conduit. A fixed horizon. You are that human vessel. Your blood has been pristinely primed to the necessary specs."

Conduit. There's that word again.

"Why me? Did you run out of fanatics at the last Evil-Con convention?"

"Each and every scar crisscrossing your body is a unique transmitter, years in the making. You will channel the magic to us, like a living, breathing power line."

Some deep-fried Tess for their Thanksgiving turkey.

"Us?" I echoed. "Who is *us*?"

"The Cult elders." His voice was smooth, seductive even, the whisper of a viper offering up its venom. "The architects of the future. The chosen. The enlightened. The ones who will wield the ultimate power."

Talk about lacking self-awareness.

"You went to a lot of trouble dragging me here, but I'm not the only one with hocus-pocus scars. Miles Donovan showed me his."

He scoffed. "Donovan. I always knew he was a chump. A useful idiot for a time, but ultimately expendable. All members of the Cult of Erasure bear similar markings, but they possess limited capacity for power transference. You, on the other hand, are a full-fledged conduit from head to toe."

"Then why not pool your resources and do it yourselves? You know, teamwork makes the dream work and all that cultist jazz."

"Because that much power transference will be... messy. You are about to be the multiverse's most magnificent lightning rod, absorbing the power of a thousand electrical storms, channeling it, refining it. I hate to be the bearer of bad news, but the conduit always burns out."

Don't sugarcoat it, you nutcase.

"How am I so lucky as to be roasted in the name of progress?"

"I wish I had a better answer," he said, his hand reaching out. I recoiled as his fingers brushed my cheek. "But you were simply there. Savian saw the opportunity and took it—a blank canvas brimming with possibility, a fledgling mage young enough to be molded into the perfect instrument with careful preparation. And now you are here, ready to fulfill his vision."

Savian. The name echoed in my mind like a gunshot, the last piece of the puzzle clicking into place. Savian was the illusion mage who had materialized in our home library that rainy night eight years ago. The monster who had murdered my parents. The one who had marked me. Savian was the architect of my nightmares and the architect of the Cult of Erasure—my tormentor then and my tormentor now.

"You better hope *Savian* has a backup plan. Because I'd rather gargle glass than help you fascist psychos rewrite reality."

"There are worse fates, Ms. Hilliard."

"Like, say, tearing a man apart piece by piece? Who killed Miles? Was it you or your lord Savian? Where would I find this monster? I want to thank them in my own special sort of way."

"Donovan had become unpredictable. When that happens,

a member becomes expendable. After he failed to deliver you at Sun Prairie, he refused to cooperate and lead you to a stronger portal. His sentimental attachment to you got him killed." He paused, his lips twisting into a cruel smile. "He insisted on ensuring your safety during the power transference, the weak fool. We acted quickly to ensure his *silence*. I see now, we were too late."

The casual cruelty of his words, the lack of remorse, twisted my gut. Murder was no more significant to him than ordering a cup of tea.

"You murdered your comrade in cold blood. Did you use thralls to do it or your Nyktian monsters?"

"Both, but their success was owed to a frostlock demon. Always a wise choice to freeze an opponent's magic, don't you think?"

"Thank you for sharing the precise details of your treacheries," I said, my voice a shard of ice. "I'll be sure to include as much as possible in my Yelp review of this charming, out-of-the-way kidnapping destination."

"It matters little now," he said, almost sympathetically. "It's far too late for regrets and it's far too late for you." He clapped his hands. "Seize her!"

Two Nyktian guards burst into the room. They were upon me before I could reach for my dagger, before I could *blink*. Their hands clamped onto my arms, pinning them to my sides, hurting me.

I writhed and squirmed, every muscle aching taut with adrenaline.

"Hold her still," the arch necromancer Kyros instructed. He stepped closer, holding a small sphere. Its surface swirled with shadows.

A mindscape orb.

Panic surged through my core. I struggled against the guards' iron grip, hissing, kicking, trying to bite anything within reach.

"Don't fight it," Kyros said as if soothing a spooked horse. "It will take but a moment. I'll extract a few memories to verify nothing crucial was missed."

"How about you take that orb and shove it—"

Kyros flicked his wrist, and a wave of dark energy slammed into me, pinning me in place. My wind magic sputtered before it could ignite.

He pressed the orb against my forehead. A jolt of pain detonated in my head. I screamed but the sound stuck in my throat. Images flashed through my mind—fragmented memories, distorted and jumbled, ripped from all context like book pages thrown into a blender.

I fought back, slamming my mental shields down with all the force I could muster, but it was like swimming through quicksand. The onslaught of the orb overwhelmed my defenses.

The door exploded, splintered wood and chunks of stone spraying in every direction. Tristan stood in the doorway for a split second, his eyes blazing like red-hot coals. He moved with a speed that defied physics, a whirlwind of fangs and bloodlust. One moment the guards were holding me fast, the next they were crumpled heaps on the floor, their limbs twisted at unnatural angles, their necks broken.

Kyros staggered back, blindsided, losing precious seconds. Tristan was on him before he could recover his bearings, the vampire's bloodied hands wrapping around his throat.

The choking necromancer raised his hand. A tendril of smoke snaked through the air, a dark, writhing serpent of necromancy. Tristan stiffened, his hands dropping to his side like his strings had been cut.

"Such a loyal pet," Kyros sneered. "Who do you belong to, vampire? No matter, even the most devoted can be persuaded to change their allegiance."

I felt the tidal wave of necromantic energy he unleashed into the vampire slam into me as if I had targeted it myself. A subterranean chill seeking to corrupt, then control.

Tristan roared, his body contorting, his movements spastic.

He got to him. The asshole is inside Tristan's head, forcing a bond.

"Tristan, snap out if it!" I yelled.

The vampire's head pivoted to me, his fangs bared and dripping blood.

Tristan, if you're in there, now would be the time for a smartass comment, followed by ripping this creep's head off.

"Secure the prisoner," the necromancer commanded.

Instinct took over. I reached out, pushing past the pain, past the fear, past the mind-numbing pressure in my skull. My illusion sensors probed the necromancer's core, hunting for a chink in his sadistic armor. I poured every ounce of will and every speck of magic into the assault until I latched onto his dark sorcery. It was my lifeline. I pulled it toward me, wrapped it around my body like a shroud.

The necromancer resisted, an angry fury crashing against my core. I pushed back, twisting his hate magic with a deafening roar, channeling it into the feeble vampire.

It all happened so fast Tristan's fangs were inches from my throat when he froze, his darkened eyes locked on mine. I felt the unnerving depths of his mind as clearly as my own, as if I was his dark maker pulling his strings.

For a heartbeat, my eyes met the stunned necromancer's eyes. He thought he had planned for everything, but he hadn't planned for Tristan.

My grip on the stolen magic teetered. "Take me out of here," I told Tristan, darkness cutting through me like a river of ink.

The vampire scooped me into his arms and bolted out the door, through corridors, past more crumpled bodies (*note to self: never piss off Tristan*), and into the streets of the citadel. Houses and silhouettes blurred past as he raced to the edge of the town, leapt over the towering glass wall and sprinted into the wild beyond.

We didn't stop until we were far from Esperia and his legs finally gave out. Tristan dumped me onto the ground, rather roughly, his chest heaving.

Kyros had been caught with his guard down. Tristan was an unexpected variable. A vampire who, for whatever reasons, came to my rescue. Hell, *I* was caught off guard by the whirlwind vampire avenger.

But it was more than that. The arch necromancer was stunned by my ability to invade his core and siphon his magic. I doubted he knew I was an illusion mage. The bastard Savian must have improvised on a whim and kept that little detail to himself.

I wanted to know. Now I knew. I had really tried to imagine the worst, but my imagination failed.

Chapter 25

"WHAT DID YOU DO to me?" Tristan demanded, finally catching his breath. His eyes turned a sickly green as he pinned me with a stare that made me feel like a bug under the microscope.

I shrugged, trying to ignore the insane hammering of my heart against my ribs and the echo of necromancy in my mind. "I don't know, I reacted on instinct, a spur of the moment, *oh-crap-we're-about-to-die,* kind of thing."

A muscle ticked in his jaw. "You hijacked my mind. Instinct doesn't do that. Instinct makes you run or fight, not harness vampires."

"I have no idea how it happened," I insisted, the memory of our linked minds more than a little disturbing. "The necromantic magic in Nyx... it's different. Unrestrained. Wild. Maybe it messed with my magic, amplified it."

"Swear you won't ever do that again." It sounded less like a request and more like a command.

The truth is I saved you, buddy, and might have to do it again.

"Trust me, the last thing I want is to return to that icy abyss you call a mind. Once was more than enough."

He grumbled, clearly not finding my answer satisfactory.

"You shouldn't be complaining," I shot back. "If I hadn't reacted, you'd be his meat puppet for all eternity, and I'd be a fucking human battery."

I'd completely lost access to the necromantic power that had given me control over Tristan, but the sticky, foul residue of that dark energy clung to me, pushing against my illusion veils. It made my skin crawl.

Tristan's head whipped around so fast I could swear I heard a crack in his neck. "Why didn't you let me loose on him while we had the chance? I could have ended that miserable swine right then and there. Ripped his throat out. Feasted on his blood."

The vicious image he painted appealed to me more than it should. That joined a lengthy list of *Things to Discuss with a Therapist Later.*

"It wouldn't have worked. Not for long. I was losing my grip on you, fast. He'd have yanked your mind back in seconds. I'm no match for an arch necromancer, Tristan. I caught him off guard, but he won't make that mistake twice."

Tristan brushed his ash-blond hair back from his face, saying nothing, but his entire tense body radiated frustration.

"Why did you come back, Tristan? Why did you help me?"

"My charge was to protect you at all costs," he said flatly as if it were a matter of little consequence.

Raven had saved my ass. That was one good thing. A vampire bodyguard with a hair-trigger temper on the other hand...

not completely reassuring, but thanks, I guess.

"Then how do you explain taking off in the first place?"

He studied the horizon as if it held the answer. "Portal hunting."

I raised an eyebrow.

"No luck," he said. "We'll have to venture deeper into this hellscape until we find a way out."

"I can barely take another step," I said, fatigue and the sharp pain in my injured hand finally hitting full force. "We need to rest. And I need water and food. I'm lagging, my body is shutting down."

He opened his trench coat, revealing an inner lining that looked like something out of a spy movie. Straps, pockets, and the glint of metal—a switchblade, a dagger, enchanted coins, a pocket watch, a compass, vials, herbs and three leather flasks.

A vampire survival kit.

He handed me a large Band-Aid. He'd noticed my injured hand.

"Snatched these from the town marketplace," he said as he pulled out a flask and offered it to me. "Hope that's water and not some local homebrew."

I uncorked the flask and sniffed its contents. I poured a few drops onto my palm. Cold water. Glistening and crystal clear.

"Tristan, you're a genius," I said before taking a refreshing gulp.

"Pace yourself. We don't know if we'll find more water."

"What about you? Don't you need... sustenance?" I hoped it wouldn't come to the point where I'd have to offer him my blood to keep him... alive... I mean, healthily undead.

They don't prepare you for this at the Academy.

"I'll manage," he said, his eyes dropping to the soft pulse of the carotid artery in my neck. "Come with me."

He led me to a nook beneath the shadow of a jutting cliff, a natural shelter from the elements and prying eyes. He spread out his trench coat on the rocky ground. Chivalry, apparently, wasn't dead. Just undead.

Tristan bent over and took a small vial out of the coat. He drew a semicircle on the ground with the blue liquid. "To mask our scent," he said. "You have thirty minutes. I'll keep watch and then wake you."

I didn't argue. I curled up in the center of his coat, careful not to disturb his treasures, resting my head on cool stone, clutching my throbbing hand.

Inhaling the leather and smoky scent of his coat, I drifted off.

When Tristan shook me awake, I had no idea how long I'd slept.

"There's something in the air," Tristan said, crouching beside me. "They're coming for us."

I rubbed my groggy eyes. "They? Who's they?"

His head snapped up like he had caught a whiff of danger. He pointed at the horizon. A crimson glow spread across the sky like a bloodstain, moving our way. Fast.

What toxic substance could turn the Nyktian sky red?

"We have a minute or two before they're here," Tristan said. "Do we fight or flee?"

"I don't suppose there's a hidden pocket portal in your magical coat?"

His fangs descended with a sharp *whoosh.*

I'll take that as a no.

"They know what they're dealing with," I said, my eyes fixed on the approaching crimson tide. "We don't know what we're dealing with."

He pulled me to my feet and shrugged on his coat like a reflex. I handed the water flask back to him to tuck away inside the coat, my stomach twisting.

We had no choice but to run and keep running till we found a portal, or Killian found us. If the Cult got their hands on me, it was over—for us and for the world we'd sworn to protect.

A growing crimson cloud sliced through the sky ahead, spreading fast like the wings of a giant eagle.

There was nowhere to hide. Whatever was hunting us approached from all directions. We were outmaneuvered and outnumbered.

I'm firing my travel agent when we get back.

The red glow shifted, swooping out of the sky in a swirling mist and pursuing us with terrifying speed. Three dark shapes hurtled out of the mist, all claws and teeth and bad intentions.

"Demons!" Tristan said, nostrils flaring.

More shapes emerged from the red haze, their ravenous eyes glowing with predatorial lust. I spotted five Nyktae standing in the distance, maybe more lurking just out of sight. Not like the Nyktian guards in Esperia. These were ferocious warriors, their faces painted with black tribal ink.

The demons closed in, their hair-raising shrieks muting my ears. They were a full foot taller than Tristan, their leathery skin a patchwork of black, gray and maroon. Their powerful legs ended in two cloven hooves that struck the ground with a resonant, menacing thud, leaving sparks in their wake.

Sinewy, lean metallic scales ran down their demon backs like some weird biomechanical experiment. Twin twisted horns jutted from their foreheads, curving forward. Their faces were dominated by two mismatched eyes—one glowing with an intense red, the other a dark, empty socket.

Tendrils of scarlet smoke warped the air around them as if they had just been forged in blood fires. They were death itself. I prepared for the end.

Horns and hooves seemed like a cosmic joke, but I suddenly remembered; horns and hooves meant these were minor demons with minimal supernatural abilities.

Okay, so I panicked a little. It's been a day.

The only way to kill these things was to remove their heads. It severed the connection to whatever infernal realm fueled their existence.

That's no easy task when the demons are actively trying to make you their new chew toy.

I felt every drop of their abysmal, oppressive power thrumming within my blood, but I couldn't tap into it, control it or even understand it—and that was probably a good thing. That way lies madness and all that.

Tristan pulled me behind him, so a nearby bluff would guard my back while he guarded my front. "Stay here," he said.

A long, ragged howl ripped from Tristan's throat, catching me off guard. Vampires were silent killers, they stalked their prey from the shadows, but he was channeling rage. His fangs glinted in the twilight as he charged headlong into their manic advance. He took down the first demon with brutal efficiency, twisting its head clean off its body with a sickening snap crunch sound.

And I immediately feel sorry for the demon, while fighting demons.

Tristan leapt over the beheaded body and slashed two Nyktian throats so fast I barely registered what had happened.

The remaining demons snarled and lunged for Tristan, their claws slicing through the air frantically.

The vampire, a silhouette of lethal grace, sidestepped with inhuman speed, landing a bone-cracking punch to one demon's ribs. The demon howled, sharp spikes erupting across his body like a porcupine from hell.

The second demon attacked Tristan from behind, its horned head lowered for a goring strike. The vampire dropped to a crouch, spinning on his heel to deliver a sweeping kick that sent the demon sprawling. He leapt onto the demon's prone form, his lengthy fangs sinking into its throat.

The first demon unleashed a burst of scarlet energy, the blast scorching everything in its path, including Tristan's coat tails. Both demons jumped on Tristan, digging their claws into the vampire's back and abdomen.

My heart pounded as I fumbled for the glass runes in my fanny pack.

"*Dynamis*," I shouted as I hurled the runes at Tristan. "Grow in strength!"

Supercharging a vampire. Definitely not a thing one should ever do, but desperate times...

Tristan exploded from beneath the demon pile-up, the front of his shirt in tatters, bloody wounds striping his face.

He hissed in fury as his skin struggled to knit together. He whirled around, eyes blazing with thirst for vengeance. His fist collided with the nearest demon's face, the impact reverberating in my energy field. The wheezing demon staggered then crumpled face first, its skull fractured.

Tristan whirled around to face the second demon, now charging with a croaking battle cry, but the vampire widened his stance to meet its charge. The sudden impact dazed the demon. In a flurry almost too fast to see, Tristan twisted the demon's arm, snapping bone and sinew, and drove his knee into its abdomen. The demon coughed up a splatter of black blood, collapsing into a heap. Tristan's boot stomped the demon's head again and again until its vertebrae were crushed, and the skull separated from its neck.

The first demon darted toward *me* with startling speed.

Oh, good gods!

I flailed my arms, channeling everything I had into a wind vortex. Adrenaline and fear mixed a hell of a cocktail of magic, or maybe the residual energy from the rune spell boosted me. Whatever the reason, I spun the biggest, baddest whirlwind I'd ever conjured. It blasted into the demon, lifting it off the ground and hurling it violently into the rocks.

Supercharged Tristan seized the opportunity, grabbing the demon's head with both hands and spinning it until the loud snap echoed like a gunshot. The demon's body went limp, slipping to the ground like a noodle.

Behind Tristan, the three remaining Nyktae hovered helplessly in midair, trapped by his levitation magic.

When did he do that? Lesson of the day: Never, under any circumstance, mess with a supercharged vampire.

Breathing heavily, Tristan stood amidst the carnage covered in demon pieces. The faint glow of his regenerative power illuminated his face as it stitched itself back together. He surveyed the fallen demons, his expression one of cold satisfaction. He flashed me a fang-filled grin.

His body jerked violently as a thick, silver bolt exploded through his chest, splintering his heart into a thousand pieces.

Tristan teetered as his smile dripped away, becoming a crimson ribbon, before his body tipped forward and landed with a thud on the ground.

Chapter 26

Kyros stood on a bluff fifty feet away, his giant crossbow fixed on me.

You won't release that arrow, you psycho. You need me.

Crimson invaded the sky. More demon hordes poured over the horizon, their spine-chilling shrieks piercing the air.

I dropped to my knees. I flipped Tristan's body over. His eyes were glassy, his mangled chest completely still. Something inside me snapped, shattering the carefully constructed dams holding back my true nature.

My concealed scars burst across my skin with a stinging pain. I roared like a wounded lion—the unearthly sound curdled my own blood. Green runes ignited on top of the scars glowing like emeralds, pulsing with a power that felt familiar and unreal at the same time.

My mother's warding magic. Why did I never imagine it was part of my inheritance?

Power churned in and around me like a cyclone gathering force. All runed up and pissed to the nth degree, I unleashed my sensors and drove them deep into the necromancer's core, siphoning his dark energy. I didn't just tap his reserves; I was draining them dry.

Mother's rune magic shielded my core from the energy backlash. Those cursed illusion marks that marred my skin activated, turning me into a conduit, a channel for raw power transference. It was a terrifying sensation, a feeling of limitless potential, like housing a nuclear reactor in my gut.

I sank huge torrents of the necromancer's magic into Tristan's chest, willing him back to life, to his eternal undeath. Energy streamed through my blood in swells of white-hot agony, flooding into him. I had no idea what I was doing, but I couldn't stop.

Heal him, damn it! Bring Tristan back to me!

Magic stormed inside me like a trapped beast, threatening to rip me open. I would not survive, I had to let it go, to break the connection before it broke me, of that I was certain. *No! Screw that! Caution be damned!* Tess Hilliard, the P.I. who valued restraint above all, had left the building. The illusion mage I'd hidden away for eight long years assumed control and she was hungry.

I fought against my own destruction, directing the overload of energy into Tristan's shredded heart, ignoring the agony in my own chest.

Let go, Tess. You can't win this battle.

NO!

Words ripped from my throat of their own volition, an ancient blood spell I'd only seen once on paper.

"Sanguis vitae renovare!"

Suddenly, I gained control, guiding the dark magic inside Tristan's body, weaving it with my own life force and the magic of my mother's runes.

I tore the bandage from my injured hand, wincing as the wound reopened. I squeezed a single bead of blood into Tristan's ravaged chest—the catalyst needed for the dark ritual.

Seconds passed; nothing. I had to let go, but before I did the ache searing my chest vanished. Tristan gasped as his eyes snapped open. He spat up blood and bile that splattered onto the ground. I watched, transfixed, as his rib bones fused together and the flesh of his heart mended.

His piercing amber eyes found me. My breath caught in my throat. He no longer gazed upon me with cool detachment. Instead, I saw the most unexpected quality... devotion... or loyalty. I had seen him like this before. Tristan looked at me now the way I had seen him look at Raven.

Not this. I didn't ask for this. Fuck my life.

Bringing him back had forged a bond, a necromantic link, a chain that tied his life, his *undeath*, to mine. Tristan was bound to me. And Raven... Raven would surely have my head for this.

Stay focused. I'll deal with that fallout later.

Right now, a demonic tsunami was falling from the heavens, a crimson tide of destruction. I had to act fast, to harness and solidify this vampiric connection, or Tristan might break free and succumb to the insatiable hunger of newborn vampires. There was one way out, the narrow path carved by Tristan when he became that demon-killing machine. The ground was bloody and full of body parts but ran away from the oncoming assault.

"Tristan," I said, lifting his face with both hands. "We gotta move."

He blinked, awareness snapping back into his eyes like a flashbulb. He scanned the horizon, senses triggering. He snatched me off the ground like a set of keys just as the first demon burst through the red haze.

Two more demons materialized... Five... Ten... Fifteen...

They all landed and then froze, held back by an invisible leash. Their mismatched eyes fixed on the lone figure on the bluff. Kyros, pale and glistening with sweat, leaned heavily on an enchanted staff—a twisted hunk of dark wood topped with gleaming metal. The necromantic energy transference I had forced on him had clearly taken its toll.

"Kill the vampire," he barked. "Take the woman alive!"

The demons, frothing at the mouth, surged forward as one, a battering ram of hellish fury.

I felt depleted, my own magic core a deflated balloon. Every spell, every trick, every pulse of power stolen from Kyros went into bringing Tristan back. I scraped together the last tendrils of rune magic to weave a green energy shield around us like my mother had done countless times.

Tristan sprinted through the chaos clutching me to his chest, weaving around the bodies and over rough terrain. More demons materialized from the crimson mist, hot on our heels, slashing at my shield with long, gnarly claws. Tristan ran straight at Kyros. A brilliant strategic move, if slightly reckless.

The necromancer wouldn't risk another shot at Tristan—not with me, his precious conduit, in Tristan's arms.

I knew the shield wouldn't hold out for long. Beads of sweat raced down my forehead into my eyes, my limbs felt heavy. My focus wavered.

The edges of the shield weakened. A crack appeared in the emerald energy, spreading like a spiderweb.

A demon's claws raked across Tristan's back, tearing through his already shredded shirt. I grew faint as I struggled to pull oxygen into my lungs.

A heart-stopping growl ripped across the battlefield, followed by the whip-crack of leathery wings cleaving the air. A swift gust of wind whipped my hair across my face. A dark shadow swept over us, blotting out the sky.

I looked up to find a massive black wyvern plunging our way, unleashing an inferno of fire that incinerated demons and Nyktians, bones and all. The ground softened with the gray ash of the dead.

Killian the Destroyer.

The demons scattered, hissing and snarling, breaking their ranks as the wyvern circled, raining down fire. One by one they retreated in panic, vanishing into their red mist.

Kyros no longer stood on the bluff.

Coward.

Killian landed like an earthquake and keeled onto his side. I scrambled to kneel beside him. He was immense, easily eighty feet long from nose to tail. His wings, extensions of his arms like those of a giant bat, were punctured with gaping holes.

The edges of the wings were ragged and torn like they'd been dragged for a thousand miles.

Oh, you colossal fool.

His huge black eyes blinked at me. A cocoon of blue light ignited around him. The wyvern form dissolved, transforming slowly into the Therian King in all his battered glory.

The wounds were more gruesome on human flesh. He winced as he pushed himself up into a sitting hunch. He tried and failed to produce a grin.

"Did you really portal-hop without any buffering?" I said.

He shrugged. "I'll live."

"While I need you, yes, you'll live, but afterwards, after this is all over, I'm going to kill you myself for being so reckless."

Tristan draped his tattered trench coat over Killian's shoulders.

"I knew you were impulsive, but this... this takes the damn cake," I muttered. The sheer scale of the last twenty minutes had taken its toll.

Killian gripped my hand, pulling me close. "We have to find cover."

Tristan flashed between us, fangs clicking into place. He squared off with Killian, hissing.

"Release her, dragon." His thoughts echoed in my head as clearly as if Tristan had said them aloud.

No way... I hear my vampire's thoughts!

Killian's eyebrows drew together. His gaze darted from Tristan to me, a puzzled frown creasing his forehead. "What's this guard dog act?"

Oh boy.

Patches of red mist still clung to the sky. "We don't have time for a pissing contest, guys," I said. "We're an easy target out here."

My vampire and I lifted our wounded dragon savior and limped as one six-legged creature to a nearby cave tucked into the base of a towering bluff. We had to squeeze through a narrow crevice single file, but once inside there was ample space to fit all three of us with relative comfort.

"Tell me everything," Killian said, short of breath. He slumped against the cave wall, his face pale, his body brutalized from the portal journey.

I knew that shifting back into his human form depleted him of nutrients and fluids. I dug into my fanny pack, pulling out the power bar and handed it to him with a flask of water.

Killian chugged it all down within seconds. He wiped his mouth with the back of his hand. "Don't suppose you have more of those?"

I shook my head. "Slim pickings out here, Your Grace."

He nodded, pensively. "Alright, Tess, tell me what happened? Why didn't you stick to the plan at the library?"

"Not a choice we made, Killian," I said, weariness overtaking my mind and body rapidly.

"I need to understand. Did the vampire do it?"

"Come on," I said. "He just carried you to this cave. He saved me countless times and he might have just saved you."

"Fine. Tell me if you want me to stop asking," he said.

"Mature. Yeah, I'm tired. Be patient. We were there at the li-

brary waiting for you. *We* were on time. And then the portal…
it just went fucking apeshit, pulled us in like a collapsing star
and then dumped us out in the middle of bumfuck nowhere
which turned out to be here, Nyx. It was a trap, Killian, obviously. They lured me to Central Library so they could pull me
into this realm. Apparently, I'm hardware, some kind of magic
conduit, the key to unlocking ancient Netherworld power, so
toxic assholes can reshape the whole damn multiverse to their
own fantasy, the creepy fucking world groomers."

The color drained from Killian's face, leaving him as pale as
a sheet of parchment. "Start from the beginning."

I gave him a condensed version of my conversation with
Kyros, leaving out the details about the scars and about Savian,
the illusion mage who'd marked me and murdered my parents,
and who was behind it all. I'd buried that too deep for too long
and I liked it buried.

Killian cursed under his breath.

Out of the corner of my eye, I caught Tristan brooding as he
leaned against the wall, arms crossed like a petulant child, his
lips pursed.

Shit. He'd seen the marks flaring on my skin, pulsating with
power. He knew I wasn't telling Killian everything. He knew
I was holding out.

I nudged Killian's arm to change the topic. "Where were
you by the way? What made you late? Why did *you* change the
plan?"

"A semi-truck overturned on I-90… sideway." He flashed a
humorless grin. "Eventually, we… moved it."

Moved it, my ass. More like flipped it over their heads into a ditch with a flick of their Therian tails.

"A convenient delay, I suspect, all part of their plan. They left every clue for us to find—the Netherworld map, the Codex page—knowing we'd rush to this moment. They directed my every step and must have laughed as they saw me standing outside the right portal at the right moment. The only wrench in their gears was Tristan jumping in after me. I'm alive because of him."

Killian turned to Tristan. "A debt acknowledged."

Tristan inclined his head and looked away.

"No snarky retort, Tristan."

He glanced up at me. *Whoa.* He heard my thoughts, too. This vampiric bond was getting creepier by the second. It felt like we shared a brain, and the thought made my skin crawl.

"There's a leak in the dam," Killian said. "Someone's feeding intel to the Erasers. I don't know if it's a Bureau rat, or someone in your Shadow agency, but someone's playing both sides."

"Maybe it's one of your goons," Tristan said, his voice quiet but the challenge in his eyes loud and clear.

It's finally here... the testosterone sponsored pissing contest!

Killian growled, his muscles coiling. Almost certainly, the sorry state of his body saved us from a bloody cave battle. "My people are above reproach," he said, his voice a low growl, reining in his temper with visible effort.

"Why don't we all just chill and remember we just saved each other's asses from becoming demon kibble? Let's not forget...

that whole *teamwork making the dream work* thing."

What am I saying? I'm so corny.

Killian's gaze lingered on Tristan then flicked back to me. "I need sleep to accelerate the healing. And we need a plan. Wake me up if you sense danger."

He stretched stiffly out on the rocky floor, pulling Tristan's tattered trench coat, more holes than fabric now, over his broad frame. He'd gone through hell to find me. An unexpected knot tightened my throat.

"The dragon is too powerful for you," Tristan said. He stood guard near the cave entrance, eyeing the sleeping Therian. "And he has an impressive knack for leaving a trail of death and destruction behind him."

I glared at him. His eyes were cold and unreadable. "Really? Killian's powerful? Like I need a lecture on dragon strength right now. I don't know if you noticed, but we could use a fucking nuclear warhead right now."

"You have me."

My skin crawled with an army of ants. "Okay, how are you doing that? How are you planting thoughts in my head?"

He scoffed. "You forged a bond with blood magic, and it didn't occur to you that it might have profound implications?"

"Excuse me, shipping was delayed on my copy of *Vampiric Bonds for Dummies*," I snapped. "I can't have you reading my mind, Tristan. It's intrusive and unsettling. And I'm weird. And you're weird. How do we shut it off?"

He looked at me with impatient bemusement. "It's not mind reading. It's projection. We only share what we choose to communicate. Your inane inner monologue is safe."

Small comfort, I guess. And... it's not that inane.

"Great. Let's keep the psychic chatter to a minimum then. Stick to imminent-death warnings and the like. It feels creepy otherwise."

I clearly annoyed him, but he held his tongue. One thing I started to notice—the deference he held for me wasn't even a sliver of the devotion he had for Raven.

Oh, goodie, a new way for people not to like me.

"And, Tristan, one more item," I said in a faint voice. "Zip it around Killian. No provoking the dragon, and don't spill secrets I haven't cleared for public consumption. I have my reasons."

His eyes were so intense I thought they'd drill a hole in my forehead. "I can't do anything you don't want. Not anymore."

"You're not my slave. You can do anything you want other than murder, mayhem, bloodsucking sprees, or any other brand of general lawlessness."

"Charming. Let's see... that leaves knitting or killing myself."

Ha! A vampire with a sense of humor.

"Once this is over, I'll release you. Raven can re-bond you. It'll be like none of this ever happened."

"You can't cancel a vampiric bond like a cable service."

"Well, that's a problem for another day, we have bigger problems to worry about now."

"I need to hydrate," Tristan said. "I lost a considerable amount of blood. With your permission, of course."

My life right now. "Just don't drain the local wildlife population and don't kill anything."

He hissed and vanished, a shadow melting into the night.

I sighed, exhaustion and doubt pulling at me again. Killian was out cold, his powerful chest rising and falling with a hypnotic rhythm, the sharp angles of his face softened in sleep.

Killian Tierney—dragon, wyvern, Reiver, unlikely knight in shining armor, ready to swoop in to save the damsel in distress (me) and barbecue all her enemies.

Gods, I'm sleepy, corny, inane and lost.

WHEN TRISTAN SHOOK ME awake, I struggled to remember anything. I must have been dreaming... a lingering warmth, sand on my feet... My parents were there with me on a sun-drenched beach, the bittersweet echo of another life.

Reality hit me like a loud slap in the form of the disconcerting weight of a muscular arm draped across my waist.

Oh, sweet merciful hell. I'd fallen asleep nestled against Killian, my limbs wrapped around him as if he were an oversized teddy bear, my head resting against his chest, his steady heartbeat a lullaby in my ears. A small fire burned by the entrance, illuminating the cave.

"Incoming," Tristan said, snapping me out of my daze.

"Killian!" I untangled myself, nearly tumbling over. I shook the Therian King, but it was like trying to rouse a mountain. "Killian, wake up!"

Tristan joined in, shaking Killian with enough force to rattle his bones. The vampire's face was a picture of utter distaste.

Two hands shot out lightning fast. One clamped my throat, the other Tristan's. A furious roar erupted from Killian that shook loose pebbles from the cave ceiling and made my ears ring.

Killian's eyes blazed, wild and feral. He came to his senses as recognition slowly dawned on him. He released us. His murderous rage shifted to groggy annoyance. He looked crankier than usual, his hair tousled, his eyes heavy, his entire demeanor aggressive.

Tristan bared his fangs, but I commanded him with a warning glare. The fangs retracted, but his tension didn't.

"You... do *not*... shake a sleeping dragon," Killian said with a dry throat.

"Oh, I'm sorry," I snapped, rubbing my throat. "Go back to sleep. The demons will be here to wake you in a few minutes."

A distant roar rang out, underlining my point perfectly.

Killian's eyes narrowed. "What's out there?"

"No idea," I said, reaching for my dagger. "But I bet it sucks."

We crawled out of the cave, cool night air tickling our skin. The sky was dark and starless. I blinked my eyes to adjust.

"Tristan, are you sure your spider senses work here?"

Killian inhaled the air deeply, nostrils flaring. "No, he's right. It's all wrong."

With a flash of light and a gust of wind, Killian shifted. A whirlwind of black scales and rippled muscles covered him.

His massive wings unfurled into an impossible span.

The giant black wyvern dragon.

Holy hell. It always surprised me how huge that thing was. His wings were less ravaged now, several wounds had scabbed over, but he still looked like he had been chewed on by a pack of giant dogs.

The wyvern lowered himself to the ground, his head dipping, one wing extended, making himself as accessible as a fifty-foot-tall, fire-breathing dragon could be.

Wait, it's an invitation.

"No way," I said, backpedaling. "I don't do high altitudes without a parachute, or at least a dozen tequila shots."

Tristan shoved me forward. With a groan, I scrambled up the wing and settled right between Killian's massive shoulder blades. His scales were smooth and surprisingly warm, but the spikes that ran along his spine were razor sharp. I clung to one of the spikes, my heart hammering against my ribs.

I immediately regret this.

When Tristan attempted to climb after me, Killian's jaws snapped shut a hair's breadth from the vampire's head.

"Hey, knock it off," I yelped. "No vampire snacks! We need Tristan."

No clue if the wyvern brain could process my words, but I knew he felt my vibe. Raven had warned me that this dragon form was extra nasty.

"Your dinosaur needs obedience school."

"Tristan, we said... imminent-death warnings only!"

Killian breathed out a ribbon of blue fire. Great. This was

going to end with my hair and face burned off. I'd look like a local.

"Both of you, cool it," I snapped. "Or I swear I'll slam the damn portal shut when we find it after I go through it and seal it. You two will be stuck here playing patty-cake with the Nyktae."

Killian snorted, dipped his head and allowed Tristan to climb onto his back. The vampire settled in behind me, his arms bracketing me protectively.

The wyvern launched himself into the air with a colossal downstroke of his wings. The wind whipped through my hair as the ground fell away. It was a dizzying, disorienting sensation I could feel in my gut. My white knuckles clung to the spikes on his back, my stomach yearned for the solid ground.

It took me a few terror-filled heartbeats to realize what was happening: the dumb dragon was flying us back to Esperia.

Tristan's whole body tensed. *"He's delivering us to the necromancer."*

"No. Why would he save us only to take us back?"

"I don't know, why was he late? He's part of it, Tess!"

"Just... unless you can fly... we'll... find out."

Silence. No retort, no sarcastic quip, not even a hiss.

Ah, right. The vampiric bond put limits on what he could say. It must have been unflattering. He didn't have to say it out loud or *"in loud"* or whatever. This beast controlled our fate now.

Instead of beelining for Esperia, Killian veered off course, circling the Nyktian town like a predator stalking its prey. The black wyvern blended seamlessly with the ink sky as he rode the air currents like a shadow.

He landed on the town's outskirts, a few hundred feet from the thick glass wall that enclosed it.

Killian shifted back into his gloriously naked human form. The transformation heat of the dragon lingered in the air. Gray eyes locked with mine. And yes, he was *naked* naked. Again.

"Why did you bring us back here?" I said, more for Tristan's benefit than my own. The answer was painfully clear.

Killian's lips curled into a half-smile. "Because," he said, "I don't like to run. And you need to walk into the center of the trap to find its trigger."

"This is hardly sneaking in," Tristan said. "We have to scale that wall."

"Zzrask mentioned a hideaway door," Killian said, scanning the towering glass wall. "Known only to a few, used for smuggling goods and…" His voice trailed off. "Shall we say, less than savory activities."

If he found the seedy details of Esperia's illicit trades unspeakable, I certainly didn't want to hear about them.

Killian traced the wall. The glass under his fingers appeared dulled amidst the otherwise flawless surface. "Here. This must be it."

"You trust Zzrask?" I said, dizzily looking up the wall, too close to see its top. "After everything that's happened? No, this is another trap."

"Would you prefer to scale this wall, Tess, and fight your way through the citadel guards? I'm sure your new bloodsucking pal would do as you command. I heard he's easy that way."

Oh, bite me, Tierney.

"Fine," I said. "Let's play it your way. The end of everything has to be better than your endless sarcasm."

"Bad things have happened, shake it off," he demanded. "Zzrask owes me a debt. He won't betray that. His honor and his life depend on it. Trust me if you can't trust him."

His attempt at reason earned him a reluctant nod.

Killian pressed his palm against the glass, applying finger pressure to a specific spot. A grinding sound whispered as the glass slid inward, revealing a slot big enough for a single person to squeeze through sideways.

"Always had a soft spot for a secret passage," Tristan said, fangs ready.

I also didn't want to hear that story.

Killian slipped through, ducking to avoid the low archway. I followed behind and Tristan brought up the rear. The wall sealed shut behind us.

The passage opened into an alleyway that reeked of pungent spices.

"Welcome to the belly of the beast, Detective," Killian whispered.

"It's my second tour, Your Grace. One was enough. Got any useful advice?"

He flashed me a grin, among other things. "Don't touch anything. This place has teeth." He glanced down at his exposed... everything. "A disrobed stranger with skin walking down the street will cause a stir."

"You think?" I muttered, surveying my own bloodstained jeans and torn jacket. "My blood-drenched ensemble will also not win raves."

"Stay here, out of sight," Tristan said and sprinted into the shadows.

"What's with you two?" Killian said, eyeing the spot where Tristan had disappeared. "Why's he so eager to help?"

I shrugged. "Raven gave him specific orders. Plus, this place is strange. Weird things happen in Nyx."

He raised an unconvinced eyebrow but didn't push. "I can wait for that story to be told in full... when you're ready."

Did hell just freeze over?

Tristan reappeared with three hooded tunics draped over his arm.

I eyed him suspiciously. "Where did you get those?"

"Acquired them from a generous donor," Tristan said, poker-faced.

"A donor?" I frowned. "Tristan, you didn't... *kill* anyone, did you?"

"Not one, three," Tristan said, licking his lips with a predatory gleam in his eyes. "Slit their throats. Drained them dry. It was a mercy considering their ugly wardrobe."

WTAF?

Killian snorted. "He's yanking your chain. Not a drop of blood on him or the robes."

"They were drying on a line," Tristan admitted. "Freshly washed."

Gods, lost in Nyx with two smartasses.

We quickly squeezed into the tunics. The course fabric made me itch and they fit about as well as potato sacks, but we had a chance to blend in.

From a distance. In shadows. Maybe.

"Well," I grumbled, tugging at the scratchy collar, "I guess it's true. There really are things worse than death."

Killian grinned. "Who wants to crash a necromancer party? See what all the fuss is about."

We slipped through tight alleyways. Most walls were carved reliefs of Nyktian mythology—creatures with six eyes and serpentine tails, battles fought with swords made of bone and shields woven with shadow tendrils, chronicles of the past and of imagination.

On the wider streets there were market stalls piled high with strange-looking fruits and vegetables. Odd that they would be unattended. Maybe Nyx had a surplus of produce, or maybe the consequences of stealing were severe.

My stomach growled loud enough to wake the dead. "Are these safe to eat?" I muttered, eyeing luminous purple orbs and green knobby pods. "I can't fight evil on an empty tank."

Without a word, Killian grabbed an iridescent fruit that looked like a giant plum and took a healthy bite. "Good enough," he declared, purple juice staining his lips.

I followed suit, sinking my teeth in whatever my hand landed on. The flavors were rich and complex on my tongue, sweet and tart and floral. It was natural but it hit my brain pan like chocolate mousse.

I shoved a crusty loaf of their bread into my pack, just in case.

"Don't get too deep into the menu," Tristan warned, eyeing the fruit warily. "Nyktian food could have adverse effects on human digestion."

Tell me before my first dozen bites next time.

The central building where I'd met Kyros looked deserted. It didn't seem right. Even at this late hour, you'd expect a guard at least.

We combed the premises methodically, floor by floor, room by room, inspecting every nook, every cranny. Empty drawers and closet doors hung open. Shelves were left bare. Random items littered the floors. A hasty but effective attempt to erase all traces of the Cult of Erasure, to wipe clean any item that could lead us to them.

I stood in the center of my interrogation room. I reached out with my sensors, probing for any residual magic, any fever-print echoes of the dark power that had pulsed within these walls.

There was nothing. No telltale hum, no prickle of unease, not even a whisper of a dying shadow.

"Kyros is gone," I said. "The bastard knew we'd be coming."

"He will be found," Killian said, eyes burning. "Even if I have to rip this entire realm apart, brick by brick."

Killian stormed out of the building, his anger blistering around him like a heat lasso. The city was quiet, unnervingly quiet. We crossed the marketplace, rounded a corner and came face to face with a group of seven guards.

Killian cracked his knuckles. "Finally, dance partners," he said.

"We need them alive," I warned. "We need at least one of them to talk."

He ignored me, of course, and sauntered up to the guards with a wide smile on his face and his hands casually tucked inside the sleeves of his tunic. "Grand evening, gentlemen. We're out for a late-night stroll. In the name of our esteemed mutual friend, Commander Zzrask, I beseech you to let us pass."

What the hell was that? A Shakespearian diss?

The Nyktae drew their swords from their scabbards. All eyes were on Killian.

Killian chuckled. "As you wish." He landed a thunderous punch on the head of the closest guard. The force of the blow cracked something and sent the Nyktae sprawling, knocked out cold before hitting the ground.

The remaining six Nyktian guards attacked in unison. They were fearless but Tristan and Killian made short work of them, their strikes calculated, somehow inflicting debilitating wounds without killing the guards.

Is it possible I got through to them?

The fight was almost over when reinforcements arrived, a whole fucking regiment of Nyktian warriors rounding the corner.

Another setup. There were dozens of them, and they were bigger, meaner and more eager than the decoy guards.

"Time to stack bodies," Killian said with glee.

I need new friends.

Reaching into my fanny pack, I rummaged for whatever

tricks I had left that might disorient the military-style assault, when a wave of numbing cold rushed through my body. The temperature plummeted. Ice spread across the ground. I stumbled. My teeth chattered.

A crystalline form materialized out of thin air. Its breath was a cloud of arctic mist. Its body was made of jagged icicles that clinked together like haunting wind chimes.

"A frostlock demon," I choked out. I reached for my sensors and couldn't access them. My magic fizzled in my core like a snuffed candle.

Killian growled. "We'll use the old ways."

He and Tristan launched themselves at the Nyktae with fists and fangs. With our supernatural essences on ice, we were down to brute strength alone, and I was no brute.

Normally, a single frostlock demon would pose little threat to a Reiver, but Killian had been reduced by the strain of the portal jumps and the energy it took to shift and fly. His dragon wings had been clipped, so to speak.

The memory of Miles hit me in the gut like a sucker punch. The Cult of Erasure had used the same tactic on him, stripping him of his power with a frostlock demon before murdering him. But unlike Miles, I had a full terror team, a cranky dragon and a snarky vampire.

Killian's blows landed with bone-crunching force, but for every Nyktae he dropped, two more sprouted from the shadows. Tristan fought by his side, shooting concerned glances my way between strikes. His strength and speed made him deadly even without his heightened vampiric abilities. Together, they were devastating and effective, but they could not stem the relentless tide.

A dark figure leaped from a rooftop like a ninja. Time slowed as he landed with catlike precision mere feet away, close enough that I could see the enflamed blood vessels in his eyes.

Commander Zzrask, in all his gelatinous glory, stood poised with a spear made of bone and metal. He raised the weapon above his head, its tip pulsing with a phosphorescent glow. His eyes, cold and calculating, swept over the scene like he was a god.

"Thissss... isssss noooot.... the Nyyyyksssssian... waaay," he rasped. His voice sliced through the chaos, silencing the battlefield.

The Nyktae hesitated, exchanging uncertain glances. Zzrask spoke again in their indecipherable native tongue.

A hulking warrior approached the Commander, his gestures growing ever angrier as he responded. Zzrask turned his face away for a moment, then plunged his spear into the warrior's chest. The hulking Nyktae collapsed into the gathering pool of his own dark blood.

Zzrask delivered his message in a language all could understand.

The Nyktian warriors grumbled but lowered their weapons and backed away. The frostlock demon vanished in a swirl of icy mist.

Magic surged back into my core with a warm rush.

"Neeeed... to... taaalk," Zzrask said, his unsettling eyes finding mine. "Deteeective." He dipped his head in what I hoped was a show of respect.

"It's my honor, Commander," I managed. "Your timing is impeccable."

Killian stepped forward. "Where are they?"

Zzrask gave him a toothy approximation of a smile. "Erassss-sure leeaderssss... aaare in... sssstooone tooower."

Chapter 27

THE STONE TOWER WAS a monolith carved out of a single massive slab of gray stone, a cylindrical monstrosity stretching into the sky. It stood alone in a desolate expanse of rocky terrain as if all forms of life had retreated from it. This was the Cult of Erasure's headquarters, their stronghold, the drab heart of their twisted ambitions.

Tristan, Zzrask and I dismounted the wyvern. My sore legs felt wobbly from the long flight. A stealth approach was no longer an option. When I'd protested earlier about charging in blind, Killian had given me a long lecture on the merits of what he called *aggressive negotiation*. Raven may have been right about the drawbacks of bringing a dragon king into hostile territory.

Interwoven wards shimmered around the tower, each thread tinted with a different color. They wouldn't have taken the time to build such elaborate defenses unless they were safeguarding something rare and powerful.

The tower itself appeared impenetrable. Thick stone and

no windows. Digging under it might work in theory, but the Erasers would probably notice us long before we finished and, of course, the bottom could also be thick stone.

The wyvern cocked his head. A torrent of fire exploded from his throat, scorching everything in its path, turning rocks into molten slag.

I staggered back, shielding my face, watching in awe as the wyvern bathed the steel tower doors in hellfire. The wards hissed and popped like firecrackers; the magical threads twisted like dying snakes before disintegrating. The reinforced door caved in and crumbled like tin foil.

Holy crap, he can fry wards and barbecue steel.

The inferno subsided. A plume of smoke curled into the twilight sky. Killian shifted back. He coughed, his skin glistening with sweat. He had used up the last of his energy. He gingerly slipped into the tunic.

"Nooowww... weee... fiiiight," Zzrask hissed, clutching his spear. He strode toward the shattered entrance, his body jiggling like a Jello mold.

I turned to follow Zzrask, but Killian caught my hand. He wrapped his arms around my waist, pulling me close. His eyes were shadowed.

My stomach fluttered. "Are you trying to get us killed?"

"I've been trying to keep you alive since we first met, Detective Hilliard." His fingers traced a path down my cheek, a trail of heat against my skin.

My body tensed. All five senses warned me of imminent danger.

"Is that smoke coming out of your nostrils, Your Scaliness?"

"Don't tempt me, Tess." His voice was rough, urgent.

What's this now? "I would never dream of it, Killian."

Tristan's voice punctured my mind like a blade. *"Say the word and I'll make him back off."*

Killian buried his face in my hair, his breath warm against my ear. The world tilted. My knees weakened. This was not the time for this, for whatever this was, but I found myself unable to move a muscle.

"We have a tower to conquer," I blurted out.

"The scent of a beautiful woman's hair," he whispered, "is a fine thing to experience before dying."

Beautiful. Something crumpled inside me, irrevocably. Primals had valued beauty throughout the ages in all forms. Ancient Greek statues, the four beauties of China, the detail and color in Aztec jewelry. Killian hadn't seen the real me. He hadn't seen the grotesque scars, the battleground of blemishes, the disfigurement of my body and my spirit. What beauty would he see then?

"Unless you want to live out your life in a Nyktian cell, we need to keep moving!" Tristan snarled in my head.

I pushed away from Killian, smoothing my hair. "Aren't we being a tad dramatic, Your Grace? I'm in it to win it."

He released me, his gaze lingering for a beat. Then his eyes laughed, his lips curving into a mischievous grin. "A woman running to the violence. Consider me impressed."

"This is no time to flirt," I said. "It's time to make Erasers disappear."

Gods, I say awkward things when I feel awkward.

We raced after Zzrask into the tower. The interior was cold and silent like we'd entered catacombs. Electric bulbs elongated our shadows on the rough-hewn stone walls and floors.

Will we ever leave this place?

"Thissss wayyyy," Zzrask said, picking up speed.

Frantic footsteps and distant voices echoed through corridors. We'd caught the Erasers off guard, but the element of surprise faded fast. This was their battleground.

The fact that we'd made it so far meant Savian and Kyros were too cocky about their defenses, or they'd already flown the coop. Defeat washed over me, followed by a grim realization. I wanted Savian dead. Obsessively. Unhealthily. More than I wanted anything.

Zzrask skidded to a halt before a wide door. Two guards took one look at us and bolted. Tristan shot after them without a word, leaving us to deal with whatever we found behind the door.

We burst in and I nearly swallowed my tongue. The room was a tech junkie's wet dream—banks of computers, humming servers, and a wall of screens that would make NASA jealous. How they'd managed this very human setup of technology in Nyx staggered the mind.

Killian raised his fist, ready to thrash the equipment punk rock style.

"Noooo," Zzrask gurgled. "Find.... ssssource!"

"The source?" I blinked. "The great and mighty Netherworld power source is in this hacker's den?"

"Yessss. Fiiiind heeere."

Zzrask was right. Smashing things wouldn't solve our problems. I stepped to the main console, studying the flickering security feeds on the wall. I might not be a tech wizard, but I'd seen enough heist movies to give it a shot.

After some fumbling with keys and buttons, I found a small lever. The camera views shifted as I toggled, giving us a whirlwind tour of Evil Tower Incorporated—labs, workshops, living quarters and enough medieval style weaponry to start World War IV or, at least, stage a reenactment of the siege of Constantinople.

"Thissss," Zzrask hissed, pointing at one of the screens.

My pulse quickened. There, on top of a crystal pillar, sat a sphere crackling with rings of energy. Both pillar and sphere were encased in a transparent dome of crisscrossing wards.

Basement Level, Room 18.

"What terrible and unholy power is contained within?" I pondered.

Tristan leaned in. I never noticed him entering the room. "Any ideas on how to pull the plug without a seismic pop?"

I glanced at Killian, who lingered in thought. "I always have ideas," he said. "Not sure which, if any, could prevent unwanted results."

Oh boy. Not sure I'm ready for him to roll the dice.

"Alright, let's go shut this thing down," I said.

We slipped out of the control room. We hadn't gone more than a few steps when the shadows ahead shifted. Six Nyktian guards blocked our way.

"Do they not know they're going to die?" Killian said. His right hand already crackled with a ball of elemental fire.

Zzrask stepped in front of Killian and addressed his fellow Nyktae. After some deliberation, the guards stepped aside to let us pass.

"That was anticlimactic," I muttered as we hurried past.

"Dooon't... woooorrrry, Deteeeective," Zzrask rasped next to my ear. "Pleeeentyyyy... mayyyyhem... ahead."

Ha, now I'm really worried.

Following Zzrask down a maze of staircases, we felt the change. The deeper we went, the more the air prickled with electric energy.

We reached a heavy door. It hummed with a smothering of wards.

Zzrask held up his hand to keep us quiet.

Killian stepped forward, his eyes narrowing as he studied the wards. He thrust both hands forward. Twin jets of white-hot flame erupted from his palms, engulfing the door. The air sizzled and popped as the wards fought back, but Killian's fire was relentless. The magical barriers crumbled like ash, and the doors swung open with a groan.

We stepped into a large, cavernous chamber. In the center stood the five-foot tall crystal pillar pulsing with enough swirling energy to power all of Nyx. A shimmering orb sat on top of the pillar, sparkling with electricity. Dozens of smaller crystals were arranged in a complex geometric pattern, amplifying the energy of the orb. Magic ran amok in that place, causing my skin to tingle and strands of my hair to float.

I inched forward, drawn by the mesmerizing display. "How do we power this thing down without igniting it? We can't play dice with the universe."

Einstein kind of said that, but these guys won't know.

A dozen grotesque beasts burst into the chamber from a sliding panel to our left and another from our right. Behind them, Nyktian warriors stormed in, followed by a wave of hooved demons.

More beasts poured through the door, enclosing us in a tight ring. They had thick, pachyderm type hides covered in coarse, bristly hair, short black tusks and were the size of a pygmy hippo.

"Ssssurenderrrr!" the Nyktian leader bellowed.

Killian's hands ignited with twin balls of flames. Zzrask's body rippled in ways that defied physics and good taste. Tristan leaped to my side, ready to defend me at all costs.

I sized up our chances. Outnumbered, outgunned, and out-positioned in a room full of enough magical juice to fry us all.

"And miss all the fun?" Killian growled. "We like these odds."

We do?

I cracked my knuckles. "Yeah."

The horde charged, a tsunami of claws and teeth.

Damn. I'm not built for this.

Killian met their charge head-on, his elemental fire blazing. His form blurred, shifting into a dragon. Not into the towering wyvern, not into the red dragon of Picnic Point.

This was something different. Smaller, more compact, but no less impressive—seven feet tall, his scales a deep blue, his eyes golden.

He roared, a sound that shook dust from the ceiling, and dove into the fray. Claws flashed. Heads rolled. Literal heads. They quickly became serious tripping hazards.

At first all my efforts centered around not dying, but the chamber thrummed with power. I whipped my wind magic to life, flinging two demons like ragdolls. I hurled blasts of compressed air, sending beasts sprawling and knocking Nyktians off their feet. I spun, my arms outstretched, summoning cyclones that ripped through the enemy ranks, tossing bodies against walls.

Zzrask gurgled something unintelligible and proceeded to smash three of his fellow Nyktians into a slushy gelatinous mass.

Okay, that's just gross.

More enemies poured in. Two necromancers with corpse-pale faces commanded a dozen skeletal vampires whose eyes glowed a sickly red.

Thralls. The Erasers know how to throw a party.

I spotted Tristan, cornered by two beasts, and flung an emerald shield his way to protect him both from the beasts and the necromantic power that had entered the scene. The last thing I needed was a Tristan-thrall.

The necromancers unleashed a torrent of dark magic, bolts of black energy that sizzled through the air. I reacted instinctively, my illusion magic flaring, a veil of shimmering energy snapping into place between Tristan and the incoming attack. The dark bolts struck the shield, exploding in a shower of sparks. The impact reverberated through my body, a jolt of pain that blurred my vision and partially blocked my hearing.

Tristan's eyes widened. "Behind you!"

I spun. Three frostlock demons. *Not these dudes again.* Their icy breath froze everything it touched.

Killian, his miniature dragon radiating a furious heat, roared and unleashed a bolt of fire, a searing orange inferno that struck the nearest frostlock demon. Its icy form shattered, dissolving into a cloud of steam and glittering shards.

The dragon took a freezing blast to the chest. His scales crackled with frost. His form wavered. He began to roar in pain as he shrunk.

"Killian!" I lunged toward him, but claws raked my back. Pain exploded across my shoulders.

We were losing this fight. Tristan bled from a dozen cuts and gashes. Zzrask's gelatinous body clouded and bubbled with injury.

"Got any more brilliant ideas?" I yelled at Killian, ducking a hooved demon's swipe.

The Therian King, human again and looking worse than ever, flashed a pained grin. "Working on it. Try not to die in the meantime."

"Solid plan," I shouted.

Through the chaos, a figure emerged. The sight made my blood run cold. Kyros, my arch nemesis since arriving in Nyx, his face a mask of death and hatred. A chill ran down my spine.

My eyes locked on the crystal pillar. The source of all this madness. I had one chance to end this or die trying. Might as well go for broke.

"Tristan!" I shouted over the din. "Clear a path to the source!"

He nodded, understanding instantly. With a howl that would make a dire wolf proud, he tore into the crowd, carving a path to the pillar.

I sprinted after him, ducking claws and dodging spells. Tristan took hit after hit, his entire body smeared with blood. But he held or at least slowed the line, a one-vampire wrecking crew.

A demon sprung at me. Sliding under its grasp, I felt claws graze my scalp.

My hair must be so wretched. I'm earning my monster card.

Finally, I reached the pillar. The orb hummed with enough power to make my teeth and bones hurt.

"Okay, you oversized car battery," I muttered, pressing my palm against the ward barrier. "Let's see what makes you tick."

I reached for every scrap of magical knowledge and skill I had, praying it would be enough. Because if it wasn't, I was about to become an actual hot mess you could read about in the next edition of *America's Stupidest Paranormal Detectives*.

Dark energy prickled my senses, drawing closer. Kyros was coming for me through a sea of dead bodies like some twisted angel of death. Across the room, Zzrask went down under a pile of demons.

I spread my arms wide, unleashing my illusion magic no

holds barred. The hidden marks flared across my body one by one like glowing dominoes.

"Here's mud in your eye," I whispered, then slammed into the wards with everything I had, leaving nothing in the tank. *"Explodere!"*

Pain gashed through me like a hot iron. The wards trembled, lines of angry red spreading like cracks on ice. They split open with a thunderous pop, and I burst through.

Kyros was feet away, his shock becoming a murderous rage as the wards snapped shut behind me. I swayed on my feet, fighting to stay conscious.

The power source loomed, a sphere of crackling energy that made every hair on my body stand on end like I'd stuck my finger in a cosmic socket.

Focus, Tess.

Kyros unleashed a bolt of dark energy that slammed Tristan into a wall. The vampire's bones snapped like twigs.

I reached for the orb. One wrong move, and we'd all be atomized. My hands jerked back instinctively.

A roar shook the chamber. Killian's eyes found mine. "TESS, DON'T!"

He ripped a frostlock demon in half, his fury palpable. Blue flames erupted from his skin as he tapped into his elemental magic. Where a man stood, a dragon now raged.

He was too late. My hands closed around the orb.

Pain. Blinding, all-consuming pain. It felt like trying to channel a hurricane through a straw.

So this is what electrocution feels like.

My body burned from the inside out. I screamed, forcing the raw kinetic energy into my scars, becoming the conduit I swore never to be.

The thralls were on Killian, Kyros pulling their strings. I ripped my hands from the orb, my skin sizzling. I hurled the energy onto the Killian-dragon, transferring the devastating Netherworld power to him.

The transformation was instant. Magic enveloped the Therian King in ripples. An armor of pure power crystallized over his scales. He roared. Thrall heads fell like bowling pins.

Kyros broke through the wards, a spear raised high. I met his gaze, lightning crackling between my fingers. His weapon bounced off the force field I tossed between us. I slammed everything I had left into Kyros. The bolt went straight through him, exploding his chest, leaving a huge hole in its wake.

Kyros went down, still glaring hate as he perished.

That's for Miles, you sick bastard.

The chamber fell silent, save for the last sparks of energy and the ragged breathing of the fleeing Nyktae. Everything distorted. My legs grew heavy and my ears rang before I slumped down onto the floor.

Someone ran toward me. *Dragon boy*—all too human now and drenched in blood, his eyes wild with concern.

Out of the corner of my eye, I caught sight of a man in the doorway, staring at me. He wore a long black trench coat that had seen better days. His features were strangely familiar. Tall with golden hair and vibrant azure eyes.

The White Librarian. *I must be hallucinating.*

His lips moved but did not make a sound. The Librarian's words resonated in my mind. *"Until next time, child."*

That voice... a memory out of reach...

Long arms lifted me. Killian did not smell of battle. No sweat, no blood, no lingering smoke residue. He smelled of marshmallows and graham crackers.

"We just need chocolate," I whispered before passing out.

Chapter 28

I OPENED MY EYES and stretched my arms over my head. Sunlight poured through an open window. Drapes fluttered with a soft breeze that carried the scent of lilac and... was that bacon?

Wait a minute. This is all wrong.

I bolted upright in bed, startled. This was not my room. This wasn't any room I knew. A suite in an upscale resort maybe, not that I knew what that looked like. Memories flooded my brain—Nyx, blood-soaked battles, a power reactor that could've fried the multiverse.

"Whoa there, tiger. Take it easy."

Killian's voice, warm and amused. I turned to find him lounging in an armchair, looking infuriatingly handsome for someone who'd recently been covered in demon guts.

His eyes smiled at me, bright and welcoming. "The healer mage said there might be some side effects from the potions. Though I didn't expect *frantic cat* to be one of them."

"Healer mage?" I said, my voice a little hoarse.

"You were in a rough shape, Tess. It was touch and go for a while. We brought in the best—a mage who could regrow limbs if she put her mind to it. She says you'll be good as new." He winked. "Maybe even toss in an upgrade."

"We won?" The question felt naive after what we'd been through.

"Yes, Detective. We won." His smile was part pride, part appreciation. "The stone tower is rubble, the power source locked up tighter than my grandma's cookie recipe. And our man Zzrask? Well, let's just say Nyx is under new management for the foreseeable future."

"That's good news." I sank back into the pillows. I closed my eyes and suddenly found myself in a prairie blooming with wildflowers.

"Okay, what's with the happy hallucinations when I close my eyes? Am I tripping on unicorn dust?"

Killian chuckled. "It's the healing potions. It will wear off."

"Does it have to?" I said, then laughed. My ribs protested, but even the pain felt good. Proof I was among the living.

"That's funny?" Killian said, leaning forward in his chair.

"No, I was thinking... two weeks ago, I didn't even know you existed. Now we're like the avengers."

He held up three fingers. "Three weeks. It's the first day of December."

The laughter died in my throat. "I've been out for a *week*?"

"On and off." He shrugged. "Your memory is fuzzy. You woke up to eat and drink. Mostly to complain about the food, the bed, the pillows. It'll all come back to you."

Reality started creeping in. "Pankowski totally must have fired me, like with extreme vengeance," I muttered.

"The Bureau took care of all that. As far as your world's concerned, nothing's changed."

I blinked. "The Bureau knows?"

"We had to loop them in. They've vowed to keep a tighter leash on the multiverse. They want to avoid extinction level battle royales."

It was all good news. We'd saved the day, I still had a job, and the powers-that-be were finally paying attention. So why did I feel so... restless?

I met Killian's gaze. "What now?"

He reached out, his hand warm on mine. "Now, you get to adjust to your new normal. You live in a world where dragons and demons are real."

"Sounds terrifying. I guess I've been living in this world the whole time. I'm just the same old Tess no matter what is out there. I'm here. I'm a Madison girl. I root for the home team and eat bratwursts when I'm drinking."

"Bratwursts are terrifying. What's in those things?"

"Life's a mystery," I said, feeling hopeful. "I'll just take it as it comes. What's next for the great Killian Tierney?"

"I'm hoping for a few chill days. Maybe catch up on some reading."

"And how about us, Your Grace? Are our destinies still aligned?" A blush rose to my cheeks. "We made a dynamic duo."

And why, suddenly, did I want him to pin me against the

bed and kiss me senseless? To run those battle-hardened fingers through my hair, pull me close against his chest, slip his hands under my veils of decency...

My veils of... What the fuck, Tess?

His smile widened and I suddenly felt very warm. "I think we are what is called friends, Tess. You have my eternal gratitude and protection."

Great. Eternal friendzone from the guy I want to...

I cleared my throat. "Okay, Lord Friend, I'm guessing we're at the Helm. When can I return to my cozy little home?"

"As soon as the mage healer clears you." He hesitated. "There is one small complication. Your vampire buddy is causing quite a stir. He refuses to leave without you. He's demanding to see you, threatening to go on a hunger strike. Which, for a vampire, is more an annoyance than a tragedy."

Oh hell. Tristan. How did I forget about him?

I sighed. "I'll talk to him."

"Sooner rather than later, please. This punk is testing the limits of Therian restraint."

I laughed. "Therian restraint? That's funny."

"It is not funny," he said, severely unamused.

"Oh, okay," I said. "I just thought. No, I get it now. These meds."

Sheesh. Therian restraint. How do you not laugh at that?

He stood up, and I had to remind myself not to stare. He wore a simple white t-shirt and dark jeans, but on him, it looked like haute couture. The fabric clung to his powerful frame in ways that made good girls bad.

"Get well, Tess," he said. "You've been an infuriating pain in my ass, but I'll miss the banter. We should catch up soon. I'm dying to hear about that whole vampire bonding you did, and those archaic illusion marks on your flesh. You have proven more than meets the eye."

What? Really? Oh shit.

I searched for words to say out loud, but only an incoherent grumble slipped from my lips.

He paused with his hand on the doorknob, a mischievous glint in his eye. "Oh, one more thing, Detective. There seems to have been a tiny mix-up with your potions. The healer might have accidentally slipped you a small dose of a love potion along with your treatment."

My jaw dropped.

He grinned. "If you want to jump my bones right now, I wouldn't object, but something tells me you might regret it in the morning."

You complete inhuman jackass!

He left the room. I grabbed a pillow and hurled it at the closing door.

I laughed despite myself. I handled the war for the multi-verse just fine but was taken down by a witch's brew.

AIDEN LED ME THROUGH the Helm's winding corridors. My legs felt like overcooked noodles, but I plodded on.

We stopped before a heavy iron door. Aiden hesitated, his

hand on the latch. "Just... be prepared. He's been quite agitated."

"Open the door, Aiden."

He complied. Tristan paced the windowless cell like a caged tiger. His usually immaculate hair was a fright; dark circles had formed under his eyes.

Gods, they actually locked him in here. Have they made him lose his mind?

"Tristan," I called softly.

He whirled, eyes wild, then sagged with relief. "Tess!"

It was the first time he had used my first name. I turned to Aiden with fury in my eyes. "Let him out."

"Are you sure that's—"

"Aiden, don't make me get the bonshek blade."

He paled and fumbled with the keys.

As soon as the cell door opened, Tristan was there, checking me over like a lost puppy. "I could feel your pain, but they wouldn't let me near you."

I gently pushed his hands away. "I'm fine, Tristan. You need to go home."

He recoiled as if I'd slapped him. "I'm not leaving without you."

Oh boy, the bond had deepened while I was swimming in potions and happy dreams. The memory of our twisted mental tango still felt creepy.

I turned to Aiden. "Give us some privacy."

Aiden retreated reluctantly.

"Yes, you are leaving without me," I told Tristan, firmly. "Go back to Raven. Act like nothing's changed. That's an order."

His face contorted with a mixture of hurt and anger. "You can't just dismiss me like—"

"I can and I am," I cut him off, softening my tone. "Tristan, our lives don't match. My world isn't your world. And I don't have any fucking coffins tucked away in a basement. I don't even have a basement."

He seemed offended. "Those things are myths, Tess."

"Yeah, I know. I'm sorry. But this is not your fight anymore. You saved me more than once. You repaid me for saving you a hundred times over. Go. Go to your people. Go home."

"Raven will know."

"Then be very convincing. That's your mission."

For a moment, I feared he might never stop arguing. Then his shoulders slumped in defeat. "As you wish."

I watched him slink away. He glanced back full of unspoken feelings. I felt a pang of guilt but pushed it down quickly. *This is what's best for him. What's best for both of us.*

I SLUMPED INTO MY creaky office chair, the familiar scent of stale coffee and old case files oddly comforting after the chaos of the past few weeks. My desk looked like it had been in the path of a tornado. Apparently, saving the multiverse didn't exempt you from bureaucratic backlog.

Grabbing a pen and a sticky note, I started jotting down my

brand-new to-do list. Because nothing says *back to normal* like organizing your impending nervous breakdown.

1. Figure out Killian's game

I tapped the pen against my lips. Friend, possible ally, or something more? And what was that business with the *accidental* love potion? I bet he slipped that in there just to mess with me. Maybe not.

2. Pacify Raven

I winced. Yeah, returning her prized vampire with a magically bonded case of puppy love was bound to ruffle her feathers if she found out. Which she would no doubt. Whatever. I owed her for many reasons, and I'd find a way to explain, at the very least.

3. Make it up to Izzy

My best friend had been through hell because of me. I had missed Thanksgiving dinner. I wouldn't miss Christmas. I scribbled *buy entire liquor store?* next to the item. It was a start.

4. Deal with Pankowski

He was convinced that my unexplained absences were part of an elaborate undercover Bureau operation I hadn't reported to him. Maybe I could convince him otherwise. Or just hope someone else would mess up, so Pankowski would be too busy yelling at them.

5. Kill Savian

My pen hesitated over this one. The psycho asshole was still out there, somewhere, ruining someone's life. A thorn in my side, a shadow looming over my world and the world. This wasn't over, not by a long shot. He'd be back and he'd find me ready.

I leaned back, staring at my list. Save the world, mend friendships, navigate interdimensional politics, and maybe squeeze in a therapy session or five. Perfect. I was on my way. A budding optimist!

A familiar voice cut through my thoughts.

"Tess! The new cases have just come in!" Izzy burst into my office, her curls bouncing with each step. "We've got everything from possessed toasters, very scary, to a guy who swears his neighbor is a chihuahua shifter, a were-chihuahua if you will. Oh, and Mrs. Abernathy's cat is missing again. I told her to check the ethereal plane this time. Cats are curious demons."

I blinked, trying to process the sudden onslaught of normalcy. "Iz, I—"

The phone rang. The caller ID made me sit up straight. Imani Harris.

I picked up, trying to sound professional and not at all like someone who'd recently been unconscious for a week. "Investigator Hilliard speaking."

"I trust you're recovering well?" Imani's crisp voice came through.

"Yes, ma'am. Thank you."

"I'm happy to hear. We have a proposition for you. The Bureau would like to hire you as a member of our multiverse bounty hunter crew."

I nearly dropped the phone. Izzy, who had been not-so-sub-tly eavesdropping, mouthed *What?!* at me.

"I... wow. That's quite an offer," I managed.

How many times had I hopelessly interviewed for just such an offer?

"Indeed. Quite earned, too. Killian Tierney has given us a detailed account of your actions in Nyx and has personally vouched for your character."

My mind raced. Multiversal bounty hunting? That sounded intense, dangerous, a little insane, probably life-threatening—suicidal, really.

I crumpled up the to-do list and tossed it in the trash.

"When do I start?"

About the Author

Stella Fitzsimons was born in Athens, Greece, and lives in Southern California with her husband and two sons. After studying economics and language arts she went on to teach both Mathematics and English before launching *Stella's Literary Bistro*, a bilingual literary journal. Her works include: *The Vanishing Tome, Luna, Winter, Silver Dust, Shadow Fall, Moonlight Mist* and *The Last Rider.*